Silver M

HAVE A COLLECTION
OF 64 GREAT NOVELS
OF
EROTIC DOMINATION

If you like one you will probably like the rest

A NEW TITLE EVERY MONTH
NOW INCLUDING EXTRA BONUS PAGES

Silver Moon Readers Service
c/o DS Sales Ltd.
PO Box 1100 London N21 2WQ

Silver Moon Books Inc
PO Box 1614 New York NY 10156

Distributed to the trade throughout North America by
LPC Group, 1436 West Randolph Street, Chicago, IL 60607
(800) 826-4330

Slaves for Sale

by

J.T.Pearce

SLAVE FOR SALE

When the cold wind at night comes down from the snow-capped mountain tops of the Andes it swoops low over the thatched rooftops of Calimba and whistles its eerie news as it flies down the narrow passageways that mark this tiny, forgotten city.

Inside the huts and hovels which comprise it lie some of the most beautiful women in the world, willing chattels to the demands of the city's malepopulation. Colombia is a rich country, but it is also one of remarkable contrasts.

Microwave transmission towers can be found next to mud adobes.Ultra-modern highways can be seen running through tiny hamlets the inhabitants of which eke a wretched existence out of an infertile, rocky ground. Its six international airports are ringed with slums and ghettos of almost unimaginable poverty.

It is a beautiful country though. A magnificent country, with the Andes range stretching along one of its flanks, their ruggedness inviting disaster and invoking awe. It is because of that range that I was there. My name is Andy and I am, or I should more accurately say, I was, a TV executive.

You see Colombia also has the world's largest network of terrestrial television transmission towers and I'd been brought in as a consultant. My stint over, I had taken five days to try my luck up the Andes range, testing myself against the mountain. Foolhardy as this may sound I've done it before. Mountains are my passion. Not my biggest one, but one I indulge in frequently.

For this one I had made sure I was fully equipped. I had provisions for double the number of days I expected to be out for and, just in case, I had also brought with me one of the new sat-phones. I could reach anyone, anywhere in the world without having to rely on transmission towers or good weather.

It was the phone too which brought me my daily weather report. It was on the fourth day, with just one to go that the blizzard came down. Blizzards are terrifying beasts. They have a voice that howls in your ears as they stream down the mountain and they have a breath that's colder than death itself. It chills your fingers as you hammer in your pitons and tugs at your clothing to find the tiniest fissure through which it can enter and suck away your life's heat.

All I can remember was that this one was colder, harder and stronger than any blizzard I had ever had the misfortune to get caught up in and I was tiring. I was about 6,500 ft up the Northwest mountain face. Each step I took down the mountain sapped a little more of my ebbing strength. The rope that held me anchored and was my lifeline, seemed to be as slippery as soap and the very act of keeping my head up and my eyes scanning the treacherous terrain in front of me was rapidly using up what little strength I had left.

I remember quite clearly the thought that I should stop a minute, try to regain some of my strength. A niche in the rock to my right presented itself as if on cue and I angled towards it, stretched like a human fly on that almost sheer rock face and then something happened. Either one of my pitons went, or my tired hand slipped on the rope, but there was a sudden kind of slack and for a moment I was falling backwards thinking that this was it; the last mistake of my life. And then the mountain face was away from me and I was in the enveloping embrace of the blizzard and everything went white and very, very still.

***

'You, wake now, need to drink.'

I was being prodded awake.

Momentarily I thought that I was back in my hotel room in Bogota, but the pungent, earthy smells that assailed my nostrils and the dark, low ceiling overhead immediately dispelled that thought.

I sat up and winced with pain. My arms, shoulders and ribs felt sore, rock-beaten. I recalled then my fall and I turned to see who had spoken. It was the most beautiful girl I had ever laid eyes upon. She had straight black hair and a light olive complexion. Her eyes were a liquid gold and she had full, pouting lips that featured a subdued, natural red in that elfin face. She was dressed in a long, straight garment that reached down to her toes. She was barefoot.

My eyes took in the suggestive swell of her breasts beneath her dress, the way it strained at her hips and outlined her thighs. It was, I guessed, an old dress she'd long outgrown. I was used to the inequalities of life in Colombia and was not unduly surprised.

'You need drink,' she repeated. 'Drink now.'

She motioned for me to follow her. I would have of course, pains and aches not withstanding but I suddenly realised that beneath the rough, smelly blanket which covered me I was naked. Entirely nude. All my clothes had gone!

'Wait!' I cried and my voice came out a croak 'My clothes. I need my clothes.'

She turned back, the movement momentarily permitting me to admire her profile. I was right, she was a stunner. Then she said: 'Clothes not now. You come.'

'I need my clothes. I am naked.' I said enunciating each word as clearly and slowly as I could. In my time in Colombia I had run into a few situations but this had to simply be the strangest of all, I thought.

'No clothes. You come. Drink now. Make you strong.'

'What happened to my clothes?' I asked.

'Clothes gone.'

'Yes, I know. Where are they now?'

'Clothes burnt.' She said matter-of-factly. 'Clothes stink!'

I must have looked stunned for she smiled, the world's most radiant smile and motioned for me to follow her again.

Still trying to comprehend the fact that my expensive

all-weather survival gear had been burnt by these simple peasants, I slowly stood up, pulling the rugged blanket tight about me. The floor was made of some kind of matting, I saw. It was only when I stood on it however that I realised just how weak I really was and how hard I had to try not to sway on my feet.

'Drink, come.' The girl motioned again, and with her tightly rolling buttocks beneath the dress as guide, I followed her slim form outside the room, to what appeared to be some kind of large communal room. A table took centre stage on it, strategically placed in front of an open fireplace. A fire was blazing and the room was warm. A large ceramic pitcher stood in the middle of the table, an earthenware glass next to it. But what captivated my attention that first time was the hirsute, naked man at the room's far corner. He was stretched out by one wall with all his garments on the rattan mat floor about him. He was about 5ft 7', and heavily built, with a thick pelt of dark hair down his shoulders and back. His head was covered in unruly, black masses of hair that flew in all directions and his face was half hidden by an unkempt beard.

When I first saw him he had a young woman spreadeagled beneath him. Her clothes, I saw, had been savagely ripped off her. He had one calloused hand clamped tight across her mouth and was busy thrusting away between her spread legs.

He grunted each time he charged at her and with his free hand squeezed and savagely kneaded her left breast.

The woman had her legs spread wide apart. Her feet were planted on the floor on either side of the hairy brute's hips, and as he thrust at her, her knees splayed farther apart with the force of his charging and her eyelids flickered. It was so surreal that it took long moments for my mind to comprehend what my eyes were witnessing. In that time the brute took hold of one of the young woman's shapely legs and pulled it up high so that the back of her thigh was now resting on his shoulder. Having positioned her so, her body in place for deeper penetration, the brute recommenced his efforts.

Each thrust now made the woman make a muffled cry and her unfettered breasts bounced up and down in time to the man's rutting. Their nipples dark and erect featured prominently upon her creamy flesh.

Dazed I looked at my young companion to gauge her reaction, but totally unconcerned, she was already at the table and busy pouring what looked like milk from the pitcher into the earthenware glass. As I looked at her I was only too well aware of the rutting noises made by the man on the floor behind me and the muffled cries of the woman whose body he was so viciously using.

Uncertain as to what I should do or how I should react I took a step towards her.

'Drink,' she motioned the glass towards me, 'llama milk, make you strong again.'

Just then the brute behind me reached his climax with a heaving roar. There were a few moments of complete silence during which I dared not turn around and look, then there was the noise of bodies shifting and the sudden slapping sound of ripe female flesh being smacked.

'Bitch!' I heard the man snarl, 'you liked him looking at you, now we'll
start again, just to tame those wild ways of yours.'

Stunned I turned around just in time to see the brute, turning the slim, beautiful woman over on all fours. I saw his thick, reddened member, glistening from the juices of her body during his recent efforts with her, part the tight, round cheeks of her behind and push itself into the tight, bud of her rear. The man's hands were like claws upon the creamy flesh of her hips. He roughly pulled her towards him, cramming himself inside her, uncaring of
any discomfort he might be causing her. The woman cried out as he invaded her deeply again and began to rock her back and forth upon his member, shoving it in and out of the tight canal

of her anus.

He caught my eye as I watched and without a break in his rhythm, nodded me towards the table near the fire.

'Drink your milk stranger,' he said, 'it'll get cold and you need it warm to help you get your strength back. Chloe will give you some clothes.'

Chloe? I half turned towards the young girl who'd woken me. She was sitting at the table, holding a glass of llama milk, extending it invitingly towards me with both hands.

Behind me, the woman's pained cries were reaching a new height as the man began to truly get into his swing, his hips making a wet, slapping sound every time they met the soft, round cushions of her buttocks.

'What is this place?' I muttered mostly to myself.

'Calimba master. You in Calimba now.' Said the girl whose name I'd just found was Chloe.

Calimba. I didn't know it at the time but I'd fallen off a mountain only to find myself waking up in legend.

***

Chapter 2

If you have never been to Bogota you cannot appreciate the true nature of inequality. The poor eke out an existence, scratching out a living on the surface of a society so opulent that most in the west cannot even begin to imagine it.

It is a rich man's world. Just like the Abba song. Money will get you just about anything and in Bogota you can have just about anything. As a westerner, a skilled westerner at that, I was afforded the kind of treatment which back home I could only have dreamed about.

My four-wheel drive Terrano, Vuitton luggage and expensive suits must, to the eyes of the locals at least, have marked me as one of those rich foreigners who come to their country attracted only by two things: the climate and the women.

Aah, the women. I am convinced that every little girl in Bogota grows up with only one dream, her meal ticket out of that place: to win the glittering tiara of the Miss World contest. Otherwise how else does one explain the sinewy bodies, the swaying hips, the glittering, magnetic eyes with their hidden, electric message, the pouting lips, inviting lusty thoughts and the fulsome, bouncy breasts able to fire up the imagination of a saint even?

The problem of course is that the competition for the beauty title is fierce and the candidates far too many, so failing to win it, they're more than willing to do anything to please the male population of the city, in particular those males with money, and the freedom it buys.

'Mr Meyer, your room.'

I was shown to my hotel room by one of these exotic creatures. She'd led the way as the lift had broken down that day and all the way up three floors I had been treated to the hypnotic movement of her round behind beneath the regulation cream-coloured fabric of her hotel uniform.

I'd noticed, as she went up the stairs, that the smooth, dusky perfection of her long, slim legs was unmarred by stockings, and she wore no panties as there was no revealing panty line every time her dress moulded itself to the comely shape of her ass.

So it was with my imagination fired up that I stood there, surveying the room, eyes scanning the large, inviting bed and breathing in the heady, intoxicating perfume of this heavenly creature I'd spent three flights of steps fantasising about.

It was a hot, bright day outside and the french windows were open to the balcony, but the drapes had been pulled, blocking out the day's glare and creating an intimate gloom that further added to the excitement of my overheated imagination.

'Nice room,' I said and let the two suitcases of luggage I had chivalrously lugged up the steps with me, thud to the floor.

Seemingly unconcerned, unaware of the fire she had started in my brain, the young woman who'd escorted me, crossed the room, those hips swaying, long black hair tossed back with a wave and her proud breasts thrust out, to go and open the drapes.

'No!' I rasped, trying to catch my breath, realising, for the first time and to my horror, that the tightness I felt in my throat, the constriction in my chest, had more to do with the pressure that was beginning to form in my loins than the three flight of steps I'd just climbed. 'Leave them,'

My escort turned round, her face now hidden in the gloom but the surprise evident in her husky voice. 'You don't like?' she asked.

'No, I like the room.' I struggled unsuccessfully to keep my voice even. 'The room's good. I also like the gloom. It's too hot outside.'

'Yes. Always too hot in Bogota senor,' she said and the huskiness of her voice made the tightness in my loins intensify. 'Always too hot,'
We stood now almost facing each other across the room. The bed on my right, and I unconsciously took a step, placing myself directly in her path.

'Anything you want senor, you call. My name's Huanita,' she said, 'I'm in charge of your welfare. Anything at all, let Huanita know.'

'Anything?' I echoed her, suddenly aware how stupid that must have sounded.

'Anything senor,' she assured me and took a few steps closing the distance between us so that I could see her face now, the flawlessly fine features and full lips I had noticed in all the women here, ever since I got off the plane. The high arched eyebrows above luminous, all-seeing eyes. The hypnotic glitter of those eyes.

Unconsciously I let my eyes travel down the slim, smooth pillar of her neck where a simple chain held a white opal in the shape of a tear drop. A cheap trinket which against the dusky smoothness of her skin shone with a brilliance that even the most expensive precious stone could not imitate.

The opalescent rock dangled mischievously above the V-neck of her uniform and drew the gaze to the very top of her deep, proud cleavage. It was with an almost palpable effort that I dragged my eyes back to Huanita's face and felt myself blush a deep red as her lips formed a simple smile.

Now it is possible that it was the smile which tipped the balance. But before you leap into any judgement of my character bear in mind that I had just come off an eight hour flight, I was hot, tired, jet-lagged and disorientated. Alone in a culture I did not understand and surrounded by sights and sounds which I found both oddly repelling and deliciously tempting.

I felt, deep down, that all the way up the steps Huanita had toyed with me, teased me with the suggestive sway of her hips and the tight roll of her ass beneath the short hotel uniform she wore. Women like her, I reasoned, knew only too well the effect they had on men and she played on it, drawing it out, using her luminous eyes and husky voice to further add to my torment.

The way I see it I had little choice.

I reached out and put a strong arm round her slim waist, pulled her roughly against me and was rewarded instantly by a surprised gasp from those, full, felatial lips which I would soon be putting to better uses.

'Senor! What are you doing? No senor!' Huanita tried to protest as I buried my face in the mass of black hair and inhaled deeply of her scent.

I held her easily with one arm, while my free hand, acting almost as if it had a mind of its own dropped down her slim back, reached the hem of her short uniform, took hold of it and with a sudden pull, bunched the fabric up at the small of her back. With her dress pulled up like that, the tight roll of Huanita's bare buttocks was exposed for me to plunder as I willed.

'Senor no!' She tried to voice her protest but I crushed her cries beneath my lips and as she struggled against me I felt her thighs part, her buttocks push against my hand and I cupped one tight roll and roughly squeezed the firm flesh.

'Shut up you little minx!' I hissed as my hand squeezed and kneaded her tight ass, delighting in the feel of her hot young flesh. 'One cry from you and I'll have the Hotel manager know how useless you are and fire you,' I threatened, my desperate sense of desire giving me new heights of inspiration.

It was as if I'd thrown a switch. A cool calculating look came over Huanita's eyes.

'Yes!' I pressed my advantage home, my hand dipping further south, diving into the opening between her legs from behind, finding the hot slit of her snatch.

I hit home. Huanita let out a gasp and her back arched. I worked three fingers in, felt the hot flow of her love juices running freely from her body.

'You are one hot bitch,' I gasped, inwardly marvelling at my own audacity. I worked my fingers in deeper, wriggled them from side to side and Huanita arched her body in response, her pelvis now pressed against me, feeling the tight bulge of my cock through my clothes and her proud breasts, nipples erect and crying out through the thin fabric of her uniform rubbed provocatively against my chest.

It would have taken a true saint to resist; and a saint I am most definitely not.

I dropped my other hand to her waist and pulled desperately at her dress, bunching it up until her mons was revealed. I had been right. Beneath the dress Huanita had not bothered with any underwear.

'On your knees.' I hissed at her and she hesitated, momentarily unsure of herself. But I was all fired up now and intent on having my way. I put a firm hand on top of her glossy haired head and pushed her down and she complied, her eyes suddenly dropping to the floor as she realised that resistance was indeed futile and would probably have bad consequences for her.

'Senor,' she said, her voice husky still, but now barely raised above a whisper. She dropped to her knees in front of me, dress still bunched round her waist. I stood back and admired the line of her thighs, the smooth, flat plain of her belly visible to me and the tiny, line of tight black curls that lay like an exclamation mark above her sex.

I reasoned that Huanita, like most Colombian women, was in the habit of spending her free time on one of Bogota's cosmopolitan beaches wearing the smallest of bikinis and was therefore used to shaving her pubic hair to the tiniest possible line.

Such was the effect of that simple, straight line of pubes that I heard a roar in my ears and I was dimly aware of my hands fumbling with the zipper of my trousers and the next moment I could feel the hot sticky softness of Huanita's accommodating mouth and hear the laboured gasping of her breath as I thrust myself hard down her throat.

'Suck it hard,' I rasped, my own breath coming in short, laboured gasps, as I sawed my erection in and out of her mouth, 'Take it deep.'

Through her gasps and choked moans I reckoned Huanita was enjoying it also. Her sexy, pouting lips, were firmly wrapped round the thickness of my cock and she was making the most debauched, slurping sounds I had ever heard in my life.

My thrusts in Huanita's willing mouth grew harder and deeper. I could feel an electric sensation as her throat constricted at my deep invasion of it. Her lips tightened instinctively round my rod and in no time at all the first solid splash of semen flooded the hot cavern of her mouth.

It caught her totally unprepared and she gasped,

coughed, desperately pulled back to get her breath and the second splash landed across her lips and chin and dripped down to the tops of her breasts.

Normally it would have been enough; this one eruption, but so worked up was I, such was the silky feel of Huanita's hot, willing mouth as she'd sucked my cock that I was far from totally spent.

This, I knew, was only the beginning.

I picked her up roughly under the arms, lifted her to her feet, her eyes dazed, full lips speckled with white from my seed and before she had any time to recover I turned her round and threw her face first onto the bed.

One more cry. A sort of half scream but I was quick. Gave her no time to voice resistance, have any second thoughts. With her dress still pulled up, bunched round her waist, her round behind was bare, vulnerable. Ready for use.

'Senor, please, be gentle. Be gentle,' Huanita gasped between short breaths, but being gentle was far from my mind at that moment.

I placed a heavy hand on the back of her neck and pressed her face against the sheets and with my knee roughly nudged her legs apart, spreading her from behind. The tight slit of her sex opened up for me, its coralled lips aroused, wet already from my handling of her hot little sex.

'I'm gonna make you beg for more,' I rasped and taking aim I threw my entire weight on her unprotected rear.

The sweet entrance to her sex was framed by one of the prettiest little asses I had ever had the pleasure of seeing bared. I parted the lips of her vulva easily, slid deep inside her until I could almost feel her womb and Huanita let out a high pitched cry in response.

'Bitch! Don't tell me you don't do this all the time!' I hissed in her ear as I started pumping viciously, driving my hips against her, feeling the hot, tight cushion of her ass against my pelvis every time I ground myself into her.

She tried to say something but it came out muffled by the sheets and I wasn't listening anyway. My whole mind was concentrated on the silky feel of her hot sex and the tightness of her cunt as I rammed myself into her as deep as I could.

To my tired mind, disorientated, jet-lagged and now firmly in the grip of passion, my brutal thrusts took on an almost otherworldly dimension where Huanita's tight sex became a channel to another world and my ramming cock the battering ram that was trying to breach the gates.

The silkiness of the compliant female body spread beneath me worked its magic. There was a white flash behind my eyelids and my whole body went rigid. An orgasm like no other ripped through me and I felt hot, sticky semen begin to fill Huanita's love canal.

Slowly I came back down to Earth. Momentarily I was horrified by my behaviour, but I say only momentarily for one look at Huanita's placid features left me to no doubt as to her enjoyment of the rough use I had just made of her body.

I pulled myself out of her and dragged myself onto the bed. Huanita lay beside me, making no attempt to cover herself.

'Senor,' she said, 'I am your slave.'

'I don't need any slaves,' I murmured.

'Senor, a man like you always needs a slave,' she said, 'man like you should go to Calimba. There many slaves. Do exactly as you ask of them and you be satisfied beyond your wildest desires.'

'What's Calimba?' I asked, but that time Huanita clammed up and would not be drawn on the subject. And though I used her again that day, made her kneel and swallow a mouthful of semen before I undressed her completely and spread her beneath me and fucked her hard until she cried out in total surrender, she said no more about Calimba.

When I dozed off that night, mind and body hovering near exhaustion and one leg thrown casually across Huanita's freshly used body, it was of this strange place that I dreamt. A place which my mind filled with glittering towers and lofty hills. A place populated by willing slavegirls ready to do anything a man ordered them to. A place where I could be king without even trying.

Chapter 3

The Chinese have a curse. It goes like this: 'May all your wishes come true'. While I spent my days in Bogota, struggling with the wretched city's labyrinthine laws regarding TV transmission towers and slots of air-time, I spent my nights prowling its streets, finding women whom I could take to my hotel and fuck for hours, and all the time, during unguarded moments, my thoughts would return Huanita's haunting words about Calimba.

Make no mistake now. I could have easily forced the answer from her if that's what I had wished to do. Already, by then, I had come to realise that Colombian women, their entrancing beauty notwithstanding, liked to be dominated. In a short time I had become, in many respects Huanita's master. Her hot, exotic body and obliging mouth mine to do with whatever I wished.

This was my first time in such an exotic culture however. And though I immensely enjoyed the sexual favours I could force Huanita to give me, I was no rake. On account of these two reasons alone, I chose not to make her tell me any more than she wanted to.

Whether her first mention of it had been a slip caused by an unguarded moment or she suddenly decided to test me to see just how far I could go on subjugating her to my will, just as I regularly subjugated her body to the servicing of my more physical needs, Huanita never again brought up the name of this strange city.

So, deep in my thoughts the half-formed image of

Calimba took root and grew and, as so often happens with these things, it started to develop into a half-formed wish. An unconscious, fuzzy image of a legendary, hidden city populated by the world's most compliant beauties. A city which was ruled by me. The thought was never fully articulated. Never did conscious words pass my lips. Nor do I actively recall mentioning it to anybody at the time. But the Chinese say the gods have ways of learning our most hidden thoughts and then, perversely perhaps, acting on them just to tease us.

This was what crossed my mind as I followed Chloe's slim back and suggestively swaying hips out of the long, low room where that brute was still busy using the comely woman, her cries and his heaving grunts fading with each step we took.

'Wait,' I said to Chloe's back but my words were low, weak and lacked the power to yet arrest her. 'Who was that? What was he doing there?'

She walked on, gesturing with one hand over her shoulder towards me. I padded softly behind her, my sense of disorientation increasing by the second.

'The man,' I persisted. 'Who is he? Tell me who he is!'

'HeÖMatthew,' said the girl in a barely audible voice. I stopped dead in my tracks. 'Matthew?' I said to myself, trying to make sense of the very ordinary name and the brutish, primitive appearance and behaviour of the man. 'What kind of name is Matthew?'

As if sensing my confusion and growing sense of inner turmoil Chloe stopped and half turned towards me and such was the impact of her beauty, the sheer force of the finely etched, elfin features of her face, that the extremis of my situation aside, I was still able to admire the perfect profile of her face and then, drop my gaze to drink in the tight swell of her young breasts as they pushed against the restraints of the cheap, thin dress she wore.

'HeÖ' she said and paused as if searching for just the

right word to make an evident stranger to her world understand, 'heÖthe Master's sonÖhe a satyr.'
And with that she turned, beckoned and once more commenced her glide towards wherever she would magically produce clothes for me from.

'A satyr?' I gasped uncomprehendingly. 'A satyr? What the hell is a satyr?'
We were by then in a long corridor, stone walls on either side, drab but smooth and a low ceiling overhead that somehow made me feel claustrophobic. It was this sense of being hemmed in from all sides that added to my disorientation and made my brain go numb and my heart beat louder in my chest.

'Wait!' I said to Chloe's receding back, 'wait!' Dimly, I was aware that I was hyperventilating. 'WAIT!'

Startled by my shout she stopped and turned. Her liquid, tawny eyes, golden like a lion's locked onto mine with a heart-stopping clarity and I found the very air around me being sucked away.

I felt then that if I did not make some kind of noise. Did not externalise my confusion and seek some answers I would forever lose every sense of who and what I was.

'What,' I said, enunciating each word slowly and clearly, 'is a satyr?'

So engrossed was I in what was happening to me, so intense was the effort required to keep me from losing the focus of myself that I had totally failed to register the low thrumming of drums, the rhythmic almost chanting of many mouths. I took two more steps towards Chloe, who now stood still - facing me, and the answer to my question became evident to me.

To my right was a door. A perfectly rectangular opening cut into the drab stone wall. Beyond it stretched a chamber, perfectly square as far as I could tell, with walls and floor covered by lush carpets. Half-hidden drummers in the shadows moved in almost perfect unison, their rhythmic movements producing a low, reverberating sound like a giant's heartbeat. These things I registered almost immediately. The new-found clarity they induced forced my mind to function again and there, inside the room I saw a tangle of human bodies. Men and women.

More men than women.

The men were of all shapes and sizes. Some thin, with arms and legs that made them look almost like stick-figures in the dancing light of the huge fire that was the room's only illumination. Others were fat, corpulent, with big hairy bellies and legs like tree trunks. All of them were hairy. They sported the same brutish, hirsute look I'd seen in the beastman who'd savagely brutalised the beautiful woman in the room I'd first woken up in.

They were all naked.

The women were beautiful. Fantastically so.

From where I stood I could see half a dozen or so of them. They had firm, golden bodies of polished alabaster. Pert, jiggling breasts and taut backsides. Their eyes were wide in supplication and low moans escaped them whenever it was possible.

I knew there were more men than women in that room because there was not a single woman in there who was not getting two or even three of her orifices plugged at the same time. There were precious few of them who did not have their mouths fully gorged with some beastman's throbbing member. As I watched, trying to take it all in, my eyes alighted upon one particular beauty who was being positioned very precisely by a shaggy-bellied man beneath her. Her firm, golden thighs were spread on either side of the man's prone body and from the expression on her face I could tell the precise moment he pushed her down, his hands like claws upon her hips, and forced the lips of her honey-liquid centre to part for him to enter her. Simultaneously another one of his cohorts was bearing down upon her from behind. His penis erect, thin, but incredibly long, like a probe, was being thrust back and forth in the woman's anal passage. As the two men worked her in unison the woman's hips rocked back and forth and her full, round breasts jiggled with each assault. Her eyes were wide, with shock and she would probably have moaned out loud at this rough use she was being subjected to. The reason she couldn't was that yet a third beastman stood with his feet astride the head of the first one. This one had wrapped a firm hand in the woman's thick, black mass of hair and he was busy pulling her head forcefully forward, her lips firmly wrapped round the thickest penis I'd ever seen. Saliva, mixed with semen dribbled out of the corners of the woman's stretched mouth and ran down her chin.

'ThemÖmen. Them satyrs,' said a low husky voce by my side and I had to force my eyes away from what was happening to see who the speaker was. Chloe had moved silently to stand by my side. Her head, I noticed, barely made it to my shoulder and her body was only an inch away from mine so that I could feel the heat it exuded on my naked flesh. I was glad then of the rough blanket I had haphazardly wrapped round me as my body responded to the animal sounds I could hear coming from the room where all those beautiful women were being ravished, and the proximity of Chloe's nubile body.

'Satyrs?' I repeated trying desperately to guide my brain upon saner shores.

'Them have women. All women. When they want.'

'I see,' I said, but I didn't and I didn't care. Right then, at that moment I knew that my sanity, if nothing else, would depend upon the speed with which I discovered exactly what kind of place I had woken up in.

'Whenever they want?' I asked.

'Yes,' Chloe nodded vigorously her eyes all lit up by the mere fact that I caught on so quickly.

Standing so close to her I could not help but notice that the sight and sounds of all those women being roughly taken by the men had also affected her. Her chest was rising rapidly up and down, pushing hard against the cheap, thin fabric constricting it and her nipples had hardened. Their puckered tips, like hard, round buttons made perfect indentations which threatened to push through the thin material of her dress.

'Satyrs have all women. They warriors.' Chloe said and there was a dreamy look in her eyes that I found strangely unsettling, not least because the image of a naked Chloe tied-up and spread-eagled, being taken by two or three men had sprung into my head. The pounding in my temples had now travelled further down, to that place between my legs and the roughness of the blanket was only aggravating my situation.

'Clothes,' I said desperately dragging my eyes from Chloe's erect nipples to the liquid golden eyes with their dreamy look.

'Huh?' she looked genuinely puzzled for a moment or two.

'Clothes,' I said, 'you were taking me to get some clothes.'

'YesÖof course,' she said and turning abruptly on her heels she resumed her effortless glide. This time I was much closer to her than before. Much closer. So I was able to see the slight darkening of her skin behind her ears and down the slim, perfectly formed column of her neck. And it was not my imagination that the insouciant swing of her hips was now deliberately exaggerated and served only to fuel a need that was beginning to light up at the base of my stomach.

Satyrs! Chloe's swaying hips and blushing neck led me to the end of that corridor of sin, past other doorways which were hermetically shut, giving no hints of light or sound as to what might lie beyond them. We passed through a number of rooms which registered in my bewildered mind as practically identical and stopped, finally, in front of an arched wooden door.

'We're here.' Chloe said and motioned with her arm for me to enter first.

'What's here?' I asked suspiciously. Her nipples, I couldn't help noticing, were no longer erect, still it was hard to disguise the exuberance of that young bosom.

'Clothes,' she said with a simple tone and motioned again towards the door. 'Go in.'

Fearing a trap, or some trick at least, I gingerly pushed the heavy wooden door open. It swung silently on well oiled hinges and I was in a bare room with a concrete floor and two full length mirrors opposite each other. The walls of the room were lined with shelves and upon them were bales of fabric. All different colours.

'Clothes,' Chloe breathed behind me.

'No, not quite,' I said and took a couple steps into the room. 'It's a start though,'

The door slammed shut behind me with a bang that made me jump. I whirled round and ran to it but there was no visible way of opening it from the inside that I could see. Experimentally I tested it with my hand. It was securely locked.

'Great,' I murmured to myself and ran a tired hand over my face.

Having nothing else to do I walked back towards the centre of the room. Natural light was flooding in from a skylight high up in the centre of the ceiling. Feeling my heart begin to flip and jump in its ribcage I let my eyes follow the rise of wooden shelves up the wall to the point where they stopped, a good nine feet from the ceiling and a jump of at least twice that towards the skylight.

If this was a test, I thought, to see if anyone could get out it was obviously meant to test angels, for without wings it was impossible to reach that skylight overhead. Just then I caught sight of my own reflection in the mirror to my right and stopped. The man facing me was bruised, with a dark weal above one eye and lacerations down one cheek. Gaunt and red-eyed. Thinner than I'd ever remembered him and dressed in the roughest blanket imaginable.

In disgust I let the blanket fall from my shoulders, suddenly aware how much colder this room was than any of the others I'd been in so far. 'What place is this?' I yelled up towards the skylight and echoes of my own voice were thrown back at me by the bare stone walls. 'Calimba!' I yelled tasting the strange name upon my lips. 'Calimba!'

'This is where we are.'

The voice, so soft, so sudden, made me jump again and turn around.

Behind me, with her back pressed against the door which had now shut again, stood a raven haired woman. She was dressed in flowing white sheets of what looked like satin that were tied to her person in a way I could not fathom. The twirls of satin fell open here and there, affording a tantalising glimpse of the smoothness of one shoulder, the top of the swell of one creamy breast and the thrilling curve of a ripe thigh. The woman's hair fell in an untidy curly mass to her shoulders in such a way that it added to the allure of the full lips and slightly slanted eyes of the half caste. Her eyes, I noticed, were fixed pointedly at my middle. I then became aware of my own nudity and my first reaction, as a European, was to quickly bring both hands in front, cupping my scrotum and hanging penis in a vain attempt to preserve my modesty. But before I could complete the motion I saw the amusement flicker in the dusky woman's eyes, felt a strange recklessness seize me, and I stopped myself.

If my action surprised her, she gave no indication, for next her eyes took in the lean muscle on my body and the telltale bruising on my face, thighs and chest, evidence of my fall in the blizzard.

'You must be the blow-in,' she said in English and I detected a slight French accent in her voice.

'Blow-in?'

'Not many of you these days. You should be honoured.' She added.

'And you are?'

'The seamstress. You need new clothes,' she indicated my nudity and I couldn't help but smile.

'I had clothes,'

'Blow-in clothes,' she said and moved towards me, the flowing fabric she was dressed in rearranging itself on her body so that I caught a brief glimpse of the fullness of one round breast, before it disappeared, then saw a glimmer of a flat, smooth belly and the fabric parted as she walked to show me the outside line of one perfectly formed leg all the way up to the hip.

Underwear was obviously one item of clothing no one seemed to put much stock in, here in Calimba.

'You are in Calimba now. Those who come here are reborn.'

'How so?' I asked.

'This place does not exist,' said the woman in all seriousness. She had closed the gap between us and now stood inches away from me, looking up. 'Calimba is only a legend told by grandmothers to their young daughters in the poor villages of Colombia senor,'

The way she said senor reminded me of Huanita. Sweet, obliging Huanita, now as good as a world away.

'But here we are.'

'Exactly senor. Here we are. You have been fortunate to survive a blizzard. It may well be that the old gods want you here, but your clothes, everything that belongs to the outside is not welcome in Calimba. Such items are destroyed.'

'Right,' I said. 'So you're here to make me new clothes?'

'Yes senor,' she smiled sweetly, and throwing her arms wide to encompass the bales of fabric in the room she said: 'choose!'

I took in the way her breasts jiggled with the movement of her arms, and then, because I was naked and now could not afford to show weakness by becoming aroused once again, I quickly followed the movement of her arms to the walls and took in the fabric I could choose from.

'I don't know much about fabric,' I said trying not to

notice the glimpses of bare flesh that were shown me every time the woman moved. 'Why don't you make the choice for me?'

'What colour would you like senor?' she asked and her voice had perceptibly softened.

I turned my eyes back upon her and saw the beaming smile on her face. The pride, I guessed, at my putting so much trust on her.

'White,' I said, 'I always fancied something white.'

'White it is then senor,' and with a confident stride that highlighted the tight roll of her buttocks beneath the flowing material that covered her hips, she walked over to a shelf, reached up on tip-toe and picked a bale of a cream-coloured fabric off it.

'Almost white. More practical senor,' she explained and I nodded.

'Almost white then,' I said. 'How are we going to do this?'

'Do what senor?'

'My new suit,'

'Suit?' she almost laughed, 'no senor, suits are blow-in clothes. In Calimba we wear other things.'

'What kind of other things?'

'You will see senor,' she said huskily and dropped the cloth at my feet. 'First however, we need to measure you a little.'

With that she produced a metre long tape measure from a hidden fold of her ethereal dress and dropped to her knees in front of me. I was left contemplating the top of her dark, curly hair.

Over the years that have passed since, I have thought about this one moment a thousand times. Had I acted differently. Had the woman behaved in a different manner, it is possible, I suppose, that things would have taken a different turn.

I didn't. She didn't. And, evidently, they didn't. So, why analyse? Mainly because I feel that I, above all else, need to understand. I need to be able to stand back and pinpoint the exact moment in time the old place worked its ancient spell upon me and stripped me of the inhibitions which marked me as a European.

It may well be that I'm wrong. It may well be that this wasn't the moment. It could be argued, I guess, that the point of no return was passed the moment I left the safety of my Jeep and, alone and without telling anybody, set to testing myself against the unforgiving mountains of Colombia.

If that is really the case. If that's when I fell from grace, literally, as well as figuratively, it did not make itself felt until the dark-haired, half-caste woman with the sensuous lips and hypnotic eyes knelt in front of me and her fingers lightly touched my inner thigh as she measured the length of my leg. Such was the electricity of her touch that I was not even aware of becoming aroused. One moment I was there, hands held protectively in front of my manhood, shielding whatever little modesty I had left and the next I had savagely grabbed the kneeling woman by the hair, had forced her head back so that her full, lips were in direct line with my erection and, in a moment of blind passion, had brutally buried my cock to the back of her throat.

'Suck it bitch!' I hissed as I started working my hips against her mouth.

I caught her by surprise. Her eyes widened. Her mouth opened to cry out. But such was the force of my thrust that it choked her cries before they were formed and blew her cheeks out as she struggled to draw in her breath.

'Don't tell me you haven't done this before?' I gasped feeling the unwilling but nevertheless obliging suck of the woman's hot mouth, the velvety grasp of her lips as the glistening length of my cock slid in and out of the hot, wet, prison of her mouth.

With each thrust my hips pushed my cock in so hard that its bulbous head, swollen to bursting point with lust, lodged deep in the back of the woman's throat and caused her to cough and splutter. Her hands came up, imploring me to stop, but I slapped them cruelly away, caught up as I was in the sensations she was producing in me as I crudely mouth-fucked her. Saliva, mixed with pre-come juices soon coated those libidinous, inviting lips and dribbled down the woman's smooth chin to stain the very top of the white tunic covering her full, round breasts. The half-choking sounds she made as I pumped myself into her mouth, served to only arouse me further so that as I rode the crest of my passion I pulled out of her mouth with a sudden, wet, plopping sound and held my member so that the first splash of thick, creamy semen was on the woman's upturned, unprotected face. She took the first burst full on and flinched and cried out; her mouth at last uncrammed. She instinctively turned sideways so that my second burst caught her hair. She tried to get to her feet as my third splashed on her shoulder and the side of her dress.

This show of fear, the flight response, goaded the maddened beast in me so much that I took one quick step forward, closed the gap which had developed between us, and seizing her by her lush hair once more, I half spun her so that she gasped and fell face down on the floor.

She tried then to wriggle away, all too aware that at that moment in time I could not be reasoned with and her only hope of escape was to run. But I was too quick for her.

With one quick leap I was astride her, my hands grabbed handfuls of her thin, white dress and pulled them away. I heard the fabric rip and gleams of honey coloured woman flesh were revealed underneath.

'I haven't finished yet, you minx,' I heard a tight, throaty voice I had trouble recognising as mine, say. 'You have yet to pleasure me in full.'

'Master no!' she pleaded, but her pleas were falling on deaf ears.

With a few more pulls of her thin, wispy clothes I succeeded in baring her back and buttocks. Underneath her wispy dress, I discovered with growing delight, she was totally naked.

The sight of her plump, woman's buttocks, defenceless and raised for me to raid fuelled the blaze of my lust until its heat reached new heights. Holding her tightly by the hair, I ran an exploring hand down the deep cleft of her spine, followed the curves of her smooth, slim back until my hand was resting on her buttocks.

'A nice piece of ass,' I said through teeth clenched with unspent passion. My hand moulded a tight, round buttock and I experimentally squeezed. The flesh was full, young and almost rubbery in its tautness.

'The kind of ass that begs for spanking,' I said and brought my hand down in a full swing giving the woman a satisfying slap on her ass. She cried out in response and her body shook, surrounded still by the torn remnants of her dress, exposed like an exotic flower framed by its white petals. Her buttocks shook with the force of the blow and went a deeper tan.

'I bet you've been servicing these heathens too,' I growled, beyond almost any kind of control, my mind suddenly fuelled by vivid images of this delicious woman being spread by some hirsute brute, her mouth and cunt penetrated, her face and breasts used for target practice by the spurts of these mountain satyrs. The tight lips of her anus spread to take some beastman's length.

'Master please!' she begged this time, but her voice lacked all conviction and her body now had stopped struggling entirely, betraying the pleasure she had received by my rough treatment of her flesh. I let my hand drop further south, until my fingers rested on the inside of her left thigh and momentarily I savoured, warm, incredibly silky woman flesh. Then the madness of lust returned in me with a vengeance and I pulled at her inner thighs until her legs fell apart.

There were tiny black tufts framing the open portals of her cunt. The soft pink insides framed by the darker-skinned coral-lips of her womanhood, parted sufficiently to reveal the glistening depths of paradise, evidence, if any were needed, of

her arousal.
With a vault, like a spasm almost, I leapt atop her and drove my knee hard between her legs so that I made her cry out. My fingers taloned cruelly at her slim hips as I raised her off the floor, on all fours. I would normally have penetrated her. Fucked her senseless from behind. Such however was the sudden urge, or better still, craving, to utterly dominate her that I didn't.

Instead, I dropped one hand down and seized the iron bar that seemed to have sprung up from between my legs, raised it slightly and spat upon it to lubricate it. With that I took aim, going for the tight rim of her anus, and with a forceful grunt plunged myself to the hilt up her rear passage. The woman's head shot back. Her back arched and she cried out.
Oblivious to any pain she may have been feeling I concentrated on working myself in and out of her ass in an effortless glide. Each time I thrust forward with all my weight I felt the depths of her rear passage open and each time the woman's head would shoot back and a guttural cry of passion would be wrenched from her lips. The very same, ripe, lips that moments earlier had been wrapped round the girth of my shaft.

As I worked myself in and out of the ripe, hot body on all fours in front of me, I let my right hand wander. I felt the smooth, round hips, the small tufty curls of the woman's pubic hair. My hand found and started rubbing the open lips of her womanhood. I could feel her juices coating my palm as I worked my hand roughly back and forth, and then I slid that same hand, wet still from her secreted juices, up the smooth flatness of her stomach, past her ribcage to her breasts. There I cupped and squeezed the exquisitely full mounds, roughly kneaded her flesh, deriving as much joy from her added cries at this fresh assault upon her, as from the feel of the taut, full mounds I was so easily plundering. Finally my efforts became too much even for me to bear and for the second time in less than fifteen minutes my hips shot involuntarily forward and my head arched back as jagged bolts of white lightning exploded behind my eyelids.

'Bravo!'

The sound of another man's voice brought me back to my senses.

'What a performance!' said the male voice and there was the sound of a single man clapping. 'What a maestro! What a magnificent beast!'

The clapping continued.

I tried to refocus my gaze, gather my thoughts. I was still buried deep inside the woman's rear. Her back canal filled to the brim with hot semen. The man I saw was a half-naked hirsute brute. He was squat, easily as wide as he was tall, with heavily muscled shoulders and a slightly bulging belly and legs so muscular that they looked deformed.

He instantly reminded me of a gargoyle and the leisurely manner in which he was approaching me, not to mention the cultured accent of his voice and the almost accentless quality of his English told me that here was no brute, first appearances notwithstanding, and that therefore I was in no immediate danger.

With a jerk, I extricated myself from the girl's anus. She let out a little yelp and collapsed on her side in front of me, her arms and legs curling up.

'You seem to have done for poor Maria here,' said the man.

He'd stopped clapping by now and as I focused my gaze on him he took several more steps until he was fully inside the room and then leant jauntily against the nearest wall.

'One quick measure with Maria here and before you know it. Bang! You get it!' he said and clapped once or twice more.

'Who are you?' I finally asked.

'Ha!' the stranger laughed. 'Who am I? A good one indeed. Still, I forgive you. You must be bewildered, though, evidently,' he indicated the prostrated naked body of the woman I'd just had, 'your strength is rapidly coming back. Good. That is good. Tonight we dine with my father. He'll be waiting.'

Nothing of what he had said to me made a lot of sense but I was willing to go with the flow. 'WaitingÖ? Your father?' I asked.

The stranger must have sensed the genuine air of puzzlement in my voice for he stopped and peered at me. 'Didn't Chloe tell you?' he asked.

'Tell me what?'

'My father - he isÖThe Master.'

Chapter 4

'My name, by the way, is Matthew,' said my hirsute companion and extended one huge paw towards me. Reluctantly I reciprocated. His hand felt dry and hot in mine, but his handshake was firm, curt and somehow formal.

Everything here was at odds, I thought. A transparent patina of modernity seemed to overlay what, to all intents and purposes, was a city firmly anchored in Colombia's legendary past.

'Andy,' I said and released the brute's hand.

AndyÖ' he savoured the word for a moment, then his eyes were lit by a mischievous light. 'Andy Meyer.' He saw the surprise on my face and forestalled my question. 'I read it in your passport. After we found you and before your clothes were burnt.'

'My passport?' I asked heart beating fast once more. Without it I knew I would have a hard time getting out of Colombia.

'Burnt also,' said Matthew matter of factly.

This fact did more to reveal the gravity of my situation

than what I was to subsequently discover. I knew instantly that I was dealing with people who were not what they seemed, lived an exotic existence in a legendary city and considered themselves beyond any law apart from their own. Given the state I was in at the time it was an astute observation for it soon turned out that my instant assessment of my predicament was a lot more accurate than I would have wished it to be.

'We can always get you another one Andy, at any time,' said Matthew, 'thoughÖ' he paused, 'whether that will be necessary is entirely up to you.'

I wanted desperately to scream. To seize him then by his long, matted hair and ask him what he meant by that. But the way he carried his bulk left me in no doubt of his ability to meet any physical threat I could pose. Instead, I decided, my best bet would be to wait; to use my cunning and intelligence to beat whatever odds were stacked against me here.

'However Andy, here's me talking, forgetting my manners.' He clicked his fingers then once and Maria stirred for the first time from the floor, since the beastman entered. 'Get this man's clothes quickly. He must be ready for tonight.'

'Yes Master,' she said, gathering the torn remnants of her clothes around her. Her lips I noticed had a raw, red look about them and on the upper slopes of her breasts welts had been raised where I'd brutally mauled her tender flesh. All the while, as she listened to Matthew issuing orders she kept her eyes riveted to the floor by our feet. An act of submission, which I must admit, coupled with the state of extreme dishabille she was now in, made her all the more alluring to me. I felt a little ashamed then, for my behaviour. But with this sense of shame also came an awareness that I was now in some real danger and this lit a slow-burning anger in my breast.

'What's going to happen tonight?' I asked Matthew.

He took my elbow and gently led me towards the now open doorway. 'Later, I shall explain all later Andy, I promise,' he said, 'for now however we must welcome you properly. A man like you, one whom the storm gods decided to spare, must not be left with poor offerings like Maria back there,' he motioned with a thumb over his shoulder. 'What you need is a real workout, one that'll tax your imagination as well as your body.'

'I could do with some rest,' I said.

Matthew stopped and looked at me, his eyes narrowing. 'Rest, of course. Before tonight. You'll need it anyway. But for now follow me. I want to show you something.'

He led me through corridors so narrow he could barely squeeze his bulk in and down passageways wide enough to hold parades in. He talked as we walked.

'Calimba, as you appreciate is very old. Older than most people think. It appears in Colombian mythology as early as the 10th century. It is mentioned then that it was a self-sufficient city trading on wisdom and rare substances with the kingdoms and principalities around it. To protect itself it relied on its remote location, known to few and its group of special warriors.'

'Warriors?' I asked, I remembered dimly that Chloe had mentioned something about warriors but I could not recollect what exactly.

'You've been around a little Andy,' Matthew said to me, 'you know as well as I that nothing survives in this world for long without protection of some kind. Whether that protection comes from having a strong deterrent, a powerful army or belonging to a special group. Whether we talk about a nation, a company or an individual, the argument is the same. If you are different, you need protection more than those who belong to the pack.'

He was, I realised, explaining something of the philosophy of the city. I listened in fascination half-repulsed and half-attracted by this odd combination of outwardly cultivated bestiality and inner sophistication which Matthew exhibited.

'Calimba of course is no different. There are forces out there which tolerate our existence only because of the essential service we provide.'

'What service is that?'

'Don't interrupt now Andy,' Matthew bared his teeth at me in a leer, 'just listen. There are far too many things to take in immediately and at any rate some you will need to find out for yourself.' He turned down yet another corridor and came to a stop before a beautifully carved and decorated pine door. The door itself was more like a portal. There were two halves adorned by wrought iron figurines of men and women coupling furiously in just about any possible position imaginable.

'The Master himself will explain some of it tonight, I am sure and you will get to hear the rest. For now though, you need both some rest and some recreation and I think I might just join you on the latter.' With those words he pushed open the two halves of the portal and led the way in.

Unlike my previous experience, this time the door shut slowly behind us. There were handles on the inside which I tested there and then. It was open.

'Trust Andy, trust,' Matthew chuckled beside me.

The room we were in was well lit and spacious. Skylights along one side of the ceiling let in a lot of natural light and a huge fireplace provided plenty of warmth. The floor was covered with soft rugs which my bare feet sank into and the walls had been painted in a pleasant lilac colour which was soft on the eye. Exotic plants here and there completed the dÈcor.

All this I took in at a glance for what caught and instantly held my attention was the suspended girl in the middle of the room.

She had shoulder length, straight black hair which partially fell over her face and a lightly coloured skin. She was dressed in a floral print dress of white with yellow flowers on it which came down to her knees. Her hands were handcuffed. The handcuffs were attached to a rope coming down from a pulley mounted in the ceiling. The rope, I saw, had been pulled taut so that the girl's body was stretched to its limit, her arms held high above her head and her feet up on tip-toes.

'Her name is Layla,' said Matthew studying me carefully, 'she's to be our entertainment before our siesta.'

Whether she heard him or not the girl gave no indication. She remained pretty much as immobile as she had been when we first entered the room. Matthew's assumptions about me. His jaunty air, only served to further fuel my anger.

'Thanks,' I said, 'but I only need to sleep.'

'Relax Andy,' he gave an easy chuckle, 'this isn't a test. Nor do I really care if you decide to avail yourself of Layla or not, but I'll tell you something about sex. It's a kind of gestalt thing. It springs not of who you are but of what you are. The use you made of Maria back then when she was trying to take your measurements, that wasn't Andy Meyer, TV executive, but a male reacting to the proximity of an attractive woman. It was instinctive though. Unplanned. To use someone in that fashion consciously, in full control of your faculties and still derive pleasure from the fact, that, Andy, that requires a certain amount of finesse and self-knowledge.' He stopped then and waited for me to respond.

I must admit I was intrigued. Vile as he was to look at, this Matthew made a lot of sense. My plan to use my cunning to beat whatever was coming to test me, resurfaced then and I made a show of considering what he'd said.

'Are you saying she's mine?' I asked indicating the suspended body of the chocolate coloured girl.

'For this moment. Layla really belongs to no one. She's communal property. Sport for whoever feels like it.'

I tried to comprehend that. A human being casually submitting to such a fate. The more I looked at the inert, helpless form of the girl however the more I was beginning to come round to the idea and my wretched body, naked as it was, betrayed all too easily the direction my thoughts were taking.

'Aah Andy, you're beginning to see the possibilities,' said Matthew with a hint of amusement, his eyes taking in the beginnings of tumescence in the treacherous piece of flesh between my legs.

I took a few steps into the centre of the room and came to stand directly behind the girl. 'I can do anything I like to her?'

'Pretty much. The trick is that with so many possibilities open it requires an inventive mind to show true appreciation,' said Matthew as he moved to join me.

We were both left admiring the slim, taut line of the girl's body. The dress she had on hugged her figure, so that as we stood behind her we could follow the straight line of her back, down to the nipped-in waist and the inviting flare of her hips. Experimentally I put my hands on those hips. Her body felt hot, resilient to my touch. I slipped my hands further down, feeling the promise of her thighs and then touched the bare flesh of her calf, just below the knee, where the dress ended.

'Layla is like a flower whose petals need to be opened,' said Matthew behind me.

Entranced by the possibilities within my grasp I slowly raised Layla's dress, revealing shapely calves, full-fleshed, curvy thighs. The dress was tight and I had to use both hands to work it up my heart hammering all the while as I reached the very tops of her thighs and saw the beginning of the secret place between them. There was the white wedge of lace panties and then, as I worked the dress up round her waist and bunched it over the small of her back, the full glory of her round ass was bared for us to see. The lace thong of her panties had worked its way into the deep valley between the full cheeks of her behind.

'She's a work of art,' Matthew said in appreciation echoing my own thoughts. 'To be savoured, not devoured.'

Layla had a peachy, round ass. Each cheek stood full and proud. It was the kind of ass that invited special attention. I ran a hand over the surface of one smooth, round buttock revelling in the feel of its softness and for the first time there was a response from the girl.

Layla's head shot up. Her body tensed a little.

'Aaahh, she knows what's coming,' smiled Matthew. He moved in beside me, his big paw reached out to cup and squeeze one buttock, his fingers wormed their way to the place nestled in the juncture of her thighs and covered by the white wedge of lace. I watched transfixed as those fingers wriggled beneath the edge of Layla's lace panties and found their mark. A low moan came from the girl.

'She speaks,' said Matthew.

He withdrew his fingers slowly, leaving a telltale trail of woman juice on the smooth, chocolate-brown flesh.

'I think she's ready for us Andy,' he said and with that he loosened the strings holding the coarse material round his waist. The garment he wore fell away to reveal an erect manhood of truly monstrous proportions.

'We need to undress her,' Matthew pointed out oblivious to the fact of his erection.

He indicated a low table I had missed, to our left. Arrayed upon it were a number of implements I found interesting: A folded flick-knife, a couple of black dildos, their tips wickedly curved and gleaming. A long, thin whip.

'Take your pick,'

Painfully aware of the throbbing of my own erect member I walked over to the low table, bent down and picked up the folded flick knife. There was a button on the handle and as I pressed it four inches of gleaming steel shot out from the handle. I hefted its weight, testing it. Then, with it in one hand, I walked back behind Layla and seizing hold of her tight dress I pressed the gleaming edge of the flick knife against it. The sharpened blade went through the fabric without resistance and within moments I had pulled it down to the level of her ass, slicing the girl's dress in half. The two pieces fell away from her and she turned her head this way and that, the jet black hair flicking about as she tried to see what we were about to do to her. Under the dress she wore a white, lace bra that matched her panties.

I walked now in front of her. For the first time I saw her face. She couldn't have been more than nineteen, with black eyes, open wide and swimming in apprehension. She had the broad flat features of the African and a pair of lips which immediately made my mind go dreamy as I imagined them being wrapped round my cock.

I took hold of her dress from the front and tugged. It came away from her body, held only by the elbow-length sleeves round her arms, which I had to cut away. When I had finished Layla's body stood revealed. She had full, round breasts with very, dark, hard nipples, their tips erect with apprehension at what was about to befall her. The round mounds of her breasts vanished in the low-cut lace cups of her bra and the darkened tips of her nipples made a clearly visible outline against the skimpy undergarment. The bra was too low-cut for the exuberance of her bosom and I let my fingers taste the firmness of her breasts as I cupped and squeezed each mound through the lace. I then let my gaze travel down the length of her flat stomach to the flare of her hips. From the front I could see that she'd been shaven. Her sex depilated so that as the lace panties moulded her flesh, the raised lips of her labia were clearly visible to me.

'Spread yourself,' I ordered her and watched as she obediently moved her feet, balancing on the very tips of her toes to comply. With her body offered thus, I repeated the process with the knife until her underwear was cut away and lay in tatters on the floor about her feet. Then I put the flick knife back on the low table and turned towards the helpless, ripe body that was mine to use.

'You put it to her first Andy,' said Matthew and indicated the defenceless opening of the girl's body from behind.

Without my noticing him he had, I realised, made his way over to the low table and picked up a thick, black dildo. He now moved to the front of the helpless girl and his eyes took in her charms. He then shoved the dildo all the way into the girl's mouth. She made a gagging, half-choking noise and her body stiffened. Impossibly she rose even higher on her toes, her slim, back arching, the taut twin moons of her buttocks tightening in response and that's when I chose to bend my knees, aligning myself carefully with the inviting opening of her body and with a quick thrust bury my penis to the hilt inside her.

The shock of my invasion of her, wrenched a muffled cry from her lips which made Matthew chuckle. As I pumped against her straining body with all my strength, Matthew took hold of the girl's full breasts and started kneading them crudely, squeezing and mauling the full, young flesh, twisting and biting the dark coral tips of her nipples.

'Pain, Andy,' he gasped between suckling and licking the full, brown mounds. 'Pain is an extension of pleasure. Transcend one and you find a deeper side of the other.' And with that he pressed himself against Layla, his erection jabbing forcefully at the smooth flatness of her belly, while he swept his free hand across her chest, slapping her breasts from the side and making them bounce painfully together. Fresh, half-choked gasps escaped from the corners of Layla's full mouth.

'Let's change, let's change,' Matthew panted from the front. 'You come here, and I'll butt-fuck her.'

Reluctantly I pulled my unspent length from the sweet crevice between Leyla's thighs its length glistening wet with her body's juices, and I moved around to the front.

Her eyes looked imploringly at me but I knew that Matthew was right. Here was something I had to experience for myself. So I cupped and squeezed and savoured her full young breasts, while bending my knees, I once again inserted myself into her cunt.

Matthew, in the meantime, had spread the proud cheeks of her ass from behind and was grunting tightly to himself. Each thrust he made forced the girl's body to be pressed tightly against me, her breasts flattening themselves against my chest. The peaks of her nipples hard as pebbles.

Wanting to hear her moan. I reached out and pulled

the thick length of dildo Matthew had buried in her mouth. The move coincided with the deepest lunge Matthew made in her ass and Layla let out a high pitched moan of pain mixed with pleasure that fired up my desire to new heights.

'Make her squeal,' I said to Matthew and he obliged by driving harder against her, so that as I plundered the depths of her cunt and felt its wet smoothness envelop me, separated only by the thin membrane of her inner flesh, I could feel Matthew's organ raiding her ass, barging its way rudely inside her.

'Wait, wait, don't let yourself come yet,' panted Matthew as we worked the girl's body like a sex toy. Alternating between back and front. Squeezing her ass and thighs and tits until she cried out. Plugging her both ends with our cocks until her squeals of pleasure and pain hit new frenzied heights. 'She needs more!' Matthew panted.

Abruptly he pulled out of her and Layla gasped as I followed suit. Behind her I saw Matthew go back to the table and pick up the whip. Layla craned her head around desperately and moaned, but then gasped again as the lash snaked out and smacked across her back. The shock made her breasts jiggle and I moved close to her again, reaching out to tease and toy with them as she shook, squealed and flinched under the lash. Her cries becoming more and more frantic as I reached down and felt her woman juices seeping from her cunt. My fingers went up her and stirred them while she danced for us. After ten, maybe fifteen strokes Matthew threw the whip down and manipulated something on the wall behind him and there was a soft whirring in the room.

The pulley to which the girl's restraints were attached, started rotating, lowering her to the floor. The instant there was slack in the rope holding her up, she fell to the floor to her knees.

'Now, now,' said Matthew stopping the rope from letting her fall any further. "Let's see if we can both stretch her mouth. He jostled next to me, grabbed the girl's hair and pulled her head back.

'Open it for us bitch,' he ordered, and Layla opened her mouth as wide as she could. 'Both of us now Andy, both together,' he said and placing a hand on the small of my back, he shoved me towards the girl's waiting mouth. At the same time he thrust his own hips forward. Almost as one, our penises penetrated the opening of the girl's lips, blew her cheeks out as she struggled to breathe in and lodged at the very back of her throat.

Obligingly she tried to suck us. She worked her tongue as much as she could. Her lips tightened around the girth of the two cocks we'd shoved into her mouth. She made a half-sucking half-gagging noise as we pumped her almost in unison. Such was the craze of our passion that we withdrew almost simultaneously, the gashes of semen splashed over Layla's face, eyes and hair. Knowing what was expected of her, she held her mouth open, taking two shots on her tongue, even as a near-miss slid down her cheek and made a creamy path on her neck. Then, we were both done.

Exhausted, confused, I stumbled from the used body of the sex toy and leaned drunkenly against one wall.

'Andy, you must be tired,' said Matthew solicitously.

'Exhausted,' I mumbled.

'I'll leave you then. There's a bed over there,' he pointed to the furthest corner of the room, where low down on the floor, a mattress and blanket had been supplied. 'Get some sleep. I'll send for you tonight. Maria will have finished with your clothes by then and my father will be anxious to meet you.'

I stood there, head bent, breathing quietly until he left. At the back of my mind, the recent sex, my disorientation and the magic of the place were working a new transformation. I realised I'd gone from human to beast and back again in the space of minutes. Slowly I raised my head and admired the view offered by the back and well used buttocks of Layla. She'd been left on her knees still. Hands held above her head. The remnants of her underwear and dress all around her and her face covered with semen. I'd made a note of the place in the wall from where Matthew had controlled the pulley that held the girl and I went there now. I pushed the hidden compartment open and pushed the button inside. Once again there was the soft whirring. The pulley span, unwinding and Layla's body collapsed on the floor. I walked over to her and untied the rope from the handcuffs. There was nothing I could do about the latter however. I bent down and picked her up. She felt light as a feather in my arms. Her body, hot and resilient, brought back the memory of the use I had just made of her.

Her eyes opened as I lifted her.

'Can you talk?' I asked.

'Yes master,' she said. She had a heavy accent to her English which I was hard-pressed to place but at least she could understand me.

'I am going to sleep now,' I said speaking slowly, 'I want you to lie with me. Keep me warm.'

'Yes master.'

Despite her recent ordeal at my hands, and Matthew's, she sounded totally unafraid and I secretly marvelled at the motivation which made her accept her role as sex toy with such equanimity. Unsure of the honesty of my own motives but determined to get to the core of my being, I lay her down gently on the mattress and placed myself beside her. I covered us both with the blanket.

The moment she lay beside me Layla, curled into my arms, her breasts pressed against me as her legs snaked around mine. She felt soft, pliant, willing and I marvelled once more at the strange twist of events which had conspired to bring me so far from my previous existence. Satiated by my enjoyment of Layla my body started, at last, to slow down and my thoughts drifted slowly this way and that without direction. Half-formed images, like flashes of thunder, sprang up behind my closed eyelids and vanished again before I had time to fully comprehend them. Some of them where wishful scenarios, I half-caught sight of myself lying naked on my back, being serviced by the voluptuous forms of three naked women. Others were firmly rooted in the past. I saw Huanita, on her hands and knees, breasts pointing to the floor, making her way towards me, mouth open. Other women, whose names I had forgotten but whose bodies had forever engraved themselves in my memory, leapt now into my thoughts. A blonde I had purchased for a night in Amsterdam, her breasts pressed tightly together as I sawed my penis back and forth between them, the tip of my cock, brushing each time against her lips.

You would have thought that as exhausted as I was, my mind would have gone blank. It was not so. Instead the demons of desire and sexual perversion which civilisation too often tames and binds in convention and usually succeeds in banishing into the darkest recesses of the mind, now came into full play. They crawled their way to the surface and found me for once, both too weak to offer resistance and unwilling to really do so.

A buxom negress I had bought for my birthday popped unbidden in my mind's silent eye. I saw her again, bound and gagged, her helpless form bent over the polished mahogany of my living room table. Her full thighs had been spread apart, the fleshy lips of her labia open, as I and my guests in quick succession entered her, her muffled gasps goading us on, until someone brought some butter from the kitchen and we set upon her in earnest, stretching her rear passage as much as we filled her cunt.

More and more. Wave upon wave of women's faces and well-used bodies washed over me until reality and fantasy, perverse dream and dreamed perversion blended into an indistinguishable whole and my brain was caught up in a delirious fever of desire that had me tossing and turning, moaning in my half-sleep.

And then, when the heat behind my closed eyelids was

almost too unbearable to take and I was about to sit up, my fevered consciousness brought release. A kind of blankness and then one form. A single form. Dressed, half-dressed. Its desire coming off her in waves. I saw myself, a supplicant now at love's own shrine, I reached up and tugged at the rugged clothing of the form and it came away in my hand, revealing the most wondrous form I'd ever had the chance to lay eyes upon.

'Please,' I mumbled in my dream, 'please' and still the form would not step out into the light. 'Please' I begged and took hold of a delicately shaped ankle.

It seemed to fill the form with alarm for suddenly it tried to escape from me, but I was quick now. With swift movements I had it down, on floor level, and I was smothering all resistance with kisses, my mouth and lips tasting young unsuckled breasts, my hands laying claim to a heavenly treasure just as my body vaulted astride the supple hips. I parted her legs with my knees, forcefully, and when I entered her I felt a coolness flourish inside me as if I had immersed myself in the fountains of paradise.

Only after I came inside her did the tender form spread beneath me move her head and in a stray ray of light I saw Chloe's tawny eyes looking right back at me.

'Chloe,' I whispered, 'ChloeÖ'

Cool, tender hands brushed against my forehead.

Without drifting up from this state of half-sleep I slowly quietened.

When sleep finally came it sucked my consciousness by degrees so that for a while I hovered in that in-between place where all sense of self is stripped from a being and all one is aware of is simply the fact that they exist.

Dimly I thought I heard crooned reassurances from Layla's mouth. Dimly I thought I felt my body move of its own volition to part her legs and bury a massive arousal deep inside her again. My hands moved over the surface of her body squeezing her breasts, clutching madly at her buttocks.

If I did, indeed, take Layla in that half-conscious state, I cannot honestly recollect.
What I do remember though before I drifted off into total darkness and oblivion, is Layla's whispered voice saying 'Master, Layla here. Layla take good care of you now.'
Chapter 5

So deep had my slumber been that I never heard Layla get up and move away. I never heard, Maria, the seamstress come in to bring my clothes, nor indeed did I hear Matthew and his companions enter the room behind her.

'Time to get up Andy,' Matthew's voice said and the kick he gave my ribs was the first warning I had that it was time to wake up.

'What?-' I mumbled. My eyes felt permanently shut, I had to blink hard to force the bleary eyelids apart and try even harder to make them focus. My mouth felt dry as sand.

'Andy, Andy,-' Matthew's voice repeated and before I could protect myself another well-aimed kick caught me in the solar plexus and doubled me over in retching spasms.

'Should never have slept so much Andy. Sleep's bad for the soul,' said Matthew.
My insides felt on fire, otherwise I would have responded.

'The time has come my friend. The Master is waiting to meet you, and me and the boys are the welcome committee about to give you an introduction.'

Through the pain in my stomach I tried to peer at those others in the room with Matthew. They were, I could make out, as filthy and corpulent looking as he was, with bare, hairy chests and bulging bellies. Hair, long, straggly and unkempt, fell down to their shoulders and their faces sported rough, ragged beards. It would have been difficult enough to make out their age, but caught up in my pain as I was it was almost impossible. Their feet, I noticed, were bare and dirty, with long, curved toenails blackened by age and grime.

'Time, Andy, time,' Matthew said once again and moved closer towards me.

Instinctively I braced myself for another kick, but it never came. Instead I felt powerful arms seize me by the shoulders and stand me on my feet like a rag doll.

'Maria has brought you your new clothes dog,' said a voice by my ear. I rubbed my eyes with both hands and looked around me a little more clearly now, my brain, slowly waking up and seeking to make sense of its surroundings once again. Maria, dressed once again, stood there. In her arms she held what to me looked like sheets of some kind.

'Your clothes master,' she whispered and lowered her head, eyes falling expertly to the floor. Even in that extremis I had time to admire the beautiful way she had been trained.

It was a momentary flash of insight that moment gave me. Calimba, my mind said to me, is a kind of training ground. A place where men grow wild and women become submissive. Useful vessels to fuck, use, and order around.

The hands holding me by the shoulders suddenly tightened their grip. Matthew then walked up behind Maria, gingerly almost he took the clothes she'd made for me and placed them carefully on the hard floor by my feet.

'My guess is you are confused right now Andy,' he said, looking up at me, a sneer creasing up his face. 'You're not quite sure how violence fits in with all this, or indeed danger. And yet, and yet, you courted danger going alone up against the mountain.'

I couldn't quite comprehend where he was heading.

'It was a calculated risk I took,' I said, 'I knew what I was doing.'

'All of life is a calculated risk my friend. We all soon enough get to know what we are doing.'

At a nod from him the brute holding me by the shoulders brought his knee up sharply so that it connected with my kidneys from behind. I gasped. All breath was driven from my lungs and my body went rigid, quite incapable of protecting itself as pain spread throughout my lower chest region.

Maria, I noticed, as I struggled to catch my breath had her eyes riveted on the floor in front of her still but Matthew, the strange, very unpredictable Matthew had now positioned himself directly behind her.

'I want you to pay close attention Andy,' he said in his hypnotic voice, 'I know you're a clever guy. Believe it or not we are all, here, clever guys. Our looks are by choice. Tonight, in the next few moments you will dine with the Master. Believe me it's an honour accorded to few. You survived the storm in the mountain so, perhaps, you're worth it. Perhaps not.'

I thought I could detect a strange tone of envy in his voice and I steeled myself for further violence. I had already made up my mind that my passage through Calimba would not be without pain and maybe even loss and I was now ready for whatever could happen. Or, at least, so I thought.

'The thing my friend,' Matthew continued and as he spoke he placed his hands on Maria's slim shoulders, 'is that you still have a lot to learn. It's true what the rescuers said. You show tremendous potential. But remember earlier I told you that sex is a tool. A very effective tool for mining the hidden depths of one's being. It is a tool when married to pain. I saw you in action and it is a tool you use too crudely my friend. I know this may not seem quite this way to you, but consider what's about to happen as a favour. My way of helping you get through tonight.'

He gave a nod again and the brute behind me pinned my arms high up behind my back so that I felt the sharp pain in my shoulders as the joints protested against the angle they were being forced to twist in. I drew my breath in sharply and tried to blank my mind to the pain. If Matthew noticed my efforts he gave no indication, for his hands were now busy with Maria.

Right in front of me, like they had a life of their own, his hands snaked over the dark-haired woman's shoulders, slipped over the thin, white dress she wore and cupped her full, round breasts testing their weight. Then those hands started kneading the full round orbs, the rough thumbs rubbed insistently, back and forth across Maria's nipples, raising the dusky flesh into twin, tumescent peaks which pressed themselves hard against the thin fabric of the cloth covering her body.

I watched as Matthew caught each nipple between thumb and forefinger and experimentally pinched it. Maria gave a little gasp and rose up on her toes a little but kept her eyes still downcast. Her body remained still. A tiny pulse began beating rapidly at the fine pillar of her neck and its beat became visible near the hollow of her throat, palpitating like a trapped animal wishing to break through the skin and free itself. Matthew's hands, like hairy spiders crawled up her chest to the pillar of her neck, momentarily wrapped themselves around the base of it and gave it an experimental squeeze and then marched over the fine plain of her features to play with the fullness of her lips. His fingers parted her lips and invaded her mouth.

'Observe Andy, observe,' Matthew said and I watched as Maria's full lips willingly wrapped themselves round the thick, calloused fingers and she began to slowly suck them.

'Watch how the body as a whole is an instrument to be fine-tuned. It operates at optimum only when confronted by exquisite pleasure or profound pain and it takes skill to indulge in either.'

Matthew, I could see, was naked. Totally. He had somehow contrived to shed the rough length of cloth he wore round his waist and seeing the outline of his hips against the girl's willowy form I could only imagine the thick hardness he was now pressing against Maria's soft, rounded buttocks as he pressed himself against her from behind. One of his hands had, somehow managed to worm its way under her dress, so that as she suckled, licked and sucked on his fingers in her mouth, his hand was busy finding and toying with her unfettered breasts, plundering the sweet round orbs, going from one to the other, testing their weight in turn, playing with their hardened peaks, plundering them lasciviously.

'You'd think that she was ready now Andy,' Matthew said, 'ready to receive her master, but you'd be wrong.'

To prove the point he tore savagely at Maria's clothing with both hands, ripped the shreds of her clothing away to reveal the lushness of her body. Maria muffled a gasp at the suddenness with which her clothes were ripped off her, but apart from that she made no other sign of resistance.

'A woman's body is always ready,' Matthew continued and while one arm snaked around the naked Maria's tiny waist to hold her fast again him, the other one travelled over the gentle mound of her belly to the valley between her thighs where her sex lay nestling, crowned by a tiny line of untrimmed dark fuzz.

He lifted the slim, ripe body off the floor with one arm, and kept it pressed tight against his body so that unwillingly Maria's legs momentarily flailed and parted, revealing more of her sex in the process, deep-seated pink folds between her legs parting to show the beginnings of the first flow of moisture.

'Watch how easy it is to part these lips,' Matthew said, and with the fingers of one hand, splayed the lips of Maria's sex to reveal to me the pink passage deep inside. 'What you do not see my friend, what is lacking right this minute, is the evidence of her love juices. The sweet flow coming from her body which will indeed tell me that she is now ready to receive me, her body prepared even against her own conscious will to be penetrated by me. Remember this Andy, remember it well, women are captives of their biology. We subjugate them because of that and nothing more.'

I must have looked perplexed for he ventured to demonstrate: He put Maria back down on the floor and bent her forward over his arm, so that her full, round breasts dangled downwards their swollen peaks pointing towards the floor. His free hand roamed over the fullness of her bottom. He savoured the silky feel of it, the womanly combination of smooth softness and taut flesh. And then, with a sudden sweep, he brought his arm high up and then quickly back down. The sound of flesh smacking hot flesh made me flinch. A cry escaped Maria's lips, her head shot up, her eyes flew wide open. Ignoring this, Matthew again repeated the sweep of his arm. The second blow sounded a lot harder than the first, the light of satisfaction smoothing out his features told me that he was really enjoying this bit.

'Watch how this hot bitch's body reacts to the forced treatment I give her,' Matthew said and swung his arm high a third time. The third blow was even harder than the first two. It made a full, satisfying sound against the fleshiest part of Maria's behind. Her head again shot up, eyes full of surprise and emotions I could not begin to fathom and then as it fell forward again, her hair flying down to cover her face Matthew turned her round, like a rag doll, and held her for me to see her ass.

The smooth round moons of her full backside were a vivid red, imprinted by Matthew's heavy hand. Maria tried this time to react to this blatant display of her body. She tried to struggle to reposition herself, bring her thighs closer together but Matthew was in full control. He pulled her this way and that until he had repositioned her directly opposite me, head bent down, her face buried at his waist, arms forcibly held on either side of his hips.

From behind, the vertical slit of her sex was beautifully framed by the curves of her hips, the fullness of her bare backside. The coralled lips of her sex had fully parted now and nestling in between the raised folds, I could see the diamond-like twinkle of the first flow of moisture that was her body's response, caught there.

'You see what I mean now Andy,' Matthew said, pulling and pushing Maria at the same time he arched his back forcefully until I guessed what he was trying to do, even as he talked to me. Maria's muffled gobbling, the suddenly choked-off gasp, told me that he had been successful.

Her face was now buried firmly in his middle and as her head started moving frantically back and forth, the half-choked groans escaping her lips signalled her attempts to get some air even as she struggled valiantly to accommodate Matthew's massive rod in the depths of her mouth. The twinkling between her legs seen from behind grew more and more pronounced.

'Watch carefully Andy. See the moment her woman's juices flow freely. That is the moment her body has won. It's shed the control her mind has over her and has decided to follow its own will,' said Matthew.

He motioned then to another of his swarthy companions. A man with thighs the size of tree trunks. He had been standing naked at the far right silently watching all this. One massive hand holding what I could only think was the thickest manroot I had ever seen. The instant Matthew motioned to him, he ponderously moved to take up station behind Maria.
He placed a heavy hand on her slim hips. His fingers hooked cruelly there.

The hapless woman realised what was about to befall her and she tried then to extricate herself, bring her head up for air, release a cry of protest, but Matthew let go of one of her arms, placed a strong hand at the back of her head and with a shove, drove it hard down, until her face was firmly buried in the rough curls at the base of his belly. The tip of his cock lodged so firmly at the back of her throat that any sound Maria made degenerated into a wet, muffled slurping noise. In the meantime Matthew's companion wasted no time at all. With one massive hairy knee he drove Maria's slim thighs wide apart and bared her centre for an easy invasion. He positioned himself carefully, took aim and then, with his hands on her hips for purchase, he charged her hard.

From where I stood I watched the massive meaty pole, prize the fleshy lips of Maria's nether parts asunder and slowly enter her body. This sudden invasion must have stretched her inner passage to the maximum for Maria's slim, shapely body went rigid. She tried in vain to dislodge Matthew's cock from the depths of her mouth. Her head tried to come up but Matthew was buried far too deep inside her mouth and his hips were pumping desperately, driving the coarse pubic curls at the base of his cock hard against her chin. His companion too drove hard against the pinioned woman's body. He slammed against the ripe cheeks of her ass making them tremble with each thrust. He arched his back so that he went inside her an extra inch each time and forced her to come up on her toes to better accommodate the depth of his thrusts.

Fascinated I watched as Matthew had instructed, witnessing indeed the magic moment when Maria's body made the decision for her and relaxed, opening its orifices more fully so that the tight passage of her cunt, seemed to imperceptibly widen and suck her assailant's cock deeper in. At the same time her moans became lower, deeper, as her face buried itself in the dense curls at the base of Matthew's cock and her head stayed there, the only visible sign to me of her oral activity, the tight movement of her throat as she sucked him deeper in, pulled at him with all the strength her mouth could muster. Such was the momentary change that both brutish men seemed to be taken completely by surprise. Matthew first stiffened, his head shot back and his hips arched violently forward and seconds later the pulling, sucking motion of Maria's throat became one of swallowing as she took in the splashes of semen he spilled in the cavity of her mouth. Her hips too, arched higher, offering easier access to the pot-bellied brute who was busy using her from behind. His bellow, when he came, reminded me of an old bull elephant. He pulled himself from the warm depths of Maria's body with a wet, sucking sound, and held his rigid cock until the splashes of milky, white fluid that erupted from its slit splashed themselves on Maria's unprotected back and buttocks.

The two men pulled back and away almost in unison

so that for a split-second Maria stood, bent over, alone and unsupported, her buttocks and back glistening with spilled semen, her lips bruised and red, flecked with saliva and tiny gobs of Matthew's eruption. Then she collapsed on the floor on her knees, her breasts bouncing with the fall. Their tips, I saw, were hard, aroused by the use her body had been submitted to and, as she turned her head this way and that, I looked momentarily in her eyes and saw captured there, the unmistakable look of the wanton. Instinctively, without needing to be told, I knew that like this, in this state, she was quite capable of giving herself, quite willingly to any number of brutish men. Submitting to any abuse, because she was caught up in the crucible where pain and pleasure met to produce a new sensation. A feeling that permitted her to transcend her own limitations of flesh and blood and, at the back of her mind, reach that sacred place where, only the gods of old can reign supreme.

'I think I see what you mean,' I whispered half to myself half to Matthew.

The latter heard me for with a curt nod he ordered his henchman to release my arms. I felt the pins and needles of returning feeling as circulation was restored to my arms but beyond that I was also aware of the tight throbbing in my temples and the tightness in my throat. Between my legs a tumescent beast told its own tale. A tale of primal need and primitive response. A cry of the species that by-passed the conscious mind.

'Take her Andy. Take her. Take her now!' Matthew encouraged and I was dimly aware of the leers and supportive nods of his group. I was looking down a dark tunnel. A tunnel with only a round point of light and at the centre of that light lay the naked, inviting, body of Maria. The gap between us was closed as if by magic. From my point of view it felt more as if the floor moved beneath my feet bringing the kneeling girl closer rather than my feet having walked upon it. I felt the perfumed yielding flesh as I grasped her by the shoulder and turned her to face my front. Her eyes were wide, uncomprehending, lost in their own secret world. With members of Matthew's group clapping their encouragement I flicked my wrist and sent her sprawling on her back. Then, in full view of everyone, I grasped a slim ankle in each hand, and spread her legs wide apart. I pushed her knees towards her chest.

The lips of her vulva opened up for me. Its depths already filled with love juice and semen, flashing a deep pink, all warmed up. I bent my knees, took careful aim, and holding Maria thus, immobilising her against the floor, I drove my full weight down on her. The tip of my penis, like a sword, parted her body, slipped inside her and then I started grinding myself hard, driving so deep that I could have sworn I felt the tip of my cock touch her womb. This assault wrenched fresh cries of anguish from the prone girl, she arched her back in response, her head was thrown back and her semen-speckled lips parted to let out her moans. The sensation of her pussy-lips as I began to violently fuck her, sliding my length in and out of her cunt shot my already enhanced consciousness into an entirely new dimension. I knew then exactly what Matthew had meant. I knew what he'd said about power, pain and pleasure. And I knew also that I was in danger. In danger as much from myself and the beast that was slowly being unleashed deep inside me as I was from Matthew, his cohorts and the mysterious Master of Calimba.

The rules I was being made to operate under, I realised, were making themselves felt. Already they were engineering changes in my behaviour. Dispassionately, inside my head, I watched myself almost from afar stab away at Maria's splayed body, dive so hard against her and so deep inside her that her cries took on a new, shriller tone. And still I pumped at her, making her body shake and move against the floor, forcing her head to shoot back with the sensations, the cords at the sides of her neck standing out. It was a power play of sorts. This tension inside each of us. I felt it rise and rise and rise higher until even I could no longer stand its build up and of their own volition my hips shot forward and for the second time that day I splashed my semen inside Maria's hot, inviting body.

My landing back into the world of man was slow, like waking from the strong grip of a dream.

'You see what I mean now Andy,' Matthew repeated from the far corner of the room. He and his companions had gathered together. 'We used to be bankers, lawyers, teachers,' he said indicating those gathered round him, 'in time this place works a certain kind of magic on you. Now we are all satyrs, ready to live, prepared to die.'

'I don't think I fully understand,' I said.

'No. I guess you don't. Not yet. Remember however the lesson you learnt here tonight. Remember that when you are at the Master's table and it will help you make the right decisions when decisions need to be made.'

I looked down on the floor by my feet where Maria's naked body lay unconscious. 'What about her?' I asked.

'Get dressed Andy,' Matthew indicated back on the floor where my new clothing had very carefully been put down. 'We will take care of Maria.'

And with that two of them picked up the unconscious woman's used body and, carrying her stretched out between them, followed Matthew and the rest out of the room.

I was left momentarily alone to contemplate the events which had just transpired there. There was an element of mysticism here, I decided, something deep and very, very seductive. It was part of the spell Calimba wove. Its attraction. I could feel it burning in the dark with the intensity of a flame, and just as a moth gets attracted to the flame, I could sense both its danger and mesmerising pull and though I knew that this secret could possibly destroy me, I also felt deep inside me that if I managed to tame it, bend it to my will, then I would be truly unstoppable.

Chapter 6

There was a time when I used to be a saint. Hard as it may be to believe I was, in the past, strictly a one-woman guy. I can remember the moment all that changed too.

The BBC have a state-of-the-art training centre in Bristol. At the time I was a lowly transmission technician, the guy who made the coffee and checked to see that everything necessary was written on the programme scheduler's clipboard. I got the job because of Jemma. Jemma was blonde, blue-eyed and honey-voiced. She had the looks and manners of a model and the ruthless instincts of a killer shark.

Jemma and I had met by accident. I was busy trawling television centres looking for a job and she happened to be in the day I came to ask if there were any openings. The gods have a warped sense of humour, that's for sure. The receptionist was about to give me the brush off. It was raining outside, the familiar leaden Bristol sky had opened up to drop its load on the mortals living beneath it and there I was wet through, my T-shirt plastered to my body, my jeans and trainers wet, hair curling at my temples, fresh-faced, young and full of ideals, asking for a job in television.

Jemma swept through the doors, flecks of rain dropping off her designer umbrella as she closed it with the flick of a switch, her Aztec brown business suit and short skirt bone dry, her hair and make-up immaculate. She happened to overhear what I was saying as she nodded to the receptionist and pressed the button for the elevator doors to open. It could have ended there and then. Nothing at all could have happened and my career in television and my subsequent presence in Calimba might have never taken place. Who knows? Karma works in mysterious ways and there are many strange days in everyones' lives which in retrospect are recognised as being pivotal.

I had just about given up hope with the Receptionist, I had left a copy of my CV in a clear plastic envelope which she had, out of pity more than anything else, put to one side and I was in the process of turning away, shoulders already slumping at the prospect of stepping back out into the wet world waiting outside. Just then Jemma looked up from inside the elevator, just as the doors were closing. Out of the corner of my eye I sensed the faint movement and I gave her one last, envious, forlorn look and our eyes met. It was electric. Thinking back, I can only recall the clichÈs, the sense that time had stopped and the elevator doors were now moving in slow motion. That Jemma's electric blue eyes had time to blink rapidly twice, their pupils dilating as she focused on me. That my heart kind of stopped and my body froze so that for that split second I was arrested in the very act of turning away. A single drop of rain-water which had been working its way through my hair, meeting up with other droplets, joining them and accumulating bulk as it went, chose that very moment to break cover. It rolled down my forehead past my right eye, down the side of my nose and onto my cheek where it rolled like a tear.

The receptionist's head bent over her work at the desk began to slowly come up and then, incredibly time was fast again and I had completed my turning away. The doors of the elevator had shut. The receptionist had looked up.

'Wait!' The peremptory woman's voice arrested my hand just as I reached for the handle of the great glass doors leading to the watery world outside. I turned to see Jemma step out of the elevator, her hips swinging as she walked towards me. 'You are qualified?'

I stood there, young and transfixed, taking in the sheer glossy beauty of her, the thrust of her breasts beneath the double-breasted jacket she wore. The ivory whiteness of her skin where it showed in the parting of the jacket and the pearly sheen of the column of her neck, framed by the golden tresses of her long blonde hair.

'Cat got your tongue?' she teased and I could feel myself going a deep red as I dragged my eyes from her breasts to the high cheek bones of her face.

'No,' I mumbled, 'I'm qualified,'

'Can you do digital or are colleges still training you on analogue technology?'

'Digital and sat time-delayed transmissions,' I blurted, 'compressed variants as well as normal wavelengths.' That had been my personal choice, going for the new technology I'd felt might give me an edge over rivals.

'Think you can take the pace?' her eyes flashed.

I nodded dumbly, heart pounding.

'Tomorrow start OK for you?'

'I-, yes. Thank you!' I could hardly believe my ears.

'Name's Jemma, Jemma Stones,' she held out a perfectly manicured hand.

I took it feeling its sleek softness, 'Andy,' I blurted, 'Andy Meyer,'

'Meyer?' she frowned, 'is that German?'

'Half-German,' I said, 'on my father's side.'

'Tomorrow then. See you at 9.00 and don't be late-speak to Paul Jones first, he needs to OK you for payroll.' And with that she turned and insouciantly walked back to the elevator, hit the button and did not look back until the doors had hissed shut behind her.

I caught the eyes of the receptionist and smiled. 'My lucky day,' I said, and turned to face the rain outside, my thoughts a confused jumble of images where Jemma's perfectly shaped legs, swinging hips and high breasts featured prominently.

Chapter 7

When you lose control of your life, when you really lose the ability to choose your actions and determine their outcome, you only think about seizing that control back the moment your mind tells you that it has stopped being surprised by what's happening to you.

I know for a fact that civilisation is like a thin veneer, a shiny patina on the surface of every man's personality. Scratch it a little and out comes a beast, oozing through the cracks. A throwback to an earlier era when the primordial slime was the only home we'd ever known and the mating instinct was the sole driving force governing survival.

Many a drunken night had been spent in London pubs arguing with friends that we have really not progressed all that much since we crawled out of the primordial soup and cast our gazes at the sky.

Every time we move a little higher up the food chain we put in place a fresh set of controls, a new set of routines, but we also take with us all the things we had before. Maybe it's Nature's way of reminding us that we are not yet gods.

Not yet.

It had taken my hard use of Maria's lush body to realise that the controls of my civilised existence were slowly being eroded in Calimba. Expertly stripped one by one. First my clothes. Then my sense of propriety. Finally I could begin to feel the otherworldly weirdness of the place work its spell on my identity.

Deep down, in the depths of my being where the embers for survival still burnt bright, I could feel a change subtly working its effect. Andy Meyer, TV executive and enfant terrible, was slowly being transformed. Changed into something which was all the more terrifying for my inability to identify exactly what I was being changed into.

I could feel, as I thought, my mind fill with images of

brutish men and gorgeous women and the multiple layers of my existence slowly being peeled back like an onion skin.
It is possible it would have happened then. I would have proved the legends right without even trying very hard. That's how confused I was. How near the breaking point.

But my thoughts were interrupted by the arrival of the strangest of messengers.
There was a brief rap at the door. I looked up, blinking stupidly, trying to clear my inner vision more than my eyes. Trying, I guess, to make sense of my thoughts.

The door swung silently open and in came six of the most beautiful women I'd ever seen. They were dressed, incongruously, in short tight dresses and knee high black boots. The boots had two-inch high thick heels. But what drew and held my eyes was the fact that their dresses, all made of the same shiny material, were cut low at the front to reveal their deep cleavages and ended just past the juncture of their thighs.

As they marched towards me in two columns, three deep. I had time enough to admire the litheness of their bodies. None could have been over 19. Of that I was sure. They had breasts which were firm and conical, riding high on their chests, full - yes, but growing still. Tiny, nipped-in waists a man could ring his hands round with ease and gently curving hips, maturing into the kind of fullness that drives men wild and inflames them beyond the reach of all reason.

They all had the same sort of round, innocent faces, skins pearly, untouched by harsh sun and eyes clear as spring water. They all had straight, brown, shoulder length hair and as they walked their hair bounced on their shoulders and their hips swung this way and that, drawing the eye of the beholder and the tight, shiny dresses, rode a little higher over their smooth, flat stomachs to the top, almost, of their round, slim thighs so that it became possible to glimpse the tiniest wisps of golden hair shimmering at the junction of their impossibly long legs.

I watched transfixed, eyes drinking in the comeliness

of these young women, taking in the anachronistic modernity of their dress, the confidence of their manner.

They came to a stop not more than a foot from me and such was the eroticism their bodies exuded that in my naked state it was obvious that I had responded.

The first one spoke in a voice like a bell: 'We are the Trinities,' she said, 'sent by the Master to prepare you for tonight's meal.'

'Trinities,' I tested the word, 'an interesting choice, and how exactly is it that you propose to prepare me?'

'The Master did not specify,' said the same girl, speaking for them all. 'The Master does not meddle,' said the same girl, as one they lowered their eyes demurely to the floor.

'So,' I said, testing the freedom I had, 'supposing I wished to prepare for tonight's meal by taking you all, one after another, and then make you pleasure each other for my entertainment?'

'If that is your wish,' she said.

'You would not put up any resistance?'

'The Master has a message for you,' she said and again refused to raise her eyes to mine.

'Let's hear it,'

'Calimba is not about restrictions. It is about the discovery of one's limits.'

She said that and fell silent. Her words touched something in me. The same something which Jemma had recognised and then helped me to shape so long ago. Many will judge what I did next as a cruel thing. Debauched and without morality. They will see it, perhaps, as the blatant abuse of power. The exercise of authority by someone who has a certain degree of power over those conditioned by training to automatically obey.

I could argue, however, that any red-blooded, mortal man who is presented with six luscious looking, half-naked women, and chooses not to take advantage of their willingness, is suspect in either his mental health or sexuality, or both. But that would be crass.

The truth is that the so-called Master's message to me had the effect of sending my brain into a higher gear and that permitted the beast which had began to gain control of my body to take the upper hand once more.

Without thinking almost I raised my arm and back-handed the girl nearest to me. It had been her who had been doing all the talking and my unexpected blow took her completely by surprise.

Her head span with the force, her hair flew about her face and she fell to her knees with a cry of pain. Sympathetic sobs were wrung from her sisters but so well had they been trained that they stood their ground and none of them moved.

The girl I'd struck had fallen on her knees at my feet, her head lowered in total submission. The top of her head was level with the swollen tip of my erection and as I gazed down at her and then up to catch the fearful glances being cast by her companions, the flames of my mad lust raged even higher inside me until all I could hear in my ears was the loud beating of my heart and the roar of blood as it rushed to my temples. The tip of my cock throbbed in time to my heartbeats and rose higher with each beat.

'Look at me,' I commanded the kneeling girl and her innocent face turned up towards me in silent supplication.

The motion brought the fullness of her innocent mouth almost in line with my manroot and as the hapless girl realised it her eyes widened and for the first time since she had entered the room she looked uncertain and without control. The colour drained from her cheeks leaving them completely white and the liquid brown eyes grew wider in that fresh face.

'Lick it!' I commanded and pushed my hips forward. My swollen erection jabbed bruisingly at her mouth and lips and realising the hopelessness of her position the girl opened her mouth and her tongue came out to dutifully wrap itself round my throbbing tool.

'Lick all of it!' I hissed as I surrendered myself to the sensations she was creating. She was good. Her tongue, hot and wet and strong with practice wormed its way all down the length of my cock until it reached its very base and then began the slow, nerve-tingling journey upwards to my pisshole which she expertly parted and delved within. Her hands cupped and squeezed my scrotum, making my balls tingle with fresh delight. The sight of their sister busy ministering to me with her hands and tongue made the other girls agitated. Their bosoms rose and fell, their cleavages displayed to an even better advantage and suddenly I wanted nothing more than to feel those young breasts in my hands, to painfully squeeze them and suck their nipples. To taste their tender fruits and take possession of them. 'You and you,' I said barely recognising the tight voice that issued the command as my own, 'come here,' I beckoned to the two girls at the back. They looked the youngest and the most agitated and there was something about their innocent looks and the fear in their eyes that made me want to turn them round, bend them over, push the short, tight dresses half way up their backs and let them have it from behind.

Instead I motioned them to my side and with a nod I picked the second of the leading girls.

'Help her,' I said and looked at her sister kneeling by my feet.

Without further prompting the girl fell to her knees also. She bent her head and I felt the warmth of her tongue as she too began to lick my impossibly hard length. I was so massively aroused all I could feel was the pressure building in my cock. My arms went round the two young girls by my side. I felt the smooth, naked curve of their shoulders, then I let my hands fall naturally down their backs, following the sexy curve of their spines, the dip at the small of their backs and then the tight swell of young buttocks, made for fondling. Their fullness promising to provide the perfect cushion for a vigorous fuck from the rear. The slinky material that covered their bodies was sheer enough to let me feel the total lack of underwear. As my hands cleared the undulating swell of their backsides their dresses finished, I felt the hem end and then I was rewarded with the silky smoothness of tender young thighs. Naked and warm.

I let my fingers run up the soft, smooth swell of their thighs until I reached the secret place hidden between their legs. Both squealed almost at once as I dipped my eager fingers past the opening of their promising pussies and let my fingers enter their cores. The one to my left came up on her feet, stretched to tip-toe but I just wriggled my fingers deeper inside her, pushing her pussy lips wide apart, feeling the heat intensify the deeper I went in her and then I felt the warm, woman juices begin to flow from her body. Such was the delight assailing me from every side that I couldn't wait to sample the rest of them. I slowly withdrew my hands, my fingers were extracted from the vaginal openings of the two young girls and I ran my hands slowly up the tight swells of their asses climbing the smooth round hillocks, relishing the feel of them, imagining what it would be like to have them on all fours in front of me, exposed and helpless, my cock in prime position for plundering their citadels. They had, I discovered perfectly proportioned rumps. Springy and smooth to the touch, deeply divided and perfectly symmetrical. The sort of backsides, in short, that made men dream of butt-fucking, of driving their hard cocks up the sweetest asses imaginable. And they were mine!

Mine for the taking!

With four girls seeing to me that left the remaining two Trinities standing at attention, their eyes darting from their two sisters at my feet whose silent, bobbing heads as they licked my cock, provided the perfect counterpoint for the squeals and gasps of the two girls on either side of me, whose nubile bodies I was busy exploring with my hands.

'You two,' I said to them, 'on the floor, I want to see you lick each other out. Now!'

They hesitated only for a moment and then they lay on

the floor, positioning themselves on their sides, ready to sixty-nine each other.

They moved their hips and parted their thighs and from where I stood, controlling the passions that were being stirred in me, I saw to my delight that both these two had been shorn. Their sexes had been carefully depilated so that nothing hid from view the vertical line of their sexes and the, pink, pouty lips guarding their entrances on either side.

'I want to see tongues enter,' I hissed.

The two young girls moved closer to each other. Their hands moved round each other's bodies until they were cupping each other's perfect buttocks and then I heard their muffled moans, and wet slurping sounds as they began to lick each other out as I'd commanded.

Such was the pressure in my cock that I stopped being content with just having it licked and disengaging an arm from the peachy ass of the girl on my right I placed a strong hand on the top of the head of one of the girls kneeling in front of me and with a sudden motion pulled her forward. The tip of my cock easily parted her lips, pushed the tongue back in her mouth, and plunged into the hot depths of the back of her throat. She made a rasping, half-choking noise and struggled for air but I was out of her mouth almost immediately. I pulled back with a wet, audible plop and then I began giving the other girl at my feet the same treatment, filling her mouth with a good length of hard cock until she too, gasped for breath and just as she was about to faint I would pull it out and stick it back into the accommodating mouth of her friend, beside her.

Each time I pulled my cock out of one of the girls' mouths it made a wet sucking noise, and then as I plunged it into the mouth of the other one of the Trinities kneeling in front of me, I would push my hips violently forward so that my pubic bone and the dark, coarse curls at the base of my cock would grind against the soft chin and lips of the compliantly sucking girls. Without thinking, my hands had travelled up the lithe bodies of the two girls in my arms and I fondled and squeezed their breasts. My fingers found the hardened nipples through the sheer material and aroused them further. On the floor, in front of me, the last two Trinities were locked in an amalgam of sinuous flesh. They had their faces buried between each other's spread thighs and they were busy working with their tongues. Slurping at the honey flow of each other's bodies, grateful perhaps that that was all they were expected to do and I was not focusing more of my attention on them.

The multitude of messages flashing through my brain. The soft, tender breasts I was now plundering with my hands, the wet, sucking sensation as the two girls at my feet sucked my cock and the visual stimulus of the two beautiful young women licking each other out were too much for me to take for long.

I felt the slow build up of the surge begin inside me. My lower abdomen tightened and my vision went all starry as a hot lava flow of semen erupted from my cock and caught both girls in the face, just as I was pulling out of the mouth of the one and was about to plunge it into the waiting mouth of the other. The white spray caught them across their upturned, young faces. It sprayed into their hair and lips. One white globule landed across a liquid brown eye and forced the eyelid to blink. Another splashed into an open mouth while yet a third speckled pale pink lips. My hands tightened in response to the fierceness of my orgasm. I hooked cruel fingers into the tight buttocks of the two girls I was fondling. They cried in unison and rose up on the tips of their toes, hands fluttering pleadingly at me as I kneaded their tight young, flesh.

Then, the madness was over, almost as quickly as it had began and I could think clearly once again.

Slowly I disengaged my arms, oblivious to the audible sighs of relief the two Trinities at my side let escape.

Almost dispassionately I looked at the six dishevelled beauties at my disposal and had time again to ponder on the words of the message the Master had sent me through them.

'I think,' I said looking speculatively down at my deflating member, 'that it's time you helped me get ready.'

I motioned to the neatly folded bundle of sheets on the floor and watched as three of the Trinities moved with alacrity to pick it up. As they bent over, the short dresses they wore, rode up the backs of their thighs and the sweet curves of their peachy asses made me regret not having used them a little more when I had the chance.

'The Master must not be kept waiting,' I intoned beginning to take my part in this fanciful charade almost seriously.

'No doubt he will have a lot to discuss with me and I, will have a lot to tell him in return,' I said and I was rewarded by silent, puzzled glances being exchanged by the Trinities. It was gratifying to know, I thought, that at least my ability to play power games, my current condition not withstanding, had not diminished in the least.

It was time, at last, to face the mysterious Master and begin to unravel the enigma that lay at the heart of the legendary and probably deadly city of Calimba.

Chapter 8

On a cold winter's day, in Bristol, Jemma and I made a piece of television history. It had been a slow day on the newsfront, and with only an hour and a half to go on the newsdesk deadline we had been brainstorming in the back, scrambling our brains trying to find a filler that would catch and hold the attention of the nation.

I had been playing round with the fax machine, seeing what was stored on memory. News is like that. Stringers in the field have no time to chase a story unless there's money to be got from it. To get round the problem of time they fax in a one-line description. If they hear nothing they go on to the next one.

Simple.

'If we don't find something soon we'll have to have statistics, talking heads and some environmental rubbish about the ozone,' Jemma said. She was wearing a short black skirt and two-inch high heeled mules on her feet. Her legs were bare, but in the air-conditioned, controlled climate of the BBC studio it may as well have been a balmy spring day in downtown Barcelona. Hence the short black skirt she wore which kept drawing my eyes to her legs, like a magnet.

As a production assistant for the famous Jemma Stones it was I who was given the task of splicing stories together, making sure that field and studio footage blended seamlessly at just the right moment. I also helped in the story sessions - acting like a springboard for the stories that would have the country glued to their TV sets come evening. Not an easy job that. Time is always against you. What usually happened was that a story would come in and a news crew would immediately fly out to cover it, or else a stringer would send a tape and write-up and we would build the story up from that.

Slow news days were the worst of all. That day had been the pits. Every piece that had come in had been rejected out of hand.

'I want a juicy story, a tear-jerker that'll have them open-mouthed and slack-jawed,' said Jemma and stormed out of the room to talk to the boys upstairs. Rescheduling had always had to have clearance and now it looked like we would have to reschedule quite a lot of the content. I knew what she was doing: when nothing momentous is happening news wise you go for the human-interest angle. You need to find the story that will pluck the heart strings. And that needs legwork.

So I was going through the listings, half-listening to the other guys argue about the impossibility of making every news broadcast as interesting as possible. And that's when I came across the single line description: "Five-year old girl in Cheshire well." It said. That was all. I was young, eager and infatuated. Jemma Stones' cool blue eyes, blonde hair and long legs had taken over my imagination since the first day she'd hired me to the point that there were nights when they were all I could think about. A little girl in trouble, I thought and reached for the mobile phone extension and dialled the stringer who'd sent it in.

'Joe,' came the bucolic voice. I knew the man. A bit of a drunkard. Loud to the point of irritation, but tenacious to the extreme.

'Andy, BBC,' I said, turning my back so that the others would not hear me. I'd been there the shortest time. I was the youngest and they would not take kindly to being beaten. 'I just read your filing, what's the story,'

'What it says Andy,' he said, 'little girl's down a well. Father's a well-to-do farmer. Firemen are trying to get her out.'

'Yes, I read that.' I said, 'How far down the well, how difficult is it?'

'I dunno,' he said, 'filed the description this morning, I'm on something else now for the Manchester Evening News,'

'I see,' I said, I knew the pressures freelances operated under, but this was critical. 'What does the little girl look like? Is she blonde? Blue-eyed?' I asked. In this business image is everything.

'Look Andy, I haven't seen her OK?' Joe snapped back.

'OK, OK,' I back-pedalled quickly. It was to my interest to keep this guy on my side. 'Perhaps you could tell me how she's doing,' I asked, 'how old is she?'

'Five. I filed it-'

'How long was she missing before they found her Joe?' I asked holding my breath. On the exact nature of his reply hung the balance of my career I decided.

'A day, day and half. The well's remote. She was found by mistake. Some kids playing I believe. Should have been at school but they took off to go fishing. They heard her crying.'

'Goddamn! A day and a half? Give me the address

and a phone number,' I said, 'I'll make sure you get credit for the tip-off.'

He thought about that. Tip-offs carried a fee. He was already working on something else and there was not enough time for him to do both anyway. Not before we went live.

'OK pal,' he said at last and reeled off the number and area code for Cheshire. 'Oh, one more thing Andy,'

'Yes?'

'I remember seeing a picture of the little girl on the mantelpiece, by the fire. She does have blonde hair and blue eyes and she's an only child.'

'Thanks.'

I was out the room as fast as my legs could carry me.

'Miss Stones! Miss Stones!' I yelled as I took the steps as fast as I could, not willing to wait for the elevator. 'We've got a story! We've got it!'

***

Jemma was wearing a thin white blouse. It looked expensive and it was so thin that if I looked I could see through it the lace pattern of her low-cut bra and the creamy swells of her breasts as the flimsy material plunged away.

She had shed her shoes, for once, and her long legs were hidden in an ankle length black skirt with a slit up one side.

'You did it Andy,' she said, 'the whole country's talking about the dramatic rescue,'

Her cold blue eyes were slightly unfocused by the wine we had drunk and on the table before us were the remains of the three-course Chinese meal she had ordered in.

'No, you did it!' I said and meant it. Her delivery had been brilliant, balancing emotion and concern in a finely tuned performance.

'What is it exactly you want Andy? What do you want out of life?' she asked.

And because I was young and innocent and full of

wine, and the lateness of the hour and the intimacy of the dinner had worked their spell, instead of replying I stood up and helped her unsteadily to her feet and my fingers found the buttons of the wispy white blouse she had on and I unfastened them one by one.

'You,' I whispered, 'I want you.'

Chapter 9

The Trinities did as I commanded. Their unfettered breasts bouncing beneath the thin fabric of their short, shiny dresses, they took Maria's handiwork off the floor and unfurled it to reveal an intricate pair of cream coloured trousers, the sort which would have looked just right for St. Tropez but which would see you get hypothermia in Colombia's rough mountains.

Working in pairs, like modern day nymphs they clustered around me, helping me into my trousers, combing my hair, putting on a vest of similar colour to cover my chest. Their delicate fingers danced like butterflies about me, their bodies exuding the unique scent of the young and sexually mature female. As they dressed me, their perfect little faces focused and intent on the task at hand, I studied them for any outward signs of what had just happened. It was difficult to believe that creatures capable of displaying such wanton acts of lust could also look so angelic.

I playfully patted a passing rear, ran my hand appreciatively up the curving length of a young thigh, or tweaked a hardening nipple through the thin fabric which covered it. Their faces flushed, their lips reddened, their eyes darted to the floor each time I touched them and they gave out delightful squeals which only served to further inflame me.

'You are ready now,' said one of them holding up a small rectangular mirror for me to see. My hair had been brushed back and slicked down. The recent ministrations, the constant sex and the expert work of the Trinities had smoothed out the shadows from my face. The man who stared back at me from the mirror looked thinner than I'd ever remembered with eyes that looked deeper than the surface and a face which badly needed a good shave.

'I need to do something about this,' I said running a hand over the rough bristles covering my cheeks and jaw.

'The Master approves of beards,' said one of the Trinities and cast her eyes to the floor. 'The Master says virile men also need lots of hair.'

There were some giggles from the rest.

'The Master says that does he?' I asked.

'Yes.'

I stretched to my full height, hardly feeling the weight of the gossamer thin clothes on me at all. 'Time then to meet this mysterious Master. Take me to him.'

The Trinities exchanged a rapid glance, eyes darting from one to another. They seemed to reach a silent agreement, and then one of them, the youngest. With a face which belonged to a Madonna and a body reminiscent of a prize whore stepped forward and took my arm. 'I shall lead you,' she said and with a small smile she curtsied.

***

You would be forgiven if by now my descriptions of the wondrous city of Calimba have led you to form a picture of one stone tunnel after another, intertwining narrow passages lined with doors leading into other rooms.

In truth, up to that moment that too had been my only impression of what the city looked like. I did not get a good look at the city proper until the Trinity took me by the hand to lead me to the place where the Master waited for me to dine with him. Sure enough we passed the usual assortment of passages and arches, rooms with closed doors and rooms with just a thin curtain covering the access to their centre. Some rooms

we passed thrummed with the tempo of drums and I recalled once again the first time I'd heard that tempo. The time Chloe was guiding me and the wild orgy I had witnessed taking place inside.
Looking at the delightfully moving two halves of the Trinity's ass as she walked in front of me, I more easily understood how it was possible for men to behave in that fashion with any number of women. Indeed, had I had time, I might have pulled this Trinity into my arms, pressed her young, yielding body against an alcove's stone wall and raising her dress high above the tiny circle of her waist, parted her thighs, raised one leg high, exposing the pink-fleshed inner passage of her cunt, and driven the length of my cock all the way in.
I fantasised about having her grovel on all fours in front of me while I plundered that sweet rear, spreading the cheeks of her ass apart and stretching the tightness of her rear passage.
Incredibly enough, my penis rose at the thought of all this. My vision narrowed until all that was in it was the Trinity's slim, swaying back in front of me and the tight roll of her buttocks beneath the short dress. I fancied I caught a glimpse of the fold of one of those buttocks as the hem of the dress rode up, and the roar in my ears was all too real. What held me from reaching out, taking hold of and fucking the young girl senseless, was an equally burning desire to finally come face to face with the mysterious Master.

It was time to get to grips with this place, finally understand what exactly it was I had got myself into and what I needed to do in order to get myself out and claim my old life back.
So it was like this, determined and aroused in equal measures that I strode to find the Master and followed the sexy Trinity out into the open.

One moment we were within the confines of solid stone. No windows anywhere and smokeless torches hung on the walls providing the only illumination, the next, we had rounded a corner and stood at the threshold of an arched doorway looking at a leaden grey sky and, across triangular, stone rooftops, the snow-capped mountains of Colombia.

'This is Calimba,' said the Trinity and turned to give me a radiant smile.

Row upon orderly row of buildings stretched out almost as far as the eye could see. Where we stood was on a rise and from this vantage point I could see streets and squares, people dressed in grey rags going this way and that. Some pushing carts.

Calimba, the legendary city was obviously thriving.

Two things I noticed immediately as I looked at the scene. First there was not a single wealthy looking or even clean person there. And secondly they were all men. There was not a single woman to be seen anywhere.

'Master waiting. Come now. Quickly,' said the Trinity and taking her proffered hand once again I followed her slim, willowy form into the outside.

The moment we stepped out I was immediately conscious of the intense cold. It was so cold that I felt my groin clench in a vain attempt to retreat inside my body, the hairs rose on end on my forearms and my teeth started chattering.

'Cold here,' said the Trinity apparently unaffected by the sudden plummet in temperature despite the skimpiness of her outfit. 'Used to it. Been here long.' She said.

It was a good opportunity. A chance for me to ask where she'd been before. Where all the other women came from. Why was there not a single female to be seen in the city scene below us. But the cold had clutched me tightly in its grip and my whole body was shaking violently and all thought of getting any kind of information from her was driven out of my mind.

'Can w-e g-g-get ins-ide?' I managed to gasp through the chatter of my teeth.

'Inside soon, Master's place just ahead,' she pointed to an imposing granite block rising above the dwellings clustered around it like a cathedral, and tugging me by the hand still, she led me past the outer gate, through two sets of doors guarded by semi-naked hirsute brutes and into warmth.

You have to fully feel the suddenness of extreme cold to realise just how debilitating it can really be. Your body begins to gradually shut down, directing blood away from the extremities to keep vital organs warm.
Your lips go blue, muscular spasms begin travelling up and down your arms, legs and spine and finally, if nothing happens to change the extreme situation you find yourself in, your core temperature begins to drop.

That's the point of no return.

It took me twenty minutes before my lips were back to their normal colour and my limbs had stopped shaking. What amazed me the most was the fact that the Trinity had walked through the same extreme cold as I had clad in a fabric even thinner than mine and had shown no ill-effects whatsoever. Once again Calimba had succeeded in surprising me, throwing in my face the fact that, at every level, there was more to it than met the eye.

This incident also warned me.

My meeting with the Master was going to be far from an ordinary dinner affair.

'You warm now?' asked the Trinity.

Her gaze was clear as the cold blue skies above the mountains of Calimba and there was no sense of irony at the tone of her voice.

'Yeah,' I said, my hands still an inch or two above the open flames of the small fireplace which provided the warmth of this foyer. 'Take me to the Master. I am ready.'

Chapter 10

I had Jemma's blouse open now and my eyes eagerly feasted on the sweet round orbs of her alabaster breasts vanishing into the low-cut cups of the lace bra she wore underneath.
She had round, pink nipples and there was the faint outline of a network of blue veins radiating from there, just beneath the skin.

I ran my hand over the soft curve of her shoulders and then down the front of her chest to her breasts. Slowly I cupped and squeezed the firm mounds through the lace of her bra. Jemma Stones let a soft sigh escape her pretty lips, her head arched back and her hips pressed involuntarily forward and she suddenly found her entire body pressed tightly against me, the bulge of my arousal pressed against her through our clothes.

One firm hand snaked round her waist, imprisoning her, while my other dropped momentarily to her hip, gave a strong squeeze to the promising curve of hot woman flesh it encountered there and then dropped down the skirt, finding the slit in the fabric and claiming the cool prize of her left thigh.

Jemma's thigh felt smooth and hard. Pampered by money and conditioned by hours of treadmill running. My hand travelled up the back of that sleek, smooth thigh revelling in its weight and firmness and then I had found the tight half moons of her ass. She had panties on but they barely covered her behind and as I squeezed and kneaded and plied her ass, my fingers slipped past the band of her underpants and I had one full, round buttock in a tight grip.

Jemma's half-drunk eyes flew open then and she cried out: 'No! I don't want this. You're just my assistant!'

But she had fired me up for so long. Her older woman sophistication and glossy patina of money and success had been in my mind for so long that I never heard the words she spoke. Instead I tightened my hold on her ass, and worked my hand hard round, so that I could grab a handful of the thin fabric of her panties and pull. Her thin black skirt had caught up with it and as I pulled there was the ripping noise of fabric parting and Jemma Stones, the newsreader extraordinaire, the woman who every night probably featured prominently in the fantasies of half the male population of the UK stood before me, her blouse open, breasts almost spilling out of her white lacy bra and her skirt in tatters round her waist. Her panties had come away in my hand and what remained of her skirt lent allure to the long, clean line of her smooth white legs and thighs.

I felt the need there and then to push her down on her back.

She lay on the carpeted floor, eyes a little wide, cheeks colouring red, and I straddled her, hands loosening my jeans so that as she opened her mouth to protest I first did it to her Florida style. The thick, bulbous head of my cock slipped past the perfect oval opening of her glossy lips and lodged itself at the back of her throat with such force that it made her cheeks blow out. Jemma almost gagged then. She made a half-coughing spluttering sound and as I pumped myself in and out of her open mouth, she sucked desperately upon my length, fighting for breath. A mixture of saliva and pre-come juices overflowed the sides of her mouth and ran down her cheek to pool on the carpet by her head. I must have pumped her two dozen times before I tired of it. I lunged one last time deep down her neck, enough to feel the tip of my cock press against the back of her throat and then I was out of her mouth with a plop and I had turned her over onto her stomach on the carpet. She made a coughing sound again and tried to get away on all fours but I had seen the light of enjoyment in her eyes and knew instinctively that Jemma, the power junkie, could not enjoy sex unless she was dominated.
I grabbed her roughly by her hips, my fingers biting hard into her flesh and I pulled her round haunches towards me.
She had wide, flaring hips, a tight ass, its cheeks big as half moons and as she slid towards me with a cry of defeat I jabbed my cock forward and parted her buttocks with its length and began to slide it back and forth. Its saliva-lubricated length made

the cheeks of her ass shake and tremble and the sight of her suddenly so vulnerable and available made my vision blur with passion.

'So, this is how you like it bitch!' I hissed.

'Let me go. Please let me go.' She begged.

'Not before I've fucked you senseless,'

'Oh no, pleaseÖno!' she cried fully aware of the sight she was presenting me with lying there on all fours, defenceless in my grasp. 'No, noÖyes!' she gasped as I thrust my hips violently forward and the bulbous tip of my cock, throbbing red and purple with unspent passion, easily parted the tight lips of her rear passage and plundered the helpless, vulnerable opening of her ass. The force of my assault made Jemma's head shoot up. Her long blonde hair flew about her face. Her lips worked, trying hard to force a sound out:

'Please! Please!' she gasped in time to my rutting.

My hips pumped hard against her and as I shafted her from behind I slapped the round moons of her ass, so that soon there were the red imprints of my open palm on the smooth cheeks of her ass, just as my cock plunged deep into her asshole.

'Oh, oh, ohÖoooooh' she cried her body stiffening in response, as the combination of stinging pain and deep-felt pleasure worked their magic on her and her body shuddered in the grip of a massive orgasm.

Moments later I withdrew in time to have my own explosion spill its juices on her exposed body. The hot splashes landed on the small of her back and cheeks of her ass and made her body jump in anticipation of more.

Long, silent moments passed. I lay there, on my knees, jeans half-way down my thighs, cock going limp. I was breathing heavily from my recent exertions and my eyes were roaming the half-exposed, sweat and semen covered body of the beautiful woman lying face down in front of me.

Finally I dropped a hand to the womanly plumpness of her ass, kneaded the raised hillocks of her buttocks and let my hand drop into the tight crevice in between, where her thighs joined. Jemma's sex was hot and wet, its lips open in anticipation. She shaved her cunt and there was now a day's growth of bristle on the skin so that as I ran my fingertips around I could feel the rasp of the bristly growth of the golden fur that would normally guard the entrance to her citadel.

'Wow,' I said working her flesh, closely observing the reactions of this hot woman. I parted the lips of her vulva with my fingers and plunged three of them as deep as I could inside her. Jemma gave a little cry and parted her legs. Her face remained turned away from me, hidden in the crook of her elbow. The silky feel of her hot sex, fired me up once more so that I felt the rigid length of me grow and expand until it was slapping insistently against her smooth, solid thigh. I removed my hand. Leant back. Took hold of her legs by the ankles and with a sudden jerk, spread them far apart.

Caught this way, legs held apart. Jemma Stones was helpless. She wriggled to escape from my grasp but this only made the pink lips of her pussy open wider. Holding her legs apart I straddled her from behind this time and with my entire weight behind it drove the length of my cock all the way up her cunt.

Chapter 11

The Trinity beckoned and I followed. The tight roll of her buttocks beneath the hem of her short dress commanded my attention. I was warm again now, my body had stopped shivering, and my mind - freed from the needs imposed by immediate survival - was busy picturing the slim body of the Trinity spread-eagled and tied down, a plaything for a dozen Satyrs. Her accommodating mouth and tongue busy pleasuring these brutes' manhoods. Her every orifice repeatedly penetrated. The clothes I had on did nothing to restrain the burgeoning push of my erection and as I walked, the tip of my cock, rubbed against the thin fabric of my clothes and further inflamed my passion.

We walked past the, by now, usual array of doors, chambers and corridors. The difference this time was that the smells were not ones I expected to come across here. The mustiness of stone was nowhere to be sniffed. Instead subtle undertones of roses, lilacs and honeysuckles pervaded the place. The dress of the people we encountered along the way was different too. There were indeed, very few who sported either the grey, drab peasant garb I had seen Chloe wear when I first woke up in Calimba or the gossamer-thin clothes which Maria and now, I too, sported. The people we encountered were dressed in jeans. Black slacks and single-coloured soft shirts. The women were in evening dress. Shimmery, shiny materials like the Trinity's ultra-short, figure-hugging dress. Dresses the cut of which hinted of huge expense and, by association, immense wealth.

'What is the Master like?' I asked and the Trinity turned her head to look at me as she walked.

'He is good. The Master looks after us all.'

'I bet he does.' I said. I recalled Matthew's strange references. The little 'lesson' he had tried to teach me in preparation, specifically for this moment. 'How did he get here? In Calimba?'

'Master here first. Before the rest of us.'

'Do you ever get the chance to leave?' I asked.

'Leave?'

'Calimba. Leave this primitive place.'

The Trinity looked sincerely puzzled. 'Why?'

'Because then you can be free. Free to do whatever you want. With nobody telling you who to sleep with, when and where.'

'No. I don't want to leave,' said the Trinity and the way she turned her back to me and resumed her quick pace told me that I had touched a raw nerve somewhere and conversation with her, for now at any rate, was over. In silence I followed her down a final, imposing looking corridor decorated with mosaics and the ubiquitous smokeless torches which seemed to be the only real source of illumination in Calimba.

The mosaics were huge, easily seven or eight foot tall, reaching all the way up to the arched, stone ceiling, high overhead and they depicted progressively more intense scenes of wild, ancient battles or orgies. In both, they featured prominently, the semi-naked, corpulent figures of the satyrs, long-haired and unkempt with mad-looking eyes and arms which were thick slabs of muscle, looking capable of beating entire mail-clad armies on their own.

The dancing light shed by the smokeless torches bounced off the individual pieces of the mosaic and made the satyrs' eyes glitter with a dangerous madness, the whites looked virulent almost. In both battle and orgy the satyrs were hugely, massively erect. Each sported a rampant fleshy spear, overbearing and threatening.

'We are here.' The Trinity interrupted my chain of thought.

We were standing in front of thick, arched portals. On either side of them stood two men, totally still. Apart from the erections they were an almost exact replica of the satyrs on the mosaics. They had no visible weapons. Their massive hands ended in crooked nails, strong-looking and dark with dirt.

They looked like some sort of hybrid between humans and vultures. There was the same covert, calculating look of the carrion eater in their eyes. The same poise that would mark the smooth transition from rest to casual violence, in the way they held their bodies.

I remembered the ease with which Matthew and his companions had held me and pushed me about and I felt an involuntary shiver travel down the length of my spine.

'The Master is waiting,' said the Trinity, 'you must be hungry.'

I was. But I did not feel it.

'You have to be invited here,' she continued, 'you have been. You are the only one who may enter.'

'I see,' I said playing for time. I studied the portal with feigned interest purposefully keeping my eyes away from the two hulking men on either side. In all this time they had not even blinked. Only the slight rise and fall of their chests told me that they were not life-sized statues of the figures in the mosaic.

'Through there,' said the Trinity with a hint of impatience, pointing at the faint outline of a much smaller door embedded in the portal.

'OK,' I said. I took a deep breath and acting on an impulse born of fear as much as recklessness I suddenly seized her, crushed her slim body in my arms and covered her mouth with my own. Deliberately I slipped my tongue between her tender, soft lips and thrust it deep down her throat. My left arm held her tight against my body while my right snaked down her back, to the backs of her naked thighs and up again, under the hem of the short dress.

This Trinity's buttocks were tight and warm.

She made a gasping noise in my arms and tried to break away but I was far too strong for her. My hand filled itself with the round shape of one small, pert buttock and I squeezed it hard, sinking my fingers deep into her pliant flesh. I held her there as long as I could, enjoying the feel and taste of her. The two satyrs, for that's what I assumed they were, standing guard, did not even change expression all this time which said a lot about their training.

When I finally broke away I gave the Trinity a resounding slap on her backside. 'Nice piece of ass,' I said casually and her eyes momentarily smouldered with suppressed rebellion before she cast them dutifully to the floor at my feet.

'The Master is waiting,' she reminded me.

'I'll be seeing you round,' I said and grinned with a confidence I did not feel.

All my life, if there's one thing I've learnt it's to trust my instincts. Instincts sometimes can tell us things our brains cannot.

Jemma was the one who taught me to totally trust my instincts. Instinct had seen me succeed where others had failed. And instinct had taught me when to take advantage of situations and when not to. Unsurprisingly it was instinct again which told me this time that on the other side of the portal lay waiting a test. A test on the outcome of which depended a lot more than my just leaving this place. Every primitive sense told me that on the other side of the portal lay waiting decisions which for me could mean either life or death.

'We'll meet again. Count on it.' I said to the Trinity with the sort of vehemence in my voice which acolytes in magic rituals use to emphasise the potency of evil spells to non-believers. And with that I turned and pushed the panel.

A section of the arched portal no taller than me swung smoothly open. I bent my head and without looking back stepped in through it.

Chapter 12

'Just because you fucked me it doesn't mean you can tell me what to do.' Jemma said.

We were lying on her bed. Both naked and sweaty, recovering from yet one more time of my having her service me with her body. This propensity for wantonness in her never ceased to fascinate me. I had never met another woman like Jemma.

There she was, a successful professional cool and collected and in control at all times. And yet when it came to sex all she wanted was to be dominated. Totally. Completely. She wanted to be made to deep-throat me until she gagged. She loved the feel of my hips pounding against her tight, round ass. My rod almost splitting her asunder as I fucked her from behind. She ached to have her arms tied behind her back with a leather belt and then have me throw her over an armchair, her unprotected pussy completely exposed to my desires. Mine to do with as I pleased.

Away from her role of a sex toy however Jemma was hard as nails. It was a duality I could not fathom. At times, indeed, it seemed that our only meaningful communication was to be found in her bed. With me using her body.

'I don't want to tell you what to do,' I tried to explain. I hated arguing with her. 'I just don't think that going on foreign broadcasts is going to do much for your career. That's all.' She sat up to look at me, her naked breasts swinging with the movement. 'You mean you're going to miss your regular fuck.'

'No, that's not it at all.'

'So, don't tell me you think you love me!' there was a sneering tome in her voice which I hated.

'It's not impossible,' I said, 'just because you're older-
'

'Ten years older!' she reminded me.

'So-'

'So, this is just sex Andy. You're just a good fuck. There is no love.'

Her cynicism always fascinated me. And the way her blue eyes flashed never failed to arouse me either. Call it a perverse part of me.

I stood up on the bed. My erection growing by the second, standing out at Jemma's eye level.

'What?' she asked, but already the hardness was beginning to seep out of her voice.

'Lick it,' I commanded and she hesitated, looked momentarily up at me, her face framed by the twin golden curtains of her long, blonde hair, seemed incredibly innocent. Virginal almost. Her lips, bruised from my recent, rough kisses, were invitingly red.

'No,'

'Lick it now!' I commanded and putting a heavy hand

at the back of her head pulled her roughly towards me. The tip of my cock, stabbed blindly against her cheek, and I felt her lips open involuntarily, her long, pink tongue snaking out to lick along the length of my erection.

'Suck on it,' I said guiding her still with my hand, and she dutifully bent her head, her mouth opened and her lips wrapped themselves around my length, warmly sucked on me, slid slowly all the way down to my scrotum where she sucked each one of my balls. If I wanted to I could have thrown her on her back on the bed. Straddled her and violently pumped myself in and out of her mouth until I spurted down her throat and her mouth overflowed with my come.

I wanted this one to last though. I was determined to teach her a lesson. Have her suck me until she could do so no more, before I mouth-fucked the hell out of her.

'Now, lick my pisshole,' I commanded and held myself rigidly as Jemma's obedient tongue, licked its way to the very tip of my cock, circled the bulbous head there, gorged with blood and swollen to almost three times its normal size, and then traced its expanded curvature to the tight slit at its apex.

'Open your mouth,' I said and she leant back, the bright red lips forming a perfect O. 'Keep still,' I said, knowing full well how hard that would be for her. I put my hands on either side of her head, to brace myself and, taking aim, I started working myself in short, quick, stabbing movements in and out of her mouth. Every time I stabbed forward my cock would hit the back of her throat and force her head back and she would moan and try instinctively to pull away but I held her fast and kept my hips pumping violently forward.
My thrusting in her mouth, brought torrents of saliva to flood her oral cavity. Busy sucking me and trying to breathe at the same time Jemma was unable to swallow it all. It started flowing out of the corners of her mouth and down her chin, dripping on the upper slopes of her breasts, where it hung from her erect nipples like rain droplets. Her mouth felt, hot, wet and slippery.

The pressure of her chin against the base of my cock every time I lunged forward and the muffled cries that escaped her, began to connect in that remote space behind my eyes. I held her even more tightly by the head and pushed harder against her, mashing her tender chin against the coarse curls at the base of my erection, revelling in the feel of her throat dilating in order to accommodate my incursions. Before too long my mind and body reached complete fusion and moments later the first uncontrolled spasm fired off from the base of my spine and all capacity for thought was momentarily wiped out from my mind as the first splash of semen shot against the inner cheek wall of Jemma's accommodating mouth.

I kept her head pressed tightly against my middle, feeling my cock shake and throb as I pumped out shot after shot of creamy come into her mouth and heard her slurp and gasp as she struggled to swallow it all

Slowly, afterwards, I pulled myself free. Jemma held on to me with her lips, reluctant to let me go. She sucked on me still until the very last moment, when my cock slipped out of her mouth with an audible pop.

'I don't want to tell you what to do with your life,' I said looking deep into her sky-blue eyes and choosing my next words carefully as my initial step into sexual power games, I continued: 'I just want to fuck you completely, whenever and however I want.'

Chapter 13

Inside the great hall, past the arched, imposing portals and the stone-still guards who stood vigil outside was yet another surprise waiting for me.

'I suspect Mr Meyer your mind has just about had enough by now,' said a soft, cultured voice.

I let my eyes travel round first, dealing with one thing

at a time. Breaking things down so that they would not overwhelm me. At the far end of the chamber, for that was the only way to describe the massive room I found myself in, was a long dining table, covered in a white linen table cloth. The chamber was lit by countless torches on its walls and between them hung lush, expensive carpets. They depicted scenes of extreme sexual depravity. Exotic looking women with slanted eyes, elaborately coiffed hair and incredibly perfect bodies featured prominently on each carpet scene. They were surrounded by naked men. The men, I saw, were blind. Their eyes had been carefully excised and their eyelids had been sewn shut. They crowded round the women in droves, pushing against other men to get there first. The women were either on their backs or on all fours. They had a wild, almost ecstatic look in their eyes, and there was a shiny, sweat-looking sheen to their skins. My mind registered the fact that there was not a single woman depicted on any carpet who was not being taken by at least three men at the same time. Some had two men crammed into their mouths at the same time, their fleshy, felatial lips straining to contain the massive, veined organs being crammed down their throats . Others were being ridden by two men from behind, their rear passages stretching to take them, while a third would be lying prone under them, his cock in her vagina.

'We call it the entrapment,' said the same soft, cultured voice and I had to now focus my gaze on the speaker. He was a man of about fifty. Slim and tanned with clear blue eyes. He was dressed in an unrelieved black robe of a shiny material with a high Chinese collar. His hair was all white and it had been brushed back against his skull, so that it made his domed forehead all that much more prominent.

'An interesting choice of word,' I said and advanced further into the chamber.

'An apt one as I'm sure you will eventually agree Mr Meyer,' said the man.

'Who are you?' I asked.

'Aaah, the direct approach. I like that. But please, let's be civilised about this Mr Meyer, please sit down.' He motioned to the empty seat at the far end of the long table.
My feet took me there of their own volition. As I walked towards it, heart hammering, I was able to discern in the shadows, beyond the table an array of servants. They were all women, dressed in the traditional black, short-sleeved top and short skirt with the white, tiara cap of the Victorian servant.

They stood there, unmoving, waiting patiently for a command to be given. Hands held behind their backs, eyes lowered respectfully to the floor.

Three magnificent candelabra lit the brilliant white table cloth of the dining table and made it hard to see into the shadows beyond it. This semblance of normality in the otherwise madcap world I had fallen into was only superficial. Standing behind the row of servants I could, through narrowed eyes, just make out the by now familiar bulks of the satyrs. There were at least seven of them, standing with their tree-trunk legs apart, hands held impassively by their sides. Eyes practically unmoving. I reached my chair and carefully sat myself down.

'In case you haven't guessed I usually dine alone,' said the old man.

'Who are you?' I repeated.

He gave a faint smile. 'Names are not all that important in Calimba,' he said, 'at least not men's names. However I understand and even share your sense of dislocation. Although it's hard to believe, I also once shared it. So, for the record my name is Thomas. Thomas Powell.'

'You are the Master?'

Another faint smile touched his lips. 'You could say that Andy - may I call you Andy?'

'Please,' I inclined my head, 'as long as I can call you Thomas.'

'For now you may,' he said and I noticed that his voice was coloured by a mixture of regret and sadness.

My instincts had not misled me. At that moment in time the inner voice of my own counsel told me that I was, at last, close to understanding the riddle that was Calimba. Here was the key I'd needed in order to unlock the meaning of everything I had seen and experienced and in order to get it I had to play my cards very close to my chest.

'You must have many questions,' he said, 'but it would be best if we answered them as we ate. You must also be hungry.'

'I am,' I said and realised that this was the truth. My recent exertions and my tiredness had left me feeling drained. My resources were at a low ebb. I needed food to revive them.

He clapped his hands and in the blink of an eye we were surrounded by the women servants.

In the brighter light thrown by the candelabras I was able to see that they were all fresh-faced and innocent looking. They were all blonde haired and blue-eyed and their tight tunics and short skirts highlighted their natural attributes in a way which was hard to ignore.

Thomas Powell did not fail to notice my interest.

'Beautiful aren't they?' he asked.

I refused to play the game. 'Why am I here?' I asked. 'Why were my clothes burnt? Where is my passport?'

'Questions, questions,' he waved a hand in front of him as if to signify the unimportance of it all, 'so many questions. Let me ask you one instead Andy. Since you came here what have you enjoyed the most?'

'Nothing,' I said.

'Nothing?'

'That's right.'

'Not even the use of our women?'

'I enjoyed nothing I could not have had outside on my own and with my freedom totally intact,' I said.

'Oh yes! Freedom. Matthew did mention he thought you set a great deal of store by that illusion.'

'Illusion?' I gasped, I was half way out of my seat with outrage.

'Please,' he motioned me back down calmly. 'No need to get over-excited. There will be plenty of opportunity for that later on. Yes, illusion. Think for once Andy - what kind of freedom did you really enjoy outside?'

'I could go anywhere I wanted to, do anything I pleased.'

'That's right, you could. You could go anywhere you wanted to, so long as money and the law would permit you to and you could do pretty much anything you pleased; as long as you broke no laws and had the money to pay for what you wanted to do. Am I correct in my assessment?'

Supercilious tone aside, when I thought about it I could find little to argue against in that. 'Something like that,' I said.

'Of course Andy, I'm aware that outside the walls of Calimba you would not be conscious of any restraints being applied until you actually came up against them, and then, one could argue, that you might never have come up against any restraints because subconsciously you knew exactly how far you could exercise this so called freedom you're on about. Ready for some dinner?'

The smooth transition from social philosopher to polite host was deliberate, designed to throw me so completely off guard that I would not be able to come back at him with anything. I did not entirely agree with Thomas Powell's judgement of freedom outside the walls of Calimba. As an overall interpretation of the rules we all have to operate under, however, it was not that far from the truth.

'What's the menu?' I asked, trying to gain some time to think. Like the rest of the place he was coming at me too fast, from too many angles, giving me hardly any time to prepare my defences.

'Soup for starters, venison, freshly baked bread and plenty of red wine,' he said.

Venison? I thought. How did venison get on the menu of an isolated mountain city? Aloud I said: 'Sounds great.'

Thomas gave an almost imperceptible nod and out of the shadows stepped one of the servant girls. As she bent over me to ladle soup into a bowl she placed in front of me I could not help but take in the lavender scent of her. My eyes raked her body, taking in the profile of her full breasts as she continued to serve me.

'Wine?' she asked in a voice that reminded me of the tiny peal of a bell.

'Please,' I responded. The pleated skirt she wore left most of her thighs uncovered. Surreptitiously I dropped my eyes to appraise the clean, full line of her legs. I watched as she moved coquettishly away, her hips swinging suggestively under her clothes.

'I believe Matthew talked to you about power. Real power. The ability to touch base with the being you really are and overcome all restraints,' said Thomas Powell.

'He did. Kind of.' I said. The soup tasted delicious.

'He talked to you about stripping the false veneer of civilisation from you, getting rid of the restraints.'

'When I woke up,' I said, 'I saw this man, he was brutally taking a woman. Just like that.'

'Did it arouse you?'

'It disgusted me. This whole place disgusts me. This and you and these coarse looking beasts that pass as a poor excuse for men.'

Thomas Powell smiled. The first real smile I'd seen him give since I had walked into the chamber to dine with him. 'Maria said you have spirit. I'm glad to discover she was not wrong.'

'You're all primitive.' I said. 'Heathens!'

'And you, my friend Andy, are a civilised man, right? A sophisticated man. One who, however, still finds it necessary to coerce poor, defenceless hotel maids like Huanita to give him their bodies. Right?'

I must have blanched at that, the shock showing on my face for the man calling himself Thomas Powell laughed and slapped his thigh. With a wave of his hand, still laughing, he bade two of the blonde women servants to clear the soup and bring the venison.

It arrived on silver platters, still steaming, smelling of exotic spices and herbs and accompanied by oven-baked bread.

'Not bad for primitives then?' asked Thomas Powell.

'Does everyone in Calimba eat like this?' I sneered. I fully expected the answer to be no.

'No one in Calimba lacks for anything. This is a self-sufficient city. Its citizens probably enjoy the last, truly democratic working model of government in the world.'

'So you're voted in every year, are you?'

'Every four years. Like any democracy.'

Had he lit up a stick of dynamite using the candelabra to light the fuse and chucked it my way, I doubt I would have been any more surprised.

'What?'

'Try the meat. It's quite good,' he forked a piece from the platter in front of him and put it on his plate. Stunned, I followed his example. One of the blonde women servants who had been standing behind me until now stepped forward with alacrity. She solicitously bent over me to refill my flagon with wine. The wine smelled sweet and fruity. Its smell mixed nicely with the heady woman smell of her ripe body. It was all getting too much to take again. The rich food and good wine. The beautiful women. The strange, other-worldly setting and now this! This man getting elected every four years so that his brutish cohorts could use and abuse any woman as and when they wanted!

'I'll show you something Andy,' said Thomas Powell. Once again he clicked his fingers. The blonde woman who was serving me moved to stand by his side. 'This is Anita,' said Thomas Powell, 'of German extraction. She is only 19. Good stock.'

To me he sounded like he was appraising a pedigree pet's bloodline but I nonetheless listened to him, transfixed.

'Anita was born here. She knows nothing else and though, hard as this may be for you to accept, until tonight she has been touched by no man.'

I looked at the blonde girl, dumfounded. There was a certain apprehension in her pretty eyes. The short, blonde bobbed hair shook a little in the candlelight, but all the time Thomas Powell talked, she kept her eyes riveted to the floor. Like every woman I'd already encountered in Calimba she was ready to show this incredible submission to what a man wanted.

Thomas Powell clicked his fingers again, only this time it was three short sharp clicks. From the far wall, to my left, two huge shadows detached themselves and strode into the light.

'Observe Andy,' said Thomas Powell, 'observe and you will understand a great deal about us here. You will also have many more questions to be answered, but at least they will be aimed in the right direction.'

The two bulky shapes stepped into the light to reveal themselves as two hairy satyrs. Like the rest of them they had large, hairy bellies and powerful limbs. Their hair was long and matted and their faces were covered by a heavy growth of beard. Loincloths covered their waists, preserving their modesty. A native, animal cunning burnt deep in their eyes. Thomas Powell nodded towards Anita who stood there, trembling visibly now, and the two shapes moved towards her. The instant they took a step, the poor girl uttered a cry of horror and tried to flee. The satyrs moved with frightening agility. One of them cut off her path of escape while the other came up behind her, trapping her. They took hold of an arm each and holding her thus between them they frog-marched the poor girl to a part of the chamber which was more raised than the rest of the floor around it. A couple more satyrs came into play then. Heavy torches were lit and the part they had taken the young girl to was better revealed as a stage of sorts. Ropes hung from the high ceiling, and great ring shackles were attached to the floor.

Holding the struggling girl fast one of them fastened her arms with the ropes, while the others took off her black, high-heeled shoes and fastened the shackles round her delicate ankles. There was something oddly pathetic and, at the same time, very arousing about Anita's helplessness. The very thought of her body being made available to anyone, just like that was sufficient to cause my already overactive mind to go into overdrive.

'Never been touched?' I said, my eyes darting between Anita who was now helplessly suspended from the ceiling, her arms and legs held in a spread-eagled X position, and the man who called himself the Master.

'Never,' he confirmed. 'Does that excite you?'

'No,' I lied.

'Have you never then Andy felt the delight which comes when you're the first to step on untrod snow?'

'That has nothing to do with her,' I nodded towards the helplessly tied up girl.

'On the contrary. Matthew told you about power. The exercise of power, real power demands a certain degree of communion with one's primal urges, otherwise one runs the risk of mistaking base instincts for noble motives. Do you understand me Andy?'

'What does all this have to do with her?' I said pointing towards Anita.

'Everything. Anita is young and attractive. Possessed of a certain power would you not say - an unmistakable allure. Every woman to a greater or lesser degree is possessed of the same power, the ability to control any man, every man through their sexuality.'

I looked at Anita standing in the dancing circle of light

thrown by the large torches. With her arms held up like that the hem of her short, pleated skirt had risen higher up her smooth thighs. My eyes followed the convergence of the gentle curves of her inner thighs until they vanished inside her skirt.

'Would you not want, Andy, to be the first to spread those smooth, young thighs apart, to drive yourself inside this woman's body, to make her squeal like no one else before you has?'

I tore my eyes away from Anita's legs. I could understand now why Thomas Powell was known as The Master. He was the master of manipulation. Consummate employer of the mind-fuck. This was what they were doing with me. What they had all been doing since the very first moment I opened my eyes to wake in this strange city.

'There is a difference,' I said, 'Anita has no choice. She is tied up. Helpless. The women I want to exercise power over have a choice. They've always had a choice.'

'You mean like Huanita,' he said.

'How do you know about Huanita?'

'Oh, we know a lot about you Andy. We know of the girls you bought. The ones you didn't. We've been watching you ever since you stepped into Colombia.'

'Why?'

'Shall we say that we have a certain vested interest in doing so? An interest I shall explain after Anita receives her first taste of a real man's cock.'

With that he motioned to the satyrs who stood waiting patiently in the wings. As I watched, four of them advanced towards the helpless, tied-up girl, like piranha towards a morsel of food. The Master then clapped his hands, four or five times in quick succession. A rhythmic drumbeat began somewhere. To our right a fire came to life. Women servants blew and blew on the coal embers in a black brazier, until orange-blue flames sprang from it.

Someone threw in an armful of kindling and soon there was the sound of crackling wood to add to everything, along with the smell of something exotic burning.

'Sandalwood,' the Master explained, 'pay attention to everything here Andy. There's a lot to be learnt.'

As the flames danced higher and higher and the smell of the aromatic wood got stronger a troupe of women sprang seemingly from nowhere. They were clad in chains at their ankles. Slim, golden chains which clinked as they ran. They wore only scraps of fabric held round their slim waists by lengths of leather strapping and irregular scraps of material hid their breasts.

They were all slim, of an elfin, exotic build that spoke of their origin. Their straight, black hair and slightly slanted eyes told me that they had all come from the Far East. These were women who spoke Japanese, or Korean. The colour of their smooth, pale skins was that of polished alabaster and there was a certain delicate quality to their movements which is unique to Oriental women.

As I watched they all started dancing round the fire, leaping higher and higher every time the drumbeat reached a crescendo and as they did that the scraps of clothing at their chests and waists would jump and dance and reveal, perfectly round pert breasts, crowned by tight dark nipples or, the vertical slit between their depilated legs, all sign of hair removed to permit easier viewing of their charms.

A female cry made me wrench my eyes from these maidens. Anita was being man-handled. One of the satyrs had ripped her blouse open so that it hung in tatters off her. Underneath Anita had no bra and as I watched, the soft, creamy flesh of her breasts seemed to glow with vitality against the torn threads of the black fabric of her blouse. All of the four satyrs around her had stripped off now and they sported massive erections. They danced too. And crouched down and jumped up, their heads thrown towards the ceiling, eyes seemingly focused on a vision only they could see. One of them moved close to the helplessly bound woman and with a swift, brutal motion slipped his hand under her skirt and I heard Anita scream again. The satyr grunted and leered and rolled his eyes with glee as his hand claimed its prize and Anita's fresh, young body went taut, struggling against the ropes that held it.

'These men are masters at this. Observe how they shall use her,' said the Master by my side and I almost jumped at the sound of his voice. He had moved to stand next to me and so engrossed I had been in what was happening to Anita that I had failed to hear him.

Indeed as I watched one of the satyrs slipped to the floor between Anita's splayed legs and lay on his back underneath her. In the orange torchlight his rampant erection glowed like a burning sword upon which the hapless girl was meant to be lowered. Immediately, another one straddled his prone friend's legs, standing directly in front of the girl. The third moved in to take his place behind her. He put his hands on her hips and ran them over the undulating curves of her body. He then took hold of the thin material and pulled at it until it ripped.

Anita gave out a fresh scream at this new development and looked imploringly our way.

'She knows well how it has to be,' said the Master.

Under her short, pleated skirt. Anita had worn a pair of thin, black, bikini panties. They were held in place by the thinnest of straps snaking over her hips and as we watched, the satyr who had positioned himself behind her now ran a rough, exploratory hand over the soft smoothness of her belly and his palm closed over the softness of her sex, grasping at it through the thin material of the panties. A fresh scream escaped Anita's lips and her body struggled against the ropes and chains which held her splayed apart. Rather than diminish her allure though, her struggles made her full breasts bounce and jiggle with every movement, the pink, round nipples at their tips hardening and darkening as a result and her cheeks and lips were tinged with a darkening glow which only heightened the contrast with her clear blue eyes and pearly skin.

As if Anita's scream had been the signal he'd been waiting for the satyr feeling her up took a firmer grip of the thin material of her panties and with a rough movement he pulled it completely away. Anita's sex had been carefully shaved. All hairs surrounding it had been meticulously trimmed away until all that remained was a tiny line of golden tufts, like an exclamation mark, poised directly above the vertical slit of her womanhood. The way her legs were held apart, pulled at the lips of her plump, tight young pussy so that the little peak of her clitoris stood exposed for us to see and the first flow of arousal brought on by the satyr's expert fondling of her, began to glisten within its bright pink, unsuckled depths.

'She's almost ready,' whispered the Master by my side, 'only she doesn't know it. Not yet. Observe.'

The satyr standing in front of Anita reached out and his hands went round her proud breasts. With a leer on his face, he cupped and squeezed and lifted the soft, supple flesh of her round mounds. As the man in front of her used her so, the satyr standing behind her clutched and pulled at the last remaining clothes on Anita's vulnerable body. There was the sound of thin material tearing and the soft gasps of a defenceless, trapped woman who finally realises what is about to befall her. When they had finished Anita stood splay-legged, arms held tight above her head. Totally exposed. Vulnerable and innocent. Her body visible to inspection.

This was possibly the moment the fourth satyr had been waiting for. He had been standing further back now and as Anita's defenceless body glimmered white and pink in the dancing firelight he started to manipulate some sort of lever in the shadows. With each pull he gave, Anita's body dropped a further inch towards the floor, but the mechanism holding her was so cleverly crafted that instead of going slack, the ropes that supplied the tension on her arms and legs automatically tightened, maintaining her position. The result was that as she was lowered to the floor her arms were still held stretched above her head and her legs were still pulled wide apart. The fleshy lips of her pink, untasted pussy held open and available, easy sport for anyone who wished to use her. Indeed such was the position of her legs that I fancied that when her body reached the floor her legs would be held in the perfect splits position and the pink, succulent depths of her hot, young woman's cunt would be penetrated by the rampant pole of the man lying prone beneath her.

'Anita is a trained dancer. They all are. Their bodies are fine instruments and flexibility and tautness makes them much more versatile to use,' said the Master and motioned with his head towards the show which was being staged on our right. The women there were dancing and leaping about, their clinking chains keeping pace with the ever increasing tempo of the drums. Amongst them now moved the graceless but powerful figures of the satyrs and as the women danced and jumped the thin, barely adequate pieces of fabric which hid their charms jumped with them to momentarily expose the totally unguarded line of a pussy shorn of cover, or a full, apple round breast, dappled with perspiration, the nipple at its very tip dark and very hard. This was a display which did not go unnoticed by the satyrs. The hairy beast men were naked, their manhoods stiff and throbbing, threatening in the very blatant manner they displayed their sexuality.

'They are free.' The Master said.

'Free?'

'Truly free.'

'How can beast men like that, enslaved to their desires ever be truly free?' I asked.

The Master turned to look at me, one eyebrow rising. 'Hmmm,' he said, 'I suppose that is one perspective to work from, but think, who else but the truly free of all constraints could display their sexual ardour so blatantly and still be totally unselfconscious about it?'

'Those who are so wrapped in their own desire that

they can exclude all other considerations?' I asked.

The Master let a chortle escape his lips and one eyebrow arched again. 'Very good, Andy. Very good,' he said. 'Do you find such men frightening?'

'Damn right I do. Such men will stop at nothing in order to appease their own drives. The right amount of motivation.....' I stopped abruptly as I realised the inevitable conclusion of my own train of thought.

'You see the beauty of it now Andy,' said the Master, 'you see, don't you?'

I did. I realised exactly how effective such brutish, mindless and yet controllable shock troops would be. But to become so by choice. By choice!

'And you control them all?' I asked.

'Totally,' said the Master and then added the final piece of information which blew my mind, 'I came across Calimba by accident.'

'How?'

'I was trying to climb a mountain.'

'Damn! The weather?'

'Oh no, I wasn't as good as you. I slipped and fell off!'

The shock I felt must have shown on my face for now I could clearly see the degree of effort it was taking him not to laugh out loud.

'The legend,' I said thinking as much aloud as directing a question at the Master, 'is that what the legend is all about?'

'Partly Andy, yes it is. Calimba has changed of course. I have seen to it. But the legend still persists and even I, regrettable as it may be, am bound by it.'

'What does the legend say. Exactly.'

Instead of answering he directed my eyes back to the women. 'You are missing the show,' he said.

'I've seen women dance before,' I said.

'Maybe. But you haven't seen anything like what is about to happen to these ones.'

Chapter 14

No sooner had the Master said that, than the tempo of the unseen drums increased and the beautiful, oriental dancing girls with their delicate bodies and elfin features and bouncing, pert breasts, had to pick up the frenetic pace of their dance. Their chains clinked and tinkled, adding their peal to the mad atmosphere and the first healthy sheen of sweat made their golden bodies glow with a light that only served to add to their allure. This was something they realised for as they danced they craned their heads and rolled their eyes in abject fear of the shadowy, stalking monstrous satyrs. Like lions before a gathering of svelte gazelles, the pot-bellied beasts, singled out a golden girl, managed with the sheer bulk of their presence to cut her off from the circle of her friends. The rest of the girls stopped their dance and fell back, shrinking into a corner, desperately seeking safety in numbers, cowering in the terror that must have suddenly struck them.

Their action left their hapless companion centre stage. The poor girl looked around her at the trio of closing satyrs. She fell to her knees in silent supplication, her arms crossed protectively across her chest where her young breasts rose rapidly up and down.

'You see the fear of knowledge that comes in her eye,' whispered the Master in my ear. 'You can almost smell her fear as she realises that the only way out of this lies through the one remaining single avenue offered by her body.'

'So you think she'll enjoy it?' I asked.

'She has no choice,' he said, 'she will become a prisoner of her own sensuality. Despite what you see taking place here Andy, none of these women have been entirely coerced into this bondage.'

I didn't believe him. Not then. 'None?'

'Not one,' he repeated. 'You've been through the streets of Bogota. Colombia is full of women like these. Desperate women. Lost. Seeking some way out.'

'And this is it?' I asked incredulously, 'their only way out is to become the playthings of these brutes of yours? This is the best they can do?'

He didn't answer. Instead he nodded for me to observe what was happening. In the centre of what moments earlier had been the dance floor, the largest of the beastmen had advanced towards the young girl. With his friends watching him, their massive erections pulsing in the most obscene manner imaginable, the brute placed a huge paw on the top of the young girl's head, took hold of her long, black, lustrous tresses, and with a swift, brutal movement pulled her head forward to penetrate her mouth with his cock. I watched in fascination as the bulbous, monstrous-looking head of the beastman's thickly veined erection penetrated the soft, moist oval of the girl's mouth and lodged itself deep in the back of her throat. The poor girl made a barely audible, half-choked sound. A muffled cry escaped past her full, young lips and then her face was buried completely in the brute's middle. He seemed to revel in the velvety feel of her lips wrapped completely around him, her throat dilating to take in his massive bulk, for he threw his head back and let out a deafening howl and his hips seemed to drive forward of their own volition, the girl's head held fast by a hairy, powerful hand.

'Watch how deep she takes him in her mouth,' said the Master excitedly in my ear.

As if the brute had heard him, he brought his other hand down, moved aside the girl's long, black tresses, swirling round his loins. That way we all had a clear view of the young girl's fresh face. Her chin was mashed hard against the base of this man's pubic bone, coarse dark curls scratched against her tender skin. Her cheeks were bulging out, her mouth engorged and she was desperately trying to control the gag reflex, draw in a breath. The sight made her sisters let out little distressed cries.

It was a mistake on their part. Their cries drew the

attention of the other two beastmen who until now had been content to just stand in the wings and watch their comrade use his chosen victim. They advanced swiftly upon the group. Too late some of the girls thought of escape. Too late they tried to crawl away on all fours. Their frenetic dance had drained them of all excess energy and the chains they wore hampered them successfully without rendering them completely immobile. The two brutes fell upon them like wolves upon unprotected ewes. They singled out a woman each, lifted them high, holding them by the waist, so that their slender, naked legs flailed and kicked out in mid-air, drawing the eye to the loveliness of their long, clean lines and then they held them easily against their chests. I watched helplessly, emotions of anger, disgust and unchecked lust warring in my breast for possession of my person.

As I watched, the beastmen tore the bare scraps of clothing covering the young women's golden bodies. Fresh squeals of terror escaped their tender lips and they flailed and thrashed helplessly in the iron grips of the beastmen. The one to my left brought his right hand up, cupping the tender, naked slit of the girl in his arms, lasciviously rubbing her sex up and down with force, savouring the silky feel of the cuntlips he would soon be spreading asunder with his rampant meat spear. The one to my right lost no time. He flung his prize to the floor on all fours in front of him. He took hold of her long hair and holding her like that, like a bitch on a leash he lashed out at the tight half moons of her tender backside. The blow was audible even through the manic, unrelenting beat of the drums. It drove the young girl's head up, eyes wide open, their whites showing the first hints of deep helplessness and fear. Her mouth was open, but such was the suddenness of the sting from the blow she'd experienced that she momentarily lost all power of speech and no noise came out of it.

Without wasting time the brute repeated the motion, slapping her hard on the ass, making her buttocks tremble. Where he'd hit was quite visible the darkening imprint of his massive, hairy hand. He seemed to be enjoying his role for he raised his massive hand and he slapped her hard again and again, making her head fly up with each blow, and her tender breasts, pointing down towards the floor, shake with the movement.

The girl choked back her desperate cries, bit her lips against the pain. Tried in vain to stop her body from shaking with each hard blow. When he'd struck her a dozen or more blows the brute put a massive hand against the small of her back and pushed her down against the floor, flattening her. Trapping her there against his bulk. The Master and I watched in total silence as the brute's expert hands prized the plump, red cheeks of the girl's buttocks apart and inserted a thick, hairy digit to the hilt up her rear passage. The girl's body stiffened. Her legs thrashed around in desperation. She tried to crawl away but she was held down too well. The brute, enjoying what he was doing, inserted another digit, stretching the lips of her anal canal, and wriggled his fingers back and forth and the girl finally cried out. Her cries were like a catalyst. The first girl, whose face all this time had still been buried in the original brute's middle, pulled her head away and gasped for breath. White trails of semen had run down her chin and the sides of her mouth and as she opened her mouth to let out a gasp for air, I saw globules of semen swirling around in its depths.

She only managed to pull her head away for a moment before it was brutally pulled back, the brute's pelvic thrusts, driving his massive cock deeper and deeper down her throat.

'Swallow it all, bitch. Lick it clean,' I heard him rasp as he drove his hips hard against the girl's soft lips. The third of the satyrs, in the meantime, had turned his girl upside down so that her breasts dangled towards the floor and her hair fell like a blanket before her eyes, and, holding her easily by each ankle had proceeded to part her legs, holding them far apart for us to see the pink, glistening depths of the golden gate nestled tightly between her tender thighs.

He brandished her thus towards the ceiling and it was as if a signal had been given for suddenly the drums stopped their beat and a steady stream of satyrs appeared seemingly out of nowhere and flung themselves upon the women. Before my eyes I watched a thin, tall, dirty specimen with the longest penis I'd seen on any man reach the satyr who had been holding the girl's legs apart, feet pointed at the ceiling. Manhandling her soft, young body, between them they managed to penetrate both the tight rosebud of her ass and the moist, pink gateway of her cunt at the same time. The girl let out shrill cries and bounced around like a rag doll with the combined force of their assault. Others still smothered girls beneath them. Spreadeagled them against the floor and drove at them with such force that I was sure before long at least one or the other of the women would pass out from the ferocity of the abuse and have to be dragged away.

I said that in my breast there was a war going on. The sight of all this brutality. The savage taking of these women, was something the civilised part of me, the cultured, western European part, found terribly abhorrent. But, being totally honest with myself, I also knew that beneath the disgust, there was part of me which found the casual, brutal taking of so many delectable women exciting. I was, even as I felt the disgust well up in me, secretly aroused. My own cock was semi tumescent, undecided as to what direction it should take, unsure whether it should be listening to my head or my heart.

'Look at Anita,' said the Master and pointed with his chin back towards the stage where, lit by the torches, Anita had finally been lowered to the floor. Her spread legs, stretched to the extreme position of the splits. The satyr who had been lying directly beneath her, I saw, was now throwing his hips up and down, his thick, veined, organ was buried deep inside her soft, white body. His erection vanished inside her.

Anita would have cried out. Her body was tense, her shoulders rigid. But the satyr in front of her had filled her mouth with his cock and he was busy trying to see just how deep he could go before the hapless girl passed out from lack of oxygen.

He let out low growls as he ground his hips into her face, her thatch of blonde hair flying back with each hard thrust.

The third satyr of that ensemble, the one who had stood behind her all this time, was busy mauling her breasts. His hard, cruel fingers were digging into the soft, round flesh of her breasts, his thumb and forefinger encircled the pink, tight nipples and squeezed them until the rigidity of the girl's shoulders and the blue veins that stood out at the lovely, long pillar of her neck, just beneath the skin, told of the pain she was feeling. This particular satyr seemed to have a very unnatural position. I squinted to see more clearly and that's when I saw that he had his knees bent low, his body angled downwards and then I realised that apart from plundering the ripe fruits of Anita's breasts with his meaty hands, he had succeeded in penetrating her rear passage. His cock was buried to the hilt in the tight hole of Anita's ass and even as I watched he was busy shooting hot, molten semen up the young girl's anal canal.

As I watched this tableau, to my consternation and horror, I realised that my own transformation, however temporary was now complete. Watching Anita being used like this, my ears full of the muffled cries of the young girls behind me being ravished by the hairy brutes, their holes plugged every possible way, had combined with the sight of Anita's fresh, unused body, spread to the extreme. Her every orifice was filled with a massive cock and her sky-blue eyes were filled with a mixture of pain, fear and almost indescribable ecstasy.
It was this last realisation of Anita's secret enjoyment of what was being done to her. Of her willingness to submit, however violently, to this forced degradation, that sent my consciousness cartwheeling not into new spheres of awareness but into some depth of hidden perception hitherto untapped by me.

I felt the connections being forged deep inside me. I had vivid images of Huanita's ripe, sexy body, a plaything, back in my hotel room in Bogota, there to be impaled by me whenever I wanted. I saw these willing, ripe women, being taken so easily by these poor excuses for men. It was as if I suddenly understood that Andy Meyer had for a very long time laboured under false pretences. He had striven very hard to dissociate himself from this base being which lived in him, and had been only partially successful.

'You must be hungry,' the Master was saying beside me, trying to gently guide me back towards the table.

I never heard him. Nor did I feel the light, but firm tug at my arm which turned me away from the carnal scenes being enacted in front of my very eyes. My mind was full of thoughts of lust and sexual power and the cries of many women being vigorously taken at night. I was dreaming of the nubile fullness of Chloe, the girl I first encountered in Calimba.
I was reliving the heat of her body as she'd stood next to me and tried in vain to explain to me the ramifications and deep meanings of the orgy I had happened to come across by accident.
My brain was fully engaged with Matthew's half-truths. The envy and fear I had detected in the tone of his voice, and the strange words of Maria, the seamstress, who, in a strangely tender, postcoital moment had said she would help me, no matter what I asked of her.

It was all that my brain was full of. Andy Meyer, the civilised man, was watching all this from afar, like a drowning man sees the round piece of sky above his head as he swims slower and slower at the bottom of a deep well. That Andy Meyer was a rapidly receding voice in me and what was taking his place was the cobra-headed god of lust who had risen of his own accord between my legs. It was that god who now filled my head with images of Chloe, of the way her hips swayed as she walked. Of the tightness of her threadbare dress, too small by far across her chest and her waist so that the twin mounds of her breasts and the double hillocks of her ass moulded themselves against the thin fabric as she walked.

It was such a strange thing to remember at that moment of all things. Chloe. Innocent, young, untouched and untainted Chloe. And with her came also the time I was first unfaithful to Jemma.

Chapter 15

Strange that the incident, long buried in my subconscious, would come to me at that precise moment in time.

It was in Bristol, at the BBC centre and it was late at night. A long, cold, dark winter night. I had been cocooned in a cubicle, safe from the elements which raged outside, head buried in the editing suite as I put together the latest documentary Jemma and the team had shot. When you work like that, with that kind of singlemindedness you put everything else on hold. You forget about food, tiredness, bodily functions.

The body can be forgiving. It will allow you to overlook a great many of its desires in order to concentrate on something that is close to your heart.

I used to live for television.

The body, however, while forgiving is never forgetful. It remembers what it gave you and asks it back with interest.

Surfacing from my work, body and mind feeling drained, I looked around me to see what time it was. It was only then that I realised that I'd been in the editing suite for the better part of half a day. Twelve hours straight had passed and now I was hungry.

One thing about the BBC headquarters, there are no chocolate bar machines. When I stuck my head out of the editing suite the corridors were all empty. I went back into the darkness of the editing suite, switched off the film viewer and sat, alone, back against the wall, listening to my thoughts. I must have stayed like that for the better part of an hour before I slowly became aware of the noise outside.

It was a soft, swishing noise. The kind of thing you'd expect to hear in haunted houses, in cheap horror films. It sounded like a monstrous amphibian had risen from some murky depth and was now busy dragging its decayed fins along the pristine floor of the corridor outside.

The normal reaction would have been to stand up, open the door and have a look. But it was past midnight and I'd been working for half a day and my mind was tired and ready to react in a far from normal way. So, instead, I sat where I was, half-amused by my own illogical reaction, telling myself how silly it was that my over-active imagination was making my heart race like that.

That's when the door handle started slowly being turned, just like in the movies. Involuntarily I caught my breath. I waited as the door slowly swung open and in peered, not the monstrous cabbage head of some anthropomorphic amphibian, as I had expected, but the tousled, pulled-back ginger hair of a young girl in a blue uniform. She had a pert face with a pushed-up button nose and tiny freckles sprinkled across her cheeks. The uniform told me instantly who she was. The BBC cleaning service was contracted to an outside firm.

Safely hidden in shadows I watched as she quickly studied the room, failed to notice me, and entered. She had a bucket and mop with her and she proceeded, as I watched, to dip the mop in the bucket and then run it over the plastic part of the floor. As the mop moved across the floor it made the wet swishing sound I'd heard coming from outside.

The girl was slim and fine-boned. I watched as she bent over her mop, my eyes taking in the slender line of her legs, the way the hem of her uniform rode up every time she bent down to scrub at something on the floor. One of the spots she was scrubbing at must have been particularly stubborn because she put her whole strength behind the mop and it slipped and overshot and hit the bucket. The bucket caught the edge of the carpet and overturned.

For a moment nothing happened. The girl stood transfixed, looking at the mess on the floor and staring at the wet carpet. And then, as if some hidden instinct had warned her, her eyes seemed to follow the shadows and alight upon me and her entire demeanour changed.

Her face went a deep, red, her blue eyes turned towards the floor and she looked incredibly guilty.

'It was an accident,' I said.

She looked at me, momentarily. There was something frightening her. That much I could tell. Slowly I stood up from the shadows where I had been reclining and closed the distance separating me from her.

'An accident,' I repeated slowly, trying to divine exactly what was happening. To my tired brain everything appeared to require a tremendous effort. 'Not your fault.'

'I'm-, I'm sorry,' she finally said.

She had a small-girl voice that captivated me instantly. Of course what fired me up, what really turned me on, at the time, was the undercurrent of fear I could hear in that voice. But back then I was innocent of such knowledge. All I knew was that it was late, I was alone and here was a girl and my body was responding.

'Sorry about what?'

'This,' she pointed to the floor and the wet carpet.

'Accident,' I repeated, 'nothing more. So what's the matter?'

'They'll fire me. I need this job.'

'Why will they fire you?'

'Third time this week. I wasn't concentrating enough.'

I had, by that time, gone to stand right in front of her and as I looked down at her I was taken by the freshness of her face, the way it was innocent of make up and how the freckles seemed to glow in the meagre light of the editing room and beneath the blue uniform she wore, rose and fell a fine pair of young breasts.

'You need the job?' I asked formulating a crazy plan in my mind, wondering if I could put it into practice.

'Yes,' she nodded very quickly.

'Badly?'

'Please,' she half-whispered and for the first time she raised her eyes to coyly look at me. I was intent. Transfixed. Listening to other voices, deep inside me, speaking more primal tongues than mere words, and my hands descended on her shoulders. She felt small and fragile in my grip. Her body hot.

'How badly do you want the job?' I asked.

'Please. I'll do anything. Anything.' She said.

'Anything?' I gave her shoulders a squeeze. I could feel, through the cheap fabric of her uniform, the shoulder straps of her bra.

'Anything. Yes, anything.'

I let my hands travel towards her neck. I traced the length of it with my thumbs, turned her head to face up my way and then rubbed my thumbs across her lips. Without further invitation I dropped my hands to the front of her uniform and very deliberately undid the first three buttons.

I had been right. Beneath it, only half covered by a white, lacy bra was a fine pair of milky white young breasts. Their upper slopes finely covered by a sprinkling of ginger freckles.

'Take off your clothes,' I ordered and took a step back.

My command took her completely by surprise and she hesitated, but having made my decision I was now in the grip of primal passion and I was implacable.

'Take them off or you can begin to look for another job.'

'Please,' she said and held her hands towards me in supplication.

'Taken them off right now!'

For a long minute she stood there, in the half darkness, wavering, weighing up her options. Then defeat asserted itself and her shoulders slumped. Her head dropped and slowly, one by one she undid the buttons which held her uniform together.

Inch by inch she let it drop to the floor where it pooled round her ankles. She had navy blue stockings on, to match the uniform and a pair of white lace panties. I stood admiring the wide curve of her hips, the filling-out of her thighs and the fullness of breasts the colour of milk.

'Take off your bra,' I ordered.

Hesitantly she complied. The move to undo the clasp of her bra raised her young breasts ever higher and I caught first sight of round, pink nipples. As the bra fell to the floor, by her feet she brought her arms up to protectively cup her breasts and shield them from my gaze.

'Now your panties,' I said.

Again, she took a few moments to comply. By now I was rigid inside my jeans. My manhood hard as iron.

'What-, what will you do to me?' she asked.

Instead of replying I walked round her. I stepped up behind her and put an exploring hand on her hip, brought it round the back to cup and lift a plump, round buttock, then up her back tracing the deep cleft of her spine. I stood there for a few moments, watching her tremble, exploring her nakedness, admiring the fact that I had had the nerve to pull it off.
Then, as the demands of my body caught up with me, I unzipped my jeans, took out my erection and bending her over, on the spot, drove myself into her unprotected cunt, from behind.

She made no sound. My sudden invasion of her body made her go stiff in my arms. Her breath was violently driven from her lungs and her whole body went stiff, but no sound passed her lips. I hooked my fingers round her hips and pulled her roughly against me, revelling in the feel of the soft cushion of her ass and I began to slide my cock back and forth inside her body. As I slid in and out of her I went faster and faster, the friction increasing, until at last there was the familiar built up at the base of my stomach and its corresponding counterpart behind my eyes and with a groan I let rip and splashed my semen deep inside the walls of her hot, sticky vagina. After I'd come I stood there for some time, slowly going soft, still inside her. Then, when my body told me that it had had enough, I pulled myself out of her with a wrench. Semen had mixed with her body's fluids to run in rivulets down the inside of her thighs, I noticed. I stood back and momentarily admired the round pillows of her ass. The raised cleft of her sex which only moments earlier I'd been ramming myself into.

'Get dressed,' I said feeling strangely satisfied.

I watched her in silence. She did the buttons of her uniform up one by one and bent down to pick up her overturned bucket and mop. The hem of her skirt rode up the backs of her thighs as she bent over and she straightened up quickly, pulling it down with a tug.

Although I worked late again on many occasions after that, I never saw her again.

Not did I really think about her until that night in Calimba, when the Master made me watch helpless women being used by many men at once.

Chapter 16

'More wine?' The Master asked and nodded towards one of the serving girls. She approached me with the same swing of hip and bounce of ripe bosom I had noticed in Anita. As she bent over me I smelt the fresh flower smell of her body and admired the candle light glinting off her bobbed, blonde hair. I could easily imagine myself burying my face in that shiny hair, my fingers hooking into her ripe flesh as I spread her for my pleasure.

'Where do you find these girls?' I asked as my wine glass was being filled.

The Master hesitated. He waited until after the girl had finished and she had moved away before answering.

'I told you before that this is a self-sufficient city,' he

said. 'I'm going to tell you a story. Treat it like a narrative - a fairy tale. One for adults.'

With that the man called Thomas Powell, now known as the Master, began his mesmerising tale.

The satyrs who had used Anita had finished their job and vanished back into the shadows. She'd been left, still tied up, her mouth looked red, her lips swollen from all the cock-sucking she'd been made to perform. Her chin was flecked with still-wet globules of semen. More semen had run down the corners of her mouth to dribble onto the upper slopes of her magnificent breasts.

Even from my seat I could clearly see the red welts raised on her breasts by the mauling the satyrs had given them and I could only imagine the red, just-been-fucked look her cunt and rear passage would be sporting. Her head was hanging low, her blonde tresses falling over her face like a curtain. I thought she'd passed out from the abuse that had been inflicted upon her, but I was wrong. As I watched she raised her head, her eyelids flickered and she momentarily focused on me, before letting her eyes drift across the chamber again. I caught the glint of a pearl-shaped drop of liquid hanging at the tip of her right nipple. Sweat and semen, glinting like a diamond. The droplet hung there, then, as I watched, it slowly slid to the underside of her breast and ran its course down her smooth stomach, picking up speed as it went, skirting the delicately sculpted pool of her navel to go, straight as an arrow, towards the junction between her thighs.

My vision went a little blurry at the thought of what I, had circumstances been a little different, would have liked to have done to her. The very thought of those full, red lips securely wrapped round the girth of my cock, made my mind go momentarily blank and my heart start pounding with lust. Anita's used body held the focus of my attention like a magnet. My mind filled with the parting of her legs, the opening of the coralled centre of her, a fruit whose time had come to be plucked.

'You're not paying attention to me,' murmured the Master with sarcasm. It was enough to snap me back to the present, my eyes re-focusing on him.

'I'm listening,' I said.

I couldn't help noticing that all this time the group of satyrs using the oriental women dancers were still at it. I could hear their subdued grunts as they pumped themselves into the women, drove their hips hard, burying themselves deep into the submissive bodies of their chattels. The heaving grunts of the brutish men were interspersed by low squeals and moans as the women responded to what was being done to them, as cunts and anal passages and dainty mouths were being stretched to the limit to admit thick, veined rods.

The Master went on like none of this was really happening.

'The story I'll tell you involves a young, foolhardy man who thought he could beat the mountain on his own,' began the Master, 'he was full of life, zest and thought little of the risks. Until the gods of fate intervened and brought down a blizzard upon him the likes of which he had never ever experienced.

'When that young man woke up he found himself in a poor city which time had literally forgotten. A city whose inhabitants still worshipped the old mountain gods. The goat-headed, horny Balduk, the thick-limbed, well-hung Satyr.

'The women in this city were chattels. Mere vessels to be pumped full of sperm and then cast aside until the next time.

'You will be wondering, of course, how it was possible for such a world to survive,' he said, reading my mind.

'It led a precarious existence. The men were brutes, the women ugly hags, aged before their time, worn down by the abuse that was heaped on them by everybody. They were, at the time, communal property. Belonging to no one in particular and open sport for anyone who wished to relieve themselves. Had I not been found by a foraging party and brought here, this place would not have survived long. That much was certain.'

'So you saved them then?' I said and tried hard to keep the irony out of my voice.

'In a manner of speaking, yes. When I came to this place, when fate brought me here,' he corrected himself, 'I too thought I was lost. Damned. I was leaving behind a young family I haven't seen in years and who think me dead along with a promising career in advertising.'

'Advertising?'

'Why does that surprise you?'

It didn't. Finally, my television training was beginning to take over and the things I saw around me, the very, very mixed cultural signifiers, now began to make a lot of sense.

To a large extent, I realised, Calimba was an artifice. Somehow this man, Thomas Powell, the so-called Master, had contrived to bring it about. To make it into what it was now.

This realisation deepened my hope and fear. Hope that since it had been constructed, its social order created artificially, it had to be maintained somehow and I, Andy Meyer, would find a way to deconstruct it. At the same time I realised that since everything that had happened to me up to that minute had been less than accidental, there was a larger, well-planned purpose behind every event and I was going to have a very difficult time getting away.

'It doesn't,' I said and had the satisfaction of seeing the expression on his face change from smugness to one of guarded apprehension.

'As I was saying,' he continued, 'I was lucky. I found a city ready to die and desperate for a miracle. That miracle was me. You see, for a long time I had busied myself with studying the sexual habits of women. They are, at a very basic level, just pleasure vessels. Their bodies are there to be used by men. A fact they know well, and use in order to secure a more comfortable existence. In their brief flowering they try to get as much mileage out of their looks as they possibly can. If they are lucky, and sufficiently shrewd, they succeed. If not, well, I think Andy,

my friend that we both know well the fate that befalls them then.'
I kept quiet, sipping my wine and thinking that any moment now his plans for me would be unveiled.

Since waking in Calimba I had been living on my nerves. Exhaustion had not even come near me, but I was under no illusion as to my limitations. I knew that the moment would come, sooner or later, when I would have to slow down. Sleep, leave myself unguarded and instinct told me that in this place, that would not be the wisest thing to do.

'So how do I fit in?'

He ignored my question. 'My idea for this place was quite ingenious. In many respects the culture existing here already helped me. All I had to do was play on it a little. We're self-sufficient here. Totally. We grow our own food. Make our own clothes.'

He noticed the slight widening of my eyes, 'oh yes,' he said, 'even the designer-looking clothes you saw the women wear in here, and the uniforms like Anita's, everything is made here.'

My initial sense of disbelief must have been obvious in my eyes for he immediately felt obliged to reinforce what he'd just said.

'Make no mistake here Andy. This city is a closed economy. If need be we can survive without the outside world.'

'So why was this place dying when you showed up?'

'It was dying because they lacked vision, not eyes. They could not see what they had.'

'Which is?'

'Freedom. The freedom to be as near their primal instincts as it is ever possible to get and still lead a meaningful life.'

'You call this,' I cast an extended thumb towards the satyrs who were busy pumping themselves into the soft, splayed bodies of the oriental dancing girls, 'meaningful?'

'That too has its place and yes, deep down there is meaning to be found. You've heard of Zen have you not Andy?'

'Zen?'

'Enlightenment.'

I nodded.

'Well, then you know that there are as many paths to it as there are men on this planet. Tire the body, exhaust the mind, deplete the spirit and what you get is a novel experience. You are then in touch with an inner self you have never been aware of before.'

I would have liked, at that point, to stand up, slap him in the face and walk away. I didn't. I sat there riveted, my heart hammering wildly in my chest. I knew exactly what he was talking about. My use of Maria, the way I had fucked the Trinities, it had all contributed to some kind of inner change. I too, had felt this sort of transition when I felt that I suddenly had all the answers inside my head. They were there, and all I had to do in order to pluck them out of the darkness and hold them in front of my eyes was try and focus on them.

'You don't refute this then?'

I couldn't. Much as I would have liked to I couldn't. I did, however, find it then hard to understand how the beastmen he commanded so easily could really be these enlightened men.

'What does all this have to do with me?'

'Fate. Everything. Nothing.'

'Stop speaking in riddles.'

'Riddles? Riddles Andy? But riddles are the stuff of life. The manna of the mind. Riddles are all we have. Ciphers. People. Each of them a riddle.'

'You're not answering my questions,' I pointed out. Somewhere at the back of my mind I registered that the steady rhythmic slapping of flesh being brutally rammed against flesh had now stopped and the rhythmic moans of the oriental girls being cruelly used had stopped also.

The satyrs had finished their sport with the dancers.

The low gasps and moans of pain and pleasure had ceased completely and the silence suddenly seemed pregnant with portent. The huge chamber stood totally quiet, a centre stage for the Master's next words.

'Calimba is closed to the world, but it does deal with the outside,' he said at last. He spoke like a man who chooses carefully his every word and I had the sense that he was deliberating very carefully about just how much he could safely tell me.

'From the very first moment I arrived here I realised that there is a commodity Calimba has which the outside world would pay very dearly for.' He paused.

I waited in silence.

'Women.' He finally said. 'Willing women. Women willing to do everything, anything a man asks of them. Women willing to become sex toys capable of pleasing even the most demanding of men.'

'You're a slaver!'

'Now, now Andy. Such an ugly term to use for a function which is, to all intents and purposes, socially useful.'

'Useful? How can you claim that what you do, what the whole filthy lot of you do is useful?' I could feel the outrage welling in my breast. I was half out of my chair. I might have got up entirely, maybe even seized the chance to launch myself at him, had I not heard the shuffle of naked feet on the cold stone floor. Out of the corner of my eye I saw the menacing bulks of the satyrs. They may have sated their primal appetites, but obviously that had not dimmed their sense of duty to their master. They still stood guard. Their bulk alone sufficient threat. I thought again of the huge murals outside the chamber. Lumbering warriors, totally fearless and capable of almost any deed.

'It's easy enough,' he said at last. 'I can understand how from your point of view you feel that these women here are degraded. But believe you me, they are willing participants in their own degradation. What we do here Andy, is take women like Huanita and the street walkers you bought in Bogota, train them in the art of submission to a man's desires and sell them to the highest bidder.'

'Slavery!' I spat out.

'Perhaps, but then again no more so than their previous existence. Their life before they came to us was hardly worth living, let alone enduring for long. No, we vet our buyers carefully. Very carefully, and, for women like Huanita it's a way into a world they could never ever even have dreamt existed.'

I thought about what he'd said, compared it to the degree of knowledge I had pooled in my brief stay as a reluctant guest of this city. Some things did not make sense. 'What about Anita?'

'What about her?'

'She didn't come from outside. She was no prostitute, you said so yourself.'

'Yes, yes, I did,' he waved one hand my way, 'there are women born here, in the city, as there are men. My own son, Matthew, a satyr himself, is one such man. Those women who are born here, need special treatment in order to become used to the degree of submission which is expected of them. It is a better life we are offering them Andy, far better than they could ever have here or outside, but they still need to work hard for it.'

'Anita will be sold then?' I asked.

'Most certainly. We have an auction not long from now and there is little enough time. You saw her perform. She will fetch a high price for us. '

'I see.' I said.

We sat there in silence a few moments longer, each contemplating what the other had said. It is hard now, to explain precisely how I felt. Too many things had happened to me far too quickly. Too many people had tried to help me in odd ways. It did not take much thinking for me to realise that in many respects my appearance in Calimba had matched that of the Master.

I too had fallen down a mountain. To those who lived in the hidden city then I must have seemed possessed of the very same qualities of uninhibited eroticism they had. I was none too slow to make use of available women. They did not know it of course, but there the similarities stopped.

From where I stood, I was beginning to understand, roughly, how all the disparate pieces fell together and I did not like what I saw one little bit. Successions to titles of any kind, my corporate experience had taught me, were never smooth. And this was no corporate succession. I was smack bang in the middle of a society with the values of a stone age enclave.

With that in mind I walked away from the Master, towards the stage where Anita still lay bound.

'I'm beginning to see some parallels here,' I said as I moved away from him. Without looking I sensed him motion to the satyrs to be on the alert. There was the shuffling of heavy, bare feet in the darkness. But that was it. He would wait, I guessed, to see what my reaction to all this would be.

'A legend that replays itself cries out for a succession of sorts. Am I correct?'

'You are astute,' said the Master and there was a certain degree of irony in his voice.

'And successions always involve some kind of test, unless of course,' I paused for dramatic effect, 'one of us was already dead.'

'You are a marvel,' said the Master. He stood with his arms crossed in front of him now, his gaze following me curiously as I made my way towards Anita's delectable, well-used and oh, ever so desirable body.

'And of course a legend has to be valid always. It can't be valid once only.'

'Indeed.'

'When there are two contenders for the same position, one must usually, somehow, prove himself to be the best man for the job.'

'Excellent, excellent.'

'So, everything that has happened to me until now has been a preparation of sorts. A show intended to warm me up, weaken me a little too perhaps. Ready me for what is really to come.'

'I knew I could rely on your incisive intelligence to work it out.'

'So,' I stopped, placing myself directly in front of the kneeling Anita. I placed a hand under her chin and raised her head so that I could look directly into her eyes. Her swollen lips were now in direct line with the bulge in front of my trousers. I longed to take out my own erection, free it in the cool air of the chamber and bury it deep into that delectable mouth. Instead I let a hand reach down the slick, long pillar of her neck, past the slight ridge of her collarbone, to her chest, where I quickly found and groped a warm, firm, round breast.
'When does the test begin?'

'Immediately,' and with that the Master clapped his hands in quick succession and even as I kneaded and squeezed Anita's luscious tits, and pinched her raised nipples between thumb and forefinger, my eyes went to the great metal portals of the chamber, which were now flung open to allow those waiting patiently outside to enter.

I caught a brief glimpse of who was coming through and felt the tension begin to grip my frame.

The test had indeed began.

Chapter 17

The doors had opened and a heavenly horde had invaded the Master's chamber. Crafty old man. He'd planned it well. He'd managed, from the very beginning to disorientate me, ply me with girls and myth and riddles. Keep me on the edge, constantly living on my dwindling store of resources, struggling to make sense of what -essentially- did not make a lot of sense. It was a clever plan. One tailor-made for me. And it had worked too.

Almost.

When the moment of the test came, my mind had been so troubled by what I had been put through that I almost gave up there and then and laid my life down, willing, in the end, to become the martyr he'd wanted me to be. But the Master was not as good at judging human nature as he thought he was. He had made one crucial mistake, and in my case this proved vital.

As I stood, however, that time, in the Master's chambers my hands feasting upon the compliant, firm flesh of Anita's full, round breasts, my body caught between fear and arousal, the only coherent thought I remember springing into my mind was one of pure, unadulterated, lust. The group of maidens being brought in now was as fresh and untouched as any I could expect to see. They were dressed in the thin, threadbare peasant garb I'd noticed in girls before. Their bosoms threatened to spill over the low-cut bodices with each breath, their milky white breasts rose and fell almost in unison with my own rapidly accelerating heartbeat. Their hips stretched across the fabric of their skirts emphasising their tiny waists. They were each blonde and blue-eyed like Valkyries, with long, alabaster pillars for necks and rosy-tinged cheeks which had not yet been strained by the girth of a man's full erection.

Subconsciously my hands clutched at Anita's breasts roughly enough to elicit a cry from her and I looked down to see her upturned, semen-splattered face looking imploringly at me.

'Use her!' the Master suddenly hissed by my ear. 'This is your chance. This is why she's here,' he goaded me and I, the fool, listened only to the roar of the blood pounding against my temples and missed the cunning hidden in his tone. Gasping for breath in my haste to seek relief for the flood of passion which swept over me I loosened my trousers, extracted my erect member, its head swollen and heavily veined, throbbing already in my hand and seizing Anita's perfect, blonde head, surged forward and felt my rampant spear penetrate the softness of her mouth and sink down the warm, wet depths of her throat.

So unexpected was this move that Anita momentarily gasped for breath. Her eyes widened her face grew red and a coughing threatened to dislodge me from her mouth. But I would not be placated. Fired up, almost to destruction, I ruthlessly pumped my cock into her mouth, fucking that orifice with a brutality I had never experienced before. Stabbing at her, feeling the soft, tender curve of her chin, grind against the hardness of my pubic bone, my balls, aching and swollen, pressed roughly against the tender fullness of her lips.

'That's it!' the Master hissed in my ear, looking over my shoulder at Anita's labouring head. 'Give it to her. This is your chance. After tonight she'll be the plaything of some wealthy magnate. She will be pampered and indulged and her whims will be obeyed and she will consider the likes of you and me as vermin, beneath her notice.

'Now's your chance Andy to stick it to her. To make her remember what it's like to have a real man in her mouth, to have a real man use utterly. Make her realise what it's like to taste a man's vigour, to take him full down her throat and swallow what he gives her.'

My eyes darted from the gasping, choking face of Anita struggling to accommodate my sudden, unexpected rutting, to the fresh-visaged innocents still arriving and back again to take in Anita's bouncing breasts her shapely thighs held, still apart, even as she kneeled in front of me, the tiny wispy line of curls, visible every time she pulled away from me, her lips pulling desperately at my manhood.

'Use her Andy,' the Master goaded, his words the only beacons my befogged mind was willing to follow. 'Treat her like a slut. Ask for help and we'll have her gang-banged. Her orifices plugged by three of us at the same time, her body a pleasure thing, for as long as you can sustain the use of it. Take this Andy, use it!' From behind he handed me a short, braided leather whip. Without thinking I took it and keeping my left hand on Anita's head I began to whip her back as I sawed my erection in and out of her mouth, its tip stabbing at the very back of her throat with each thrust and the whip cracking across her in the same rhythm.

A muffled, gasp escaped her each time I lunged forward and whipped her, tiny flecks of saliva bubbled at the corners of her distended lips as she worked at me, sucking and licking eagerly.

'I shall help you Andy, together we'll do her my friend,' the Master suddenly said and good as his word he undid his own garments. Through the haze that obscured my mind I registered his penis as being thin, white, but easily the longest I'd ever seen on a human being. I stopped flogging the girl and watched as he dropped to the floor behind Anita, hooked his fingers into her hips and positioning himself carefully, pressed his erection, an inch at a time up her anal passage.

Anita's body, used as it had been by the satyrs must have been tender, wet, for she went rigid and her eyes bulged and she tried to release my penis from her mouth but I held her fast. Pulled her savagely forward so that her laboured breathing stirred the coarse, tight curls at the base of my penis, and continued to pump myself in her, thinking only of the sensations she was producing as she fiercely sucked upon my rod. Meanwhile, the Master drove himself at her, his eyes on me all the time, ranting about how we would use her. How we would be joined together in her flesh. How we would become one through her. There are a few moments in everyone's life when you sense that a turning point has been reached and that a final, irrevocable, decision has been made.

At that moment I felt that such a decision was indeed there for me that night. As I pumped myself empty into Anita's oral cavity, as I half-listened to the Master's ranting, the crystal clear thought which crept into my head told me that I had been tricked. They had put something in my wine to make me react like this and that I had been tricked into becoming exactly what they expected of me. Exactly what the Master had wanted me to become.

It was a galvanising thought. A thought which, perversely enough connected with me at the very instant I felt a whiting out at the back of my mind, as Anita's accommodating mouth and lips, her firm round breasts rubbing against my thighs, her half-choked gasps and muffled moans, and pleading eyes, suddenly worked their magic and I released a flood of semen down the long passage of her throat. I shot and shot and shot myself, pouring more liquid into that avid, well-used, bruised-looking mouth than I had ever remembered myself capable of before.

Not even Jemma Stones had ever succeeded in eliciting from me such a physically draining response and Jemma could suck with the best of them, she had once spent twenty-five minutes on her knees pushing me on a roller-coaster ride of excitement as she'd worked at my cock with her mouth and when I had come, she had struggled valiantly to swallow the load I had shot into her mouth.

This time, however, it was extraordinary. It was like a long, narrow tunnel had opened up between me, the Andy Meyer standing there, and an ethereal Andy Meyer, a mad, tireless, being filled with light and lust and down this tunnel my essence flowed, emptied itself into Anita's struggling mouth, swamped even her capacity to swallow, overflowed out of the corners of her stretched lips and dripped down her chin and onto her breasts, to slide down the smoothness of her belly to the almost-shorn valley between her legs.

Such a draining should have left me exhausted, feeling vacant, but such was the potency of whatever I had been given to drink in the wine, such was the power of the mad, impossible connection I had made deep inside my head that as I pulled out of Anita's mouth and shot my final spurt full onto her face, my thoughts were already embroiled in the use I would put her cunt to. I wanted, there and then, to lay her flat down on her back and spread her legs wide apart, push them so that all her lower orifices presented themselves to me equally, displayed themselves for my pleasure, and I wanted to drive myself so deep down inside her that she would squeal with the sensation.

I would have done it too. That's how far gone I was. That's how good the spell the Master had woven had been. But at that moment two things happened almost simultaneously and they arrested my mind in mid-flight. The final few people of the throng that had been filing into the chamber walked in and a couple of satyrs brought in more lights. We were being watched by girls. Girls of all sizes and shapes. The blonde ones who had first come in had given way to slender dark nymphs, with almost adolescent bodies and small breasts, their pouty mouths painted a deep, glistening red, inviting further attention. Behind them were others. Some with hair long and wavy, falling in cascades down to their waists. Others with hair so short their heads looked like they'd been shaved. All of them had bodies any man would die for.

My gaze took all this in an instant, my mind still caught in the grip of the Master's spell, my body feeling like it could go on forever and then, as the light brought in by the satyrs played over the gathered women I saw Chloe's innocent face, her eyes full and round, looking at me with apprehension. Her mouth half-open, glistening lips, innocent yet of any make-up, her high, young breasts, untasted and untested by a man's touch, rising and falling as they pushed against the constraints of the same threadbare dress she had worn when I first saw her.

Chloe's gaze, the elfin face framed by the straight black hair, the flawless olive complexion arrested my careering mind. My eyes locked in on her and then I realised that behind her, standing still, stood a tall man. Dark and fierce looking, with rich dark locks which flowed down to his shoulders, and he was looking at me with an expression which chilled my blood.

'That is the Governor,'

The Master had finished his use of Anita, and had come to stand a step behind my left shoulder. So engrossed I had been in that moment of revelation when my eyes fell upon Chloe and I remembered who I had been, that I had failed to notice the instant Anita, pushed to the limit of her reserves by our combined use of her bound, submissive body, had taken the Master's load up her rear passage and quietly fainted. Her head had slumped forward, her gold tresses falling like a curtain over her perfectly proportioned face. She was held in place still by her shackles and, as I cast my eye over her, I realised that her body, unconsciousness notwithstanding, could take still further use. We could really now work on her, stretch every orifice to the limit, force her to take three or more of us at a time. But the Master's words held me still, forced my eyes away from Anita's maddeningly inviting body to the wildly staring, hirsute black man standing behind her.

'Who is the Governor?' I asked.

'He is the administrator of the Test. The one who'll see that all the rules are obeyed.'

My confusion was melting by degrees.

'What test?'

'THE Test, Andy. THE Test,' said the Master, 'there's only one Test to be applied in Calimba, only one Test an outsider, a blow-in, can be allowed and that is whether you can survive the next 24 hours without any of the help we've given you so far.'

It was like I'd been shot with a thunderbolt through the heart. Every nerve-end in my body tingled with dread. I must have gone pale, but I still managed to keep my face blank.

'What are you talking about?' I whispered.

The Master put a solicitous arm round my shoulders and bent his head towards me, speaking, almost, like a father.

'We've helped you every step of the way until now Andy,' he said, 'we gave you innumerable opportunities to understand what's going on here. How this place works. Now's the time for the Test. The Test which only one may survive.'

It was like a pit had opened up under my feet. Like a drowning man, in my mind's eye, I saw the experiences I had been through since I'd woken up in Calimba. The moment Chloe had confused my senses, the sex I'd had with the seamstress and then, the Trinities, my being beaten-up by the satyrs. It had all been a long, drawn-out ride into oblivion. I had had too much sex and not enough sleep, too many revelations about who I really was and not enough time to understand them all, use them to give me strength rather than weaken me.

The Master's plan had been perfect. Here he was faced with the need to get rid of the outsider but bound still by the very rules of the mythology he had put in place himself. He had been forced to play the game, test me indeed, but not before first making sure that I had no reserves left. Physically, mentally and emotionally I was, finally, standing at the nadir of my strength.

'What form does this Test take?' I could barely force the words out of my mouth.

Perhaps the Master did, at that moment, feel sorry for me. Perhaps he did feel a little guilt at all the tribulations he'd put me through. Then again maybe he was a consummate actor. He had won, he could afford to be magnanimous. He held me tighter still around the shoulders, brought his other hand up to affectionately, almost, rub my shoulder and said:

'We'll give you a headstart, one hour, then the Governor will come after you, with the satyrs. You have until sunrise to either escape from this place or take it over.'

It was that simple.

I felt my knees weaken. I was sure I would collapse. My new-found strength, the passion-mad energy which had fired me, evaporated leaving me incapable of dreaming of putting up even a token resistance.

Calimba was terra incognita to me. It really was a foreign place. Same planet, another world. Had I had time to think, to recover from my ordeal when I fell down the mountain, achieve again a mental equilibrium, I might have then had a chance. I might have considered taking the Master up on his challenge. As it was, I had been given no chance, indeed I had, craftily, been made to squander the meagre resources I had had until I stood now, at the threshold of the Test, incapable of surviving a moment longer.

'What if I don't play along?' I whispered.

The Master seemed genuinely disappointed. The heartless monster had actually been looking forward to me suffering. 'We will kill you now. Slowly. Test to see if indeed you are the Chosen one.'

'I see.'

At that moment, while I weighed up everything in my mind, death was an option I was taking seriously. I eyed-up the satyrs who had shuffled out of the shadows and now stood watching with an expectant look on their face, I looked at the women, so many women, about to be used and then sold off to be playthings for men who would not really appreciate what they had bought. And then my eyes fell upon the Governor and his murderous gaze.

'Why is he so intent on killing me?' I asked.

'Nothing personal. The Governor is chosen exclusively to administer the Test Andy. That is his function. His status will rise immeasurably for your having been here. Until you came there was little for him to do.'

I understood then. The Governor thought he should have more benefits, enjoy more of the pleasures life in Calimba had to offer, and the only way he could get that was by killing me.

'Well?' the Master asked.

'Not much of a choice,' I mumbled.

'It's all you get.'

I was seriously considering death then. I was thinking how easy it would be to seize a flaming torch, wave it about, force the satyrs to kill me.

'Don't I get a last wish?' I asked.

The Master's eyes glinted. 'Of course you do. Name it.'

Call it the imp in me, the little devil of mischief making himself felt even at a moment of as much extremis as this. Call it what you will, but at that moment in time I lifted my hand, extended a finger and unerringly pointed at Chloe and said:

'I want her. I want to fuck her.'

I know you think it deplorable, pitiable even. Standing at the threshold of death all I could think of was sex. But I had almost made up my mind. I would fuck Chloe six ways into next week and then submit, at last, body and mind satiated, to whatever fate the Master had chosen for me. All previous resolutions about besting them had vanished. I was at my wits' end, physically and mentally defeated, and I was now reaching for a final comfort. It would have been that easy. It was that close. Had he been as good a judge of character as he had thought he was, the Master, would have agreed to it there and then and I would not now be here telling you this tale.

'You can't have her,' he said.

'Why not?' I felt the disappointment like a palpable throb inside me. I had been looking forward to feasting on Chloe's ripe body, being the first to taste her delectable charms.

'She was your guide when you first came here, her fate is tied to yours. She is ours first to use, then to sell. No selling to a wealthy merchant for her. She is a slave for sale. She shall go to a whorehouse, to service men like you ten times a day.'

Had he hit me with a mace there and then I doubt I would have been more shocked. My field of vision narrowed into a dark tunnel until at the other end all I could see were Chloe's suddenly imploring eyes. I had a momentary vision of her ripe, young body, held down, spread-eagled, a plaything for thousands and I felt a roar in my ears at the sudden injustice of it.

'Surely there's some leeway here,' I said, 'she does not have to be treated like that.'

'It's part of the Test,' said the Master, his voice final.

Had he laid down a very careful plan to help me revive he could not have hoped to come up with a better one. The very thought that an innocent was to suffer because of me was suddenly odious to my being. Not only had they manipulated me, used me but now they were making me a cause for someone else's suffering.

'The Test?' I said.

'Yes, the Test. She and you are tied together. She was your guide.'

'Aaaah.' Had he been more alert the Master would have realised the change in my attitude. The almost imperceptible raising of the head, the straightening of the shoulders. But he really thought he had won. He was confident the way only victors can be, and that confidence made him cocky, and it made him careless. I took a step sideways towards him and checked to see where the nearest flaming torch was. Then in a flash, I had grabbed the Master by the throat, dragged him over by the torch and before anyone could recover from their surprise and react, I was holding the flames only inches from his face.

'Not a move any of you!' I hissed. 'Make a move and he goes blind, his face a burnt out mess!'

I must have sounded like I meant it because they all stood rooted to the spot.

'Do as he says!' the Master screamed and the magisterial tones were now gone from his voice.

'We will kill you!' hissed the dark-haired Governor, 'There's no place for you to go here. Nowhere to hide blow-in,'

He sounded tough, his eyes alight, testing me, testing his own self in a manner of speaking. I felt sorry for him, because he too was trapped, no less than I, but I was also going to be damned if I was going to let him catch me unaware. I let a smirk play on my lips. A smile of sheer bravado. A bravado, needless to say, which I did not feel. But it had its desired effect. It undermined the Governor's untested confidence and momentarily he looked confused. The feral light went out of his eyes and he stood there looking uncertain, lost.

'What's that you said?' I asked, pressing my advantage home, 'did I hear you say "kill"?' I brought the flame of the torch nearer to the Master's face and he stiffened and gasped with terror, his voice gasping to make itself heard.

'Back off! Back off! All of you! Do you want this madman to burn my eyes out?'

Reluctantly the satyrs and the Governor fell back, receded into the shadows where I had to squint hard to make out their individual shapes. It was not a good situation to be in. The chamber we were in was large enough for one of those thugs to flank me in the darkness and then risk creeping up on me from behind. It was clear that I had to get out of there.

But how?

That's when my eyes fell on Chloe again. The sweet creature stood on her own amongst the girls. Head hanging down. accepting her fate without complaint. I guess I should not have expected anything more. You can't train women to submit to your every sexual wish and then also instil a sense of rebellion in them. That's when the thought was finally driven to me that if I wanted to escape, I would have to enlist the help of someone, and no-one presented themselves more to me, then, than Chloe, my so called 'guide'.

'You!' I hissed at her, nodding towards her. 'Come here!'

My command caught her momentarily by surprise. It seemed to snap her out of whatever lonely reverie she had fallen into and bring her back to the present.

'Come here!' I repeated and simultaneously tightened my grip on the Master's throat.

'Let the Master go,' cried out the Governor from the shadows, but I had bested him. I had won, however temporarily, and the memory of that victory was fresh still upon his mind and that was sufficient to rob his voice of all authority. I knew that in the short-term the Governor was not my main worry. I still could not see the satyrs clearly and I could swear I could hear the sound of bare, calloused feet, scraping the chamber's floor.

'Remember how easy it'll be for me to burn him!' I yelled, and hefted the flame nearer the Master's eyes again. 'Chloe come here!' I had to yell to make her obey but the effect was as if I had suddenly slapped her.

Her eyes went very, very round and focused totally on me.

'Come the fuck here!' I hissed for the last time, and she obeyed with alacrity. 'Master,' she whispered and lowered her head so that her eyes were on the floor.

'Get behind me,' I hissed, 'guide me to the door.'

Something in my tone must have driven home to her the extremity of our position here because she did immediately as I'd told her. She moved behind me, put an arm on my shoulder and gently started guiding me towards the door. Locked thus, the three of us, Chloe, the Master and I, made our way, step-by-step towards what I thought would be an escape.

Step, by step, the torch waving in front of me, never far from the Master's face, the three of us made our way to the great metal portal behind me.

'Open it!' I hissed at Chloe and.heard her struggle with the metal catch. There was the cold scraping of metal on metal. Then the creaking of the door as it slowly swung on its hinges and opened outwards. My brain in that instant, caught up with the hyperalertness of my body and I remembered the two guards outside in time to tighten my grip around the Master's throat.

'Order those two goons to come in!' I said and he complied.

The two guards came in, their faces all uncertain. I smiled, knowing that in all their life they had never come across a scenario like this.

'Join the others gentlemen if you please,' I said and motioned towards the mute, helpless throng at the far side of the chamber who stood looking at me still.

'You won't get away with this,' said the Master trying to twist his head round far enough to look at me.

'Well, you did say I have an hour old man,' I said. 'A whole hour. Your rules, remember?' I raised my voice as I said that, thinking aloud, improvising, and the Master went very still in my grasp. I realised then that my instinct had been right. They had been his rules and I was now using them against him.

'So, you will undertake the Test?' he asked, the incredulity in his tone was all the confirmation I needed. He had never intended me to make a run for it. Never. He had been prepared to kill me in the chamber. That meant that he was not prepared for my next move. Suddenly, I had a chance. A slim chance, but a chance nevertheless!

'Yep!' I said and with a shove I sent him head flying towards the floor.

Without pausing to see how the throng was reacting, I turned, grabbed Chloe by the elbow and propelled us both towards the open doorway of the metal portal.

'One hour now old man. Try not to forget that.' I yelled, and with that Chloe and I were through, bolting the door behind us.

Chapter 18

With the big metal doors to the chamber firmly shut behind us I had time to check where we were. Ahead of us opened a narrow corridor, all marble floor, leading into darkness.

'Do you know where we are?' I had not yet released Chloe's arm and the soft feel of her skin in my grip was a pleasure I was not about to relinquish.

'No, master. I do not.'

She would not raise her eyes to look at me, which I liked, and she did not complain about the tightness of my grip on her arm, which I liked even more. I was under no illusions about the Master's honour here. That promise he gave me about having an hour was not worth much, not if his other dealings with me had been anything to go by. Already I could imagine the throng behind the metal doors, melting away through hidden doorways. The bloodlust upon them, goaded by the Governor's barked orders.

'I saved your life back there,' I reminded Chloe.

'I am yours,' she said with a disarming simplicity which even at that moment in time, made my heart race a little.

'We shall see,' I gave her a feral grin and tugged her towards me so that she lost her balance. She gave out a little cry and reached out with her free had to clasp onto me.

I caught her and held her against my chest. Since Jemma I had held many women in my arms. Some were professionals and some were not. Some I paid and some I didn't. But by the time I pulled Chloe into my arms I was somewhat of an expert at the way a woman's body should feel.

Nevertheless nothing in my past had quite prepared me for the way Chloe felt as I held her. Her head barely came up to my chest, and I could feel the twin, firm mounds of her breasts as they were pressed against me. Through the thinness of her dress I could clearly feel the heat exuded by her body. A heat that built almost to a conflagration near her loins as the wide cradle of her hips pressed itself against me, her thighs hard against mine. Almost beyond my volition, I swept a quick arm round her body and dropped my hand to steal a touch of her behind. The twin, full moons of her buttocks were like the rest of her: ripe and firm. Tight with youth and supple to the touch. Hot like a furnace.

I became immediately aware as my hand closed round a buttock that she had no underwear. Under that thin dress she was naked. Indeed, the thought sprang into my mind that I had only to push her against a wall, sweep her wide peasant skirt up and with a thrust I could be inside of her, giving her her first fuck. No sooner had the thought popped into my head than I had dismissed it. Whatever spell Chloe's ripe, young body was weaving upon me, survival was a stronger need still and right then we were both in extreme danger. I gave her proud, deeply divided ass one last squeeze and she whimpered.

'There'll be a time for that later,' I said, aware that my lungs were labouring like I had just run a mile. Carefully I set Chloe back on her feet and let go of her arm. 'Is there anywhere we could go which would be safe for us now?' I asked.

She nodded vigorously. 'I know a place master. I do.'

'Let's go then,' I said and with those words I entrusted my fate entirely upon the notions of a sexual innocent.

***

When you run for your life you haven't always got time to think. The world around you breaks down into kaleidoscopic images, barely glimpsed. What you are most aware of is the fact that your heart is labouring to power your body. You know that it's working hard to help you remain alive and to begin to think about being tired, or out of breath is to betray it.

Chloe and I ran like devils. We turned and turned again, running past deserted corridors, passages and tiny alleys with a dozen or more doors opening to them. Finally, Chloe signalled that we were to turn and we found ourselves in a cul-de-sac. Smooth walls surrounded us on all sides.

'Quickly, this way,' she said and touched something at the base of one of the walls and a doorway appeared to our right, as if by magic. We both squeezed through it.

'Nice little hideaways the Master has,' I grunted as I bent my knees to accommodate my height.

'Oh, this is not the Master's doing,' Chloe said. 'Calimba is far older than the Master thinks,' she ventured, 'there have been troubles in the past. We all know how to hide.'
Her words lit a fresh spark of hope inside me. 'You mean that not everyone here is on the Master's side?'

'Masters come and go,' she said enigmatically.

We walked on for about ten minutes, in total darkness, the sweat cooling on our bodies and our breaths getting back to normal, before I asked: 'so what remains?'

'Huh?'

'What remains the same Chloe, if Masters come and go? What is it that does not change?'

There was a pause. She stopped abruptly in the darkness and I walked right into her. Instinctively, my arms went round her body to stop myself from falling and I found my left hand cupping the roundest, firmest breast it had ever held. She made no move to get away.

In the dark, she stood still, trapped in my arms. I dropped a casual hand to her thigh and began to gently rub it up and down through her dress, feeling its firm promise, the ripe curve of its line. The passage we were in was narrow. Too small for me to even contemplate turning Chloe round and spreading those ripe thighs wide, but the beast of my desire was out of its cage. The danger we'd just escaped from and our recent exertions had only served to whet its appetite. It needed to feed and Chloe was more than a casual morsel. I brought both hands up to roughly cup and squeeze her breasts. Her nipples felt hard, and hot to the touch, and my fingers found them and tugged at them through the thin fabric of her dress. Chloe whimpered. 'Quiet now,' I said. 'I know it's your first.'

I did. I could only imagine the tight silkiness of her pussy.

Pushing her forward, feeling my way in the dark, I managed to turn us both so that Chloe was now pressed against one of the rough, walls on either side of us. With desperate hands I fumbled with her dress, brought it up, bunched it at her waist and let my hands roam over her.

Full, round hips flared out from the tiny circle of her waist. I ran my hands on either side of her hips, down to the outside of her thighs, then back up again, coming to feel the smooth roundness of her proud ass. In the dark, I squeezed her pliant flesh, parted those plump cheeks and finding the opening of her rear passage pushed my index finger hard up her. Chloe's body stiffened at this. She tried to wriggle away, escape my attentions, but pressed against the wall as she was, with me right up behind her, this was impossible.

I wriggled my index finger, pushing it further up her rear orifice. She was as I'd expected, hot and tight and silky to the touch. Looking back at that first, incredible experience with her, I sometimes marvel that in the midst of life-threatening danger I had had sufficient energy and concentration to do what I did to her. But then, perhaps it was the very fact that I knew, at the time, that there was a good possibility that I would not come out alive from that situation, which prompted my actions.

I have a dim recollection of fumbling with my own trousers, but my first clear memory of the time in the passage with Chloe is of the electric feel of the inside of her naked thigh as I rubbed my engorged penis up her leg. She was by now fighting me, trying to escape my grasp.

'No master, no!' she gasped.

Her efforts were no match for my strength.

'You are a slave for sale,' I reminded her, 'if not for me you would be sold to a brothel where you will have a dozen cocks a day up your tight little pussy,' I hissed. I punctuated my words with little slaps to her rump. Each time I struck the hot flesh, I felt it jump and quiver beneath my open palm. So intoxicating was the sensation that I pressed Chloe harder against the wall and turned my body sideways, giving my right hand free access to slap her thighs and hips as well as her ass. Each smack made a fleshy, satisfying sound, warming the flesh it struck, readying it for my pleasure. Even as Chloe struggled and cried out, the lushness of her body was betraying her. As I held her, I pushed my knee up between her legs from behind, prizing her thighs apart, opening her up for me to use. I could feel, against my knee, the incredible heat from between her legs, where the centre of her tightly nestled in the diamond between her thighs and, as I paddled that magnificent behind, I felt the first hint of moisture come from her. A heated wetness, as her body, magnificent love-vessel that it was, made the decision for her.

'You choose which you would rather have,' I kept admonishing Chloe in the dark, 'You can be either my toy. Here to pleasure me, or a fuck-thing for men who don't care about you. Men who see you only as an object to come inside of. Men who will fuck you senseless, two-three at a time and then discard you.'

Whether it was my admonitions or my continuous slapping I cannot tell, but the desired effect was achieved. Presently Chloe stopped struggling and lay there, pressed up against the wall, in total darkness, her skirt bunched up round her waist, legs apart, waiting to be penetrated for the very first time. It was as if a supplicant who'd been surviving on scraps had been suddenly given the keys to a restaurant. An incredible feeling of power filled the moment. Suddenly, there I was, master of this magnificent, exotic creature who was submitting to my will. Purposefully I rubbed the swollen head of my erection up and down on the tender inside of Chloe's ripe thighs and, involuntarily, she shivered. The head of my cock nudged against the swollen lips of her pussy, felt the heat there, the wetness. I savoured the moment, saving every second of it, itemising it in my head for a time in the future. The instant Chloe's body submitted, I felt her slump forward, the action raising her hips slightly higher, giving me easier access to her body. But I was not yet ready to finish with her. Even in that moment of extreme danger, my mind told me that this was a rare opportunity, not to be wasted. I pulled away from her so that in the dark, for a second or two there was no contact between us.

'Master?' Chloe's voice sounded small and now, a little frightened.

It drove home to me the strange bond that had developed, the duty I felt towards her.

I lashed out and slapped her naked, raised rump again. Felt satisfaction at the sound it made, and the squeal of pain she let out.

'Shut up!' I said, 'Talk only when you're spoken to. Understand?'

There was silence.

Again I slapped her rump, felt the fingers of my right hand bite deep into the plump, tender flesh of her buttocks. I longed at that moment for a light, a torch to show me the red marks I must have been leaving on her soft, smooth skin. The redness that must be creeping into the worked flesh, looking hot and inviting, ready for a rear-fucking that would leave her feeling drained.

I slapped again and this time she cried out more loudly.

'Answer me!' I said, 'Do you understand?'

'Yes, yes master,' she replied.

In the dark my hands groped until I felt the soft tresses of her straight black hair. My fingers took hold of it and I pulled her away from the wall which she had slumped against.

With the heightened senses brought on by the absence of light I felt the delicate, elfin features, the full, ripe lips. I held her by the hair with one hand, shuffling towards her so that the tip of my cock, hard and sensitive, jabbed like the blunt end of a spear at the softness of the flat plain of her stomach.

'Master?' Chloe's voice was questioning, uncertain. I felt soft hands touch my raised erection and the sensation sent electric sparks shooting in my nerve ends. I slapped her again, this time making unerring contact with the softness of her left cheek.

'Do only what I tell you!' I hissed and put increased pressure on her hair, where I held it, on top of her head.
Guided by my hand, in the dark and narrow passage, Chloe dropped to her knees in front of me.

'Take it in your mouth,' I ordered and pulled her towards me, jabbing at her with my hips, totally blind in the dark. The first jab missed her mouth, brushed past her lips, pushed against the soft smoothness of her left cheek, already hot where I had hit her. The second, struck her hard on the chin, drove her head back so that she cried out.
Desperately, I pulled back, corrected and lunged forward again with my hips. This time my aim was true. I felt the gasp of shock as the head of my cock, swollen, distended, flushed with blood at full arousal, found the softness of Chloe's full, innocent lips, pushed past them, parting them with force and rammed itself to the hilt in the back of her throat. Her moan of surprise was choked into a muffled groan and then a gasp as the muscles of her throat constricted involuntarily at the intrusion and she instinctively sucked on me.

In the narrow confines of the dank passageway we found ourselves in, I learnt the greatest lesson of all and the irony is that I learnt it at a time when I should have been beyond learning anything.

There, in the dark, with Chloe's invisible, accommodating mouth working away at me, her lips sucking and suckling and making wet, slurping sounds as I rammed myself into her again and again, mouthfucking her silly, I felt as if the essence of me, the thing which made me feel and think and act like Andy Meyer, somehow became separated, divorced. What was left was a machine. A superbly made sex machine which could not help but pump itself into Chloe's mouth, in preparation for penetrating and fully using all her other orifices. What made it wondrous for me was the fact that the machine, my body, slave as it was to its primitive impulses, was also a facet of what I was. It was the handle through which the world could grasp me and make me human.

It had taken the almost transcendental sensation of Chloe's sucking to make me realise that. If we both died that moment, our essences, though diminished, would still go on. What we would lose would be our capacity to interact with the world.

I have since experimented with a variety of ways, trying to find the most reliable to recreate this sensation. Nothing comes near sex.

The revelation was over in an inkling, a micromoment, and then, like a rubber band had pulled me back, with a snap I felt myself being immersed back into my physical body and all the sensations and sounds and smells became very real again and I grabbed Chloe's head with both my hands and thrust my pelvis forward violently so that her nose was scrunched tightly against the coarse curls at the base of my cock. The motion pushed me far inside her mouth and this time she knew enough to relax her throat muscles to take me deep inside her.

The sensation this produced was maddening for me, it fed my lust to next ravish her virginal, tight pussy and I pulled myself out of her mouth, feeling the strong tug of her lips as she desperately tried to hold me in. After the wet heat of Chloe's mouth the cool air of the dark passageway made all the nerve ends of my erection tingle with excitement. In the dark I felt its massive, aching, tumescence and was consumed by the need to put out the flames of passion rising inside me as quickly as possible. I dropped my hands to Chloe's shoulders and fumbled about in the dark, looking to see exactly where she was. Then, bending my knees, I picked her up by the arms and raised her to her feet. Chloe let out a gasp as I pressed her against the wall, pinned her there, beyond any hope of escape and with sure hands squeezed and kneaded the fullness of her magnificent breasts, through the thin fabric of her dress.

What I really wanted of course was to rip that threadbare dress off her, to have some light to see her, to read the expression in her eyes as I pushed her on her back, mounted her and breast-fucked her. I wanted to see her features contort as I next spread her legs wide and savagely pumped myself against her. But fully expecting that these few moments with her were to be my last, I was taking what I could. With one arm I held her pinned against the wall and with the other one I pulled her dress up from between us, baring her lower body. I then drove my knee up between her legs, parting her thighs.

'Lie still you minx!' I hissed, 'remember who I am,' I gasped as I spread her legs, revelling in the tender, supple feel of her inner thighs, the flesh there smooth and firm, a real pleasure to touch. I bent my knees, taking aim, guessing at my target in the dark and, when I was reasonably sure of success, I lunged. My first thrust, missed its mark, stabbed a little high instead and Chloe cried out in pain. But I had found what I wanted now and as I came up again I found the gate of her coral-lipped womanhood and with a stroke as old as mankind, tore its fleshy, wet portals aside and her virginity and slid effortlessly all the way into the depths of her.

Such was the force of my first incursion that Chloe was lifted bodily off the floor, legs flailing helplessly in the dark. I felt her hot pussy open up, its love canal hot and tight, stretching to encompass my girth and I let go of my hold on her and dropped both arms to grasp her round behind. My fingers hooked into the soft, pliable flesh of her ass and I lifted her bodily off the floor, supporting her weight with my legs and involuntarily Chloe's legs were raised, her thighs wrapping themselves around me in the dark.

Thus centred I charged her repeatedly, grunting with each massive stroke and Chloe screamed and gasped and thrashed in my arms, her tight ass wriggling and as I fucked her, plunged deep into her cunt, I worked one hand beneath her, until my index finger rested on the tight button of her anus, its flower closed.

I pulled back, momentarily, and then thrust again, feeling my hips crash against Chloe's centre, I heard the breath being forcefully driven from her lungs and as yet another involuntary gasp escaped her lips I chose that moment to push my finger into the tight hole of her ass. Chloe let out a high pitched cry and her body went rigid, caught in the throes of a pleasure she'd never expected and that's when my incessant pumping into her bore fruit and I felt at last the familiar white out begin behind my eyes. The spasm that seized my body threw my head back and I felt the mass of semen splash into the receptive cunt walls of Chloe's tight pussy.

Gently, I put her back down on her feet and felt her legs give way and her body slide down the wall, so that once again, she was pretty much where we had started, kneeling at my feet.

'Get up,' I ordered in the dark and my voice was hoarse, my lungs labouring as if I had just run a mile. The madness which had seized me was seeping out of me now, my passion satiated and I was beginning to realise the urgency of our situation, 'Get up now.'

I heard furtive rustling in the dark as Chloe rearranged her clothes. I again regretted the lack of light at that moment. I would have given anything for a glimpse of her bruised-looking mouth and lips, or her ripe, round thighs and the hot little nest between her legs.

'We must go,' I told her. At the back of my mind, like a spark, lay my new-found awareness and although I was conscious of the fact that our chances were slim, I also knew that fear was a luxury I could ill-afford.

'Master?' Chloe's voice sounded small and distant, coming from a long way away.

'Snap out of it,' I said, 'We need to get somewhere safe.'

My words got through to her, for she picked herself up. Her hand hunted for mine in the dark and then, she led the way, walking in total darkness with a confidence born of practice.

'You've been here before,' I said.

'Many times.'

'So you know where this passage will lead?'

'There are several exits,' she said as we walked in the dark, 'some are bound to be watched. The Master's satyrs have a way of finding out about these things.'

'So where are we going?'

'Somewhere safe,' she said.

With that we each concentrated on placing our feet on the slightly uneven, beaten earth floor of the passage without tripping. A few times I thought I heard distant cries. Women's voices. Once a baby crying. But Chloe did not slacken her pace and I was too much caught up in my thoughts to stop and ask.

'I think we're here,' she said at last.

I don't know how she knew, how she could possibly know in that complete darkness.

'Where's here?' I asked.

'We are,' she said, 'very near where you first met me master. We are near the house where I grew up.'

Unbidden, the image came in my mind of the monstrous man I had first laid eyes upon, the one who had so casually told Chloe to look after me while he was busy fucking that hapless woman spreadeagled beneath him.

'I see,' I said, 'I thought we were going somewhere safe.'

'We are. Not far from there there's a place where we can find help.'

I could hear her fumbling around in the dark again. Her hip brushed against me as she put her hands on the wall behind me and started to methodically search for something.

'What....?' I began to ask when there was a clear, audible click behind me and suddenly the dark passage was suffused with cold, clear air and the light of the stars. So accustomed to the darkness had my eyes become that I had to blink several times to clear them. Beyond the dark opening of the portal Chloe had activated lay the silent outline of a dozen or so houses; more to the right. It was a village neighbourhood scene, except that in Calimba it was probably colder than in any other neighbourhood on the planet and the houses looked like something out of the previous century.

'We must go now! Quick!' Chloe hissed at my side.

'Lead the way.'

She took hold of my hand and at a crouch, both of us broke cover and ran like rabbits in the dark, towards the row of houses on our right.

We should have made it. We would have. Except that Chloe's exertions, my cruel use of her and even the temperature difference of the cold night air, all played their part and she misjudged her footing. Her left ankle twisted as she ran and she fell with a cry of pain.

'Get up,' I was by her side, hands grasping her to pull her up and then, suddenly there was the dancing light of burning torches all around us and from beyond the shadows, bounding towards us were the unmistakeable figures of four massive satyrs.

'We're lost! We're lost!' Chloe cried. 'Leave me, master. Save yourself.'

She needn't have urged me. I already knew that the best chance for her survival was for me not to get caught. I vaulted over Chloe's prostrate body and ran as hard as I could.

From my left, from the deep shadow between two rows of houses rose a figure and flung itself at me. I felt strong hands grasp the thin fabric of my tunic and tug; there was the sharp ripping sound of it parting. Blindly I struck out with my elbow, connected with something hard more by chance than by design and heard a muffled groan. Then something incredibly hard hit me on the back of the head and almost took my legs out from under me, but I somehow kept on going, staggering, squinting to make out the path I was taking through the tiny lightbulbs going off in front of my eyes.

Behind me voices raged.

There was a tiny, sharp cry which I recognised as belonging to Chloe and I almost stopped and turned back. My legs though betrayed me at that crucial moment and I tripped, lost my balance entirely and went down in an untidy heap, rolling as I fell until I came to a stop at the very base of a tiny house.

There was deep shadow thrown by the house opposite and as I lay there, feeling the throbbing pain at the back of my skull and trying to assess whether anything had been broken I saw a tight band of four satyrs and six other people march past torches held high.

The torchlight did not penetrate into the shadows, where I lay, and from my position I was able to clearly see Chloe being marched past.

The top of her dress had been ripped to shreds so that her proud breasts lanced the air, bouncing saucily with each step she took. I guessed that one of the satyrs had backhanded her once because her left cheek was a deep, bright red, visible to me in the torchlight even from where I was hiding. A rope had been fashioned into a noose and placed round her neck and her hands had been tied behind her back so that her breasts rode even higher. One of the attendants to the satyrs held the rope. He walked behind Chloe and, as they passed me, I saw him reach out with one hand and take a feel of her round behind. Chloe let out a squeal and jumped forward, he tugged on the noose round her neck, unbalancing her and making her breasts jiggle. There were hoots of laughter from the men around her and one of the satyrs snorted with derision.

'Do you think the Master will let us have her?' I heard

him ask his companion.

'Not a chance,' said the other man and I recognised the cultured tones of Matthew, the Master's son, 'this one is as good as dead, but first I hear she belongs to the Governor.'

'The Governor, of course! He won't be pleased the man has escaped.'

'He got lucky, but he's on his own now and he doesn't know Calimba. It won't be long before we get him.'

'Will we have some sport with him?'

'The Governor said he wants to make him an example. He is convinced the man's a charlatan. A false prophet and he will not survive the Test.'

'Matik says he hit with all his strength and yet the man just walked away like it was nothing.'

'Matik has a broken nose. His pride's hurt.'

'But there was blood on his bolo.'

Bolo! I put a hand to the tender spot on the back of my head. The bastard had hit me with a bolo. I was lucky I had not been brained. My hand came away all sticky. I guessed there was a gash there, but because of shock and the cold I was beyond feeling any pain.

'Maybe,' said Matthew and I suddenly realised that there was palpable uncertainty in his voice. 'Let's take this hot womanflesh to the Governor and we'll then be able to search for the stranger properly. If Matik did hit him with his bolo he won't go very far.'

'Then maybe we could play with him a little before handing him over to the Governor.'

'Maybe.'

Chapter 19

When you are dealing with danger, sometimes the safest place is right in the centre of it. Feeling a little woozy still from the blow on the head this Matik had dealt me, I padded, as silently as I could after the massive form of Matthew and his friend. Glimmers of moonlight as we passed by blocks of dark houses, allowed me to see Chloe, her hands bound tightly behind her back, her round haunches, rolling tightly with each step, moulding the thin material of her dress.

A couple of times the troupe in front of me stopped and a discussion seemed to take place but their tones were too hushed for me to make much sense of it. During one of those times Chloe must have muttered something for suddenly Matthew turned and backhanded her without any warning. She fell to her knees with a cry, her bared breasts bouncing, her nipples erect from fright and the effect of the night air. Such was that momentary allure of her helplessness as she was on her knees, looking up in silent supplication at her captors, her full lips parting pleadingly, that even I felt a stirring in my groin. The sexual message exuded by this delightful creature did not go unfelt by Matthew and his companions. A quick look was exchanged amongst them and suddenly the entire atmosphere of the troupe was transformed. Matthew cast one quick look around, saw no sign of any danger and then looked back at the men he commanded. Imperceptibly almost he nodded to them and they started milling about, talking softly amongst themselves, hands fumbling with their clothes.

Chloe instantly sensed the change in their mood. She realised what was coming and tried to get up on her feet, but with her hands tied behind her she was quite helpless and another backhanded blow, casually dealt, sent her sprawling on her side, legs flailing under her. Helplessly, my mind seething with anger and a dozen half-formed plans I watched as Matthew shouldered his men aside, bent down to hook his fingers in Chloe's dark, straight tresses and with a jerk that made her cry out again he pulled her up. Once again she was kneeling on the ground, her vulnerable mouth and lush lips at crotch level to the troupe.

As I had feared, Matthew lined himself up directly in front of her. In a sudden shaft of moonlight I saw his massive organ, exposed, erect and heavily veined, pointed threateningly at Chloe's face, its thick, bulbous head almost directly lined up with her lips.

Chloe let out a gasp of fear and surprise and turned her head away. She made a move to get up on her feet. Matthew must have been expecting it. He nodded again and two goons fell upon her from behind, put heavy hands upon her shoulders, immobilising her and dropped their greedy, grabbing hands to roam the round expanse of her ass and cup the sweet round orbs of her breasts. Fondled thus, her body played with, bound and helpless, Chloe was no match for Matthew's insistent hand that took hold of her chin, turned her head up, face and mouth vulnerably exposed, and, with one massive surge of his hips, drove his organ past her lips to the very back of her wet, warm throat.

Chloe's dark skin turned a shade darker, the change visible even in the pale moonlight. Her eyes went wide open, threatening almost to pop out of their sockets as she felt the massive invasion of her mouth, an invasion of a thickness unlike anything she had experienced up to that moment. A half choked moan escaped her lips and then her mouth was totally filled, her cheeks blown out as she was forced to suck Matthew's cock. The big brute let out a howl and placing a massive, hairy hand at the back of Chloe's head pulled it forward, burying her face into his middle just as he pumped his hips back and forth. Chloe's moans turned into splutterings as she struggled with all her might to take a breath between Matthew's ceaseless pumping and the sucking she was being made to perform.

Such was the force of his thrusts that in the glittering moonlight and the cold night air I could clearly see glistening flecks of spittle fly as Matthew forcefully arched his back and drove his hips forwards. Each time this happened Chloe's moans would take on a deeper, more agonised quality and the veins in her lovely, long neck would swell as she struggled to accommodate the meaty pole he was feeding her.

Then, suddenly, Matthew's massive form went rigid. His head arched up towards the night sky, eyes totally unseeing and Chloe made desperate gobbling noises as he splashed his load of semen against the inside of her cheeks.

Spent, he withdrew from her mouth.

No sooner was he out of her than the goons holding her down changed positions and one of them quickly moved to replace Matthew. Their fondling of her ripe, young flesh had driven them to extreme arousal and they all now sought release so each in turn grabbed her head with both hands burying themselves to the hilt in Chloe's warm, wet, accommodating mouth.

It went on for some time.

Hidden in the shadows I could only watch and listen, helplessly, as each of those goons in turn made free use of Chloe's sweet mouth to gain release for their arousal.

Her muffled, half-choked cries soon became gasps and sobs as she tired of sucking them. And still they drove at her, one after another, mouthfucking her until her face, despite the cold, was covered with a fine sheen of sweat, her chin and lips awash in splashed semen.

Tired as she was, exhausted by her ordeal, the run we had made, my use of her and now this, Chloe would have been easy sport for the whole lot of them. The entire troupe could have spread-eagled her there and then, laid her out on the cold stones of the narrow street and by the naked moonlight, gangbanged her until she passed out.

Surprisingly they didn't.

One by one they emptied themselves into her mouth and then, as if by tacit agreement, they straightened out their garments and, with Chloe once more in their midst, resumed their march.

Once again I followed them. Cold now and numb, my feet hurting from all the running.

My mind struggled to cope with all the revelations I had had about myself, the sudden flashes of insight which had helped me transcend my old self. But these very same insights however now filled me with dread. The cold dread of failure. I knew, instinctively, why the Master's so-called Test called for me to run for my life, to try to survive in an environment I knew next to nothing about and which was hostile to me. I also knew that the very insights which had filled me with strength, now allowed me to see all the possibilities for mistakes. They permitted me to see exactly how I could fail, and to contemplate failure allows the possibility of it occurring.

As I followed the now silent troupe ahead, it was this last thought which filled my mind.

The men and Chloe, led by Matthew, went through narrow streets and under archways where the darkness was so complete that I had to slow down and feel my way through, hands touching the cold stone of the buildings we passed. Their steps were sure, unfaltering as they led the way and then came to a stop in front of an imposing stone structure. It had many windows, all narrow and tall and only one was lit.

'The Governor is expecting us,' said one of the men and Matthew shushed him with a sharp hiss.

'None of you realise what's at stake here,' he said, 'none of you!'

His outburst stopped the joviality of the men and they bad-temperedly jostled and pushed Chloe, slapping her rump and pushing her ahead of them. So intent was I in watching all this that I failed to notice the changing nature of the light around us. The deep shadows which until had given me total protection were lessening. The sky overhead was clearing and the moon, now unfettered shed its silvery cold light with renewed vigour, a final gust of wind, high overhead, blew the last wisps of cloud away and it was like night turned into day. Everything was outlined with a painful clarity and I was left, by the edge of some low-lying buildings, hugging the cold, hard ground and praying like I had never prayed before for Matthew and his troupe not to notice me. Indeed, Matthew had approached the door and some sort of signal had been given, for suddenly from inside the stone building there was the noise of activity and a lot more windows were suddenly lit. This contributed to the brightness of the moonlight so that suddenly the hammering of my heart at the thought of being discovered became greater than the chattering of my teeth. As I watched and hugged the ground and prayed, I heard the sound of marching feet from another narrow street to my left and one more troupe of men appeared, led by two massive satyrs.

One of them I recognised instantly as one of the brutes who had so cruelly used the dancers, back at the chamber. Gritting my teeth, trying to instil a semblance of control over my unruly body I started crawling back. Inch by inch I tried to make my way into deeper shadows. The new troupe were carrying torches held high overhead and long glimmers, like the tendrils of a monster intent on seizing me and killing me found their tantalising way towards me.

Just then I felt a draft in the darkness behind me. A movement in the air as if something large was in motion behind me. Unable to move without blowing my cover and drawing the unwanted attention of the satyrs I froze. Held my breath.

For long, agonising moments nothing happened.

Then, suddenly, there was a massive explosion of light behind my eyes and then, everything grew first dim and then slowly, very, very dark.

***

When I opened my eyes I realised that somehow, I had managed to come full circle.

'You, wake now, need to drink.'

I was being prodded awake.

Momentarily I thought that I was back in my hotel room in Bogota. I thought that indeed, it had all been one long, terribly ugly dream, but the pungent, earthy smells that assailed my nostrils and the dark, low ceiling overhead immediately dispelled that thought, just like before.

I sat up and winced with pain. My arms, shoulders and ribs felt sore, rock-beaten. I recalled then my fall and I turned to see who had spoken.

'You need drink,' repeated the voice. 'Drink now.'

She was a slim, blonde haired girl, her skin tinged with the light, golden cast that comes only from exposure to the sun at high altitudes. Her hair was short, cropped, almost like a man's and her features spoke of extreme youth. Tired, exhausted and in pain, as I was, I hazarded a guess that she was no more than eighteen. She motioned for me to follow her. I would, of course, pains and aches notwithstanding but I suddenly realised that my feet had been tied together, my ankles bound by a length of rough rope no more than two foot long.

'Wait!' I cried and my voice came out a croak 'My feet are tied.'

She turned back, the movement momentarily permitting me to admire her profile. I was right, she was a stunner, not quite in the same class as Chloe was, nowhere near as exotic, but beautiful nevertheless.

She said: 'Oh yes. Forgot. Had to tie you, no use you running away. The satyrs would have killed you. They make a sport of you. Test then would be over.'

As she spoke she worked at my ankles, her nimble, young fingers pulling and tugging at the knots and presently I felt my legs being released. Still trying to comprehend what she had just said I slowly stood up, pulling the rugged blanket tight about me. My body still felt sore and bruised, and the room I was in was cold. The floor was made of some kind of matting, I saw. It was only when I stood on it however that I realised just how weak I really was and how hard I had to try not to sway on my feet.

'Drink, come.' The girl motioned again, and with her tightly rolling buttocks beneath the dress as guide, I followed her slim form outside the room, to what appeared to be some kind of large communal room. A table took centre stage in it, strategically placed in front of an open fireplace. A blaze was in and the room was warm. A large ceramic pitcher stood in the middle of the table, an earthenware cup next to it. But what captivated my attention was the hirsute, naked man at the room's far corner. He was stretched out by one wall with all his garments on the rattan mat floor about him. He was about 5ft 7', and heavily built, with a thick pelt of dark hair down his shoulders and back. His head was covered in unruly, black masses of hair that flew in all directions and he had an unkempt beard.

When I first saw him he had a young woman spreadeagled beneath him. Her clothes, I saw, had been savagely ripped off her. He had one calloused had clamped tight across her mouth and was busy thrusting away between her spread legs. He grunted each time he charged at her and with his free hand squeezed and savagely kneaded her left breast. The woman had her legs spread wide apart. Her feet were planted on the floor on either side of the hairy brute's hips, and as he thrust at her, her knees sagged outwards with the force of his charging and her eyelids flickered. It was so surreal that it took long moments for my mind to comprehend what my eyes were witnessing. In that time the brute took hold of one of the young woman's shapely legs and pulled it up high so that the back of her thigh was now resting on his shoulder. Having positioned her so, her body in place for deeper penetration, the brute recommenced his efforts.

He drove himself at her, his thrusts forcing deep, guttural cries from her. He was totally oblivious to my existence and as I watched he pulled himself out of the writhing, straining woman, turned her over so that she was now face down, her round ass exposed and reaching behind him he picked up without even looking a long, thin piece of leather thong. It was thin and black. Toughened by high-altitude sun.

'Bitch,' granted the brute. With one hand he held the woman easily down. With the other he wrapped the thin whip round his fist, getting a good grip on it.

That's when he noticed me, standing there, wrapped in my blanket with the thin, blonde girl by my side. He looked my way and to my amazement, the sense of dÈj‡ vu returned as I recognised the same swarthy, hirsute brute I had encountered when I first woke up in Calimba. I felt the ground sway beneath me and reached out a hand on the thin, blonde girl's shoulder for support.

'You awake. At last,' he grunted totally unconscious of the fact that his erect member, wet and glistening had just been pulled out of the netherparts of the naked woman lying prostrate in front of him. And with that he raised his right arm high above his head, took careful aim and brought the leather lash down across the woman's buttocks. Instantly her body was galvanised. A cry escaped her lips and a thin, red welt was raised across her plump buttocks, like a furrow. Unmoved the brute repeated the move. Again the woman cried out. Again she strained without avail to escape the hand that held her, so securely, to the matting. Across her rump now lay two red welts, marking an expanse of prime female flesh no more than the breadth of a man's palm apart. The brute cast one last look my way, grunted something which I did not understand and then studied his handiwork with the intensity of a sculptor about to attempt a particularly difficult work of art.

'Observe,' he said at last, 'how she lies, waiting for me to subdue her so she can pleasure us both.'

I did not know what to make of that. My hand however, which rested still on the shoulder of the thin blonde girl, closed almost involuntarily and squeezed the small bones and soft flesh I felt there.

The girl did not move.

'Women,' continued the brute, 'the cause of our downfall. Also our saving grace.'
With that he suddenly began to lash, driving his whipping arm down at full strength, furrowing the marked area on the woman's plump behind with precise, carefully measured strokes that tinged it a deep red, tenderised it in a way I thought would cause her a delicious kind of pain were she to be taken from behind after the brute had finished working on her.

Almost as if he'd read my thoughts he said: ' Andy, you come a long way now. Long since you woke up here. Thought I'd killed you last night.'

'Last night?' I said inanely.

I felt once again disorientated.

'You good Andy. You very good,' said the brute still furrowing the woman's arse with savage lashes, making her cry out in a hoarse, pleading way which told my new-found instincts that she knew what was coming next and she would welcome it.

'Had to hit you. You might have cried out.'

Subconsciously I rubbed the back of my head where a painful bump had developed.

'Hit me? You nearly killed me,' I cried.

Instead of replying immediately he lashed the captive woman's backside once again. She let out one final cry and went limp. The brute paused, put the leather strap down and inspected his handiwork with the same intense air as before.

'Had the satyrs heard you. Had you made a noise we'd both be dead,' he finally announced.

He looked up to see what effect his words had on me.

'They got Chloe,' was all I could think to say in return.

'I know. They're going to sell her. She now, sex slave for sale. Not a toy no more. But you are under test. Not any test. The Test. The Master's Test, Andy, and the grapevine says you already better than them now.'

'But my time is not yet up. They're still after me and you can't hide me forever.'

'True, true my friend. When you first came here I thought you were just a blow-in, one of the ones we get who do not last long, but you have proved me wrong Andy, very wrong. I had to hit you to get you here last night. It was the only way to save you.'

He grinned wickedly and there was a sudden glint in his eye, as if that explained everything.

'I don't understand,' I said.

'It's simple. Not everyone in Calimba happy with the Master's rule and his stupid goons. There are cells. Resistance cells. We have been quiet for too long, working in small ways, waiting for the right moment.'

'And you think that that moment is me?' I was incredulous. Suddenly I was being hailed as a messiah, a leader out of the wilderness to liberate a captive people.

'Yeah,' he said and brought the flat of his hand down with a resounding slap on the woman's furrowed backside. She let out another yelp and this time I actually let go of the blonde girl's thin shoulder and took a few steps closer to examine her better. The woman was young, somewhere in her mid-twenties with shapely legs and plump thighs and a round behind that had been fashioned just for fucking in the rear-entry position. Her face was turned away from me, but as she lay, face down, I could see her profile and it was pretty, and noble. She had small, round breasts which rode high on her chest.

'She good,' the brute said again and slapped her backside again hard enough to make her buttocks shake. 'She now warmed up, ready for more fucking,' he indicated the red welts on her arse, where he had used the leather lash on her.

'I don't think we have the time,' I ventured, reluctantly. I must admit I was kind of warming to the idea of ramming myself up this woman's readied arse, stretching the little, tight button of her rear passage.

'Women caused the problem first,' the man said and his free hand roamed over the plump, round cheeks of the woman's behind. He caught a moon shaped buttock and squeezed painfully eliciting a further cry. She tried to wriggle beneath his grip but he effortlessly maintained pressure on her back, between the shoulder-blades, pinning her down, as he talked.

'If not for them the Master would have gone back, but no, they go crazy. They see the chance to get out of Calimba,' he slapped the woman's arse again. 'They see the chance to go fuck foreign men. So the trade gets started and the training of these hot wenches and the satyrs with their strength and speed and bulk.'

I was beginning to get the picture. 'How many of you are there?' I asked.

'Enough,' he said cryptically. 'You in then Andy?'

'Will you help me get Chloe back from the Governor?' I asked.

'Yeah,'

'Then I don't see what choice I have,' I said and held out one hand.

He looked at my outstretched hand for a few moments as if he was trying to work out what to do with it. Then he looked at me. 'No,' he said, 'We use old ways.'

'Old ways?'

'Before the Master, man's agreement sealed in man seed joined in a woman's body,' he said, and slapped the perfectly round backside of the woman he held pinioned down.

'I see,' I said.

I cast my eye quickly round the bare room we were in. During all this the blonde girl had not gone away. She stood there, looking at me, a feverish look in her eyes.

'She first,' the man said and it suddenly occurred to me that the young girl actually wanted to be the first to be used by me. She saw me as this strange hero who had come from outside to change the situation in Calimba and for her it would be an honour to give her body to the man who would deliver them.

'You meanÖ'

'She warm you up,' the man said, 'then we take this one here, ' and he brought his hand up and slapped the ripe backside of the woman he'd been lashing. Her body jerked with the blow and her head came up and she cast a quick look my way and I saw then in her eyes the look of the wanton which told me that the pain she had received had only prepared her for the ecstasy of the fucking which was to follow.

The strange spell of Calimba had taken firm root in me, for suddenly I felt a fierce flame in my loins. I turned towards the blonde girl, seized her by the hair and with my other hand reached out and ripped off the thin dress she had on. Her breasts were high and pointy, the nipples pink and unsuckled still. I put out a quick hand and squeezed and fondled her flesh, letting the blanket which covered me slide from my shoulders. I had time to think that I had indeed come full circle. Here I was, exactly at the same place I had first woken up in, only this time I was in charge. I caressed and moulded her sweet breasts, ran my hand down her flank, over her slim, girlish hips to heft and squeeze a pear-shaped buttock and then I was roaming in that secret place between her legs. She had not yet been shaved and my fingers parted the tight coarse curls guarding the pearly gate of her citadel and then I was making her gasp as I thrust my longest finger up the wet, slippery passage of her cunt.

'You're a little bitch, ain't you?' I said to her and proceeded to turn her over my arm, exposing her bared backside and then I gave the same treatment to her arse.

Her rear passage was really tight and as I pushed my finger up her she kicked out her legs and let out small cries, but I was now in the full thrall of arousal and beyond any reason.

Distantly I heard the rhythmic, meaty slap of flesh on flesh as the man I'd been talking to ploughed himself between the spread legs of the woman he had lashed. I ignored it, my attention focused exclusively on the girl. I pulled my finger out of the tight plug of her arse and grabbed her by her long blonde tresses. I forced her onto her knees in front of me and holding her head tight so that she would not avert her face I thrust my hips forward. My first lunge caught her on the chin and pushed her head back, eyes wide. My second filled her mouth to the full, stretching her lips and plugging her throat so that the only noise that came out of her pretty, young mouth was one of wet slurping as she sucked me.

'Andy, come on,' the man behind me was motioning. He had the woman on her side now, one leg held high and he was busy thrusting himself into her from behind. 'This is the one we clinch our deal on,' he said.

He was right.

I gave one final thrust into the blonde, young girl's mouth, heard her cough and splutter as I went in deep and then I had my member out of her mouth and was kneeling down on the floor, in front of the prone woman, feeding the length of my erection past her full, round lips.

She opened her mouth wide to take me in, her cries now choked by my load. I dropped my hands to her breasts and started sampling their delights.

'Harder, harder, man' the brute panted redoubling his efforts with her, so that with each thrust her body danced and flailed like a rag doll.

'Give it to her harder, make her squeal,' he said.

I complied, thrusting hard and such was the intensity of the first lunge into that wide open throat that I felt my penis overflow and the first spurts of semen splashed into the woman's mouth. I pulled myself out of her in time to catch the secondary bursts, which splashed across her pretty face, right across one of her eyes, forcing her to close her eyelid against the sting of it.

'Now, let's do her this way,' my new found friend and ally said and he lay on his back on the floor, dragging the woman towards him. She was compliant, submissive. She moved as he arranged her, lowering her onto his rampant cock so that she was astride him and her cuntlips were being spread wide to swallow his thick length.

'Now man, stick it to her, from behind,' he ordered me and I moved to comply with this. I positioned myself so that I lay on the man's legs. As the woman began to be raised and lowered I grasped hold of her hips, took careful aim at the little arsehole, winking at me, between the red welts of the lashing, and plunged forward and downward. The woman let you a high pitched squeal as she felt me penetrate her body, stretch the rim of her arse and plunge into the dark depths of her rear passage. In the full throes of my rutting, intoxicated by the feel of that tight orifice yielding itself up to me I slapped the woman's haunches as I began to ride her and with my free hand pinched and squeezed the hard little kernels of her nipples. Such was the invasion of the woman's body, so deep was this double-fucking we were inflicting on her as we sealed our pact that when the moment of explosion came, when the man lying beneath her shot his load up her spread, pliant cunt and filled it to the brim, and when I followed suit and filled her rear passage with my second molten load, she let out one final squeal and collapsed in complete exhaustion between us.

Moments passed. Moments of complete silence during which sanity claimed us back for itself. From the corner of my eye I caught a glimpse of the young, blonde girl, on her knees still, her lips looking raw and bruised and the expression in her eyes told me that whatever happened next this moment would be remembered in legends long after I was gone.

***

From the very first moment I'd set foot in it, Calimba had thrown up a spell which had totally confused my senses. Brutes spoke in cultured voices and acted in a brutish manner. Women submitted themselves totally, in a manner undreamt of by any man. The past and the present, the real and the imagined seemed to blend seamlessly into the fabric which formed Calimba's social structure.

Of course, in retrospect, it was easy to see that I was the proverbial fly in the ointment. The Master had made himself Master and created a complex legend to justify and consolidate his position. He had never counted on the freak occurrence which brought him into Calimba repeating itself, at least not in his lifetime. Irony, of course, pays no heed to timelines. I was in television and I could have instantly told him that.

There is an adage however which goes, to paraphrase just a little, "he who lives by a myth, dies by a myth." The Master had created the myth to rule unchallenged, governing the existence of these hapless men and women as he willed. But no populace, however outwardly docile, is ever entirely so. Sooner or later there comes a time for reckoning.

The time was now.

'The Master's rule has not been entirely without incident,' said the hirsute brute opposite me.

We had disentangled ourselves from the well used body of the woman and were now sitting cross-legged on the floor, dressed in grey peasant garb and being tended to by the blonde girl. As we sat and talked she brought us hot, revitalising drinks that chased fatigue away and made my body thrum and doughy pancakes cooked in large stone ovens and filled with dried, cooked meat. For the first time I realised just how tired and hungry I had been and ate ravenously as the man sitting across me explained the quiet but deliberate oppression of the menfolk of Calimba by the satyrs.

'They take our women to use as they will, gangbanging them for sport and entertainment, they set up whole games where the object is to see which woman from which area will first pass out from too much use.'

The blonde girl, her serving duties finished, next brought a bowl of hot water and began to gently cleanse the wound at the back of my head. Every time I winced with the sting of the balms she was putting on it, she would pause and

bend to gently touch it with her lips.
My mind was concentrating on the plan being laid out by my new companion. A plan as desperate as it was dangerous, my right hand, however unconsciously reached out and found the young girl's calf. I traced the long, slim line of her leg under her skirt all the way to her hip where, to my delight, I found her body free from all restrictive underwear.

Then, as I listened and thought and nodded, where appropriate, I guided my hand to the twin, tight rolls of her young ass, and proceeded to work and squeeze and pinch the flesh, reaping its loveliness for my benefit. If my companion minded what I was doing to the blonde girl while he was talking he gave no indication.

'So, you are really, our only chance. You want to go ahead Andy?'
He stopped then and looked at me, an expectant look on his face.

'It is a dangerous plan,' I said.

He remained silent.

The fingers of my right hand now parted the cheeks of the blonde girl's arse and darted between them, finding the puckered opening of her rear passage.

'We could all die,' I said and thrust a finger deep into her arse.

The blonde girl's willowy body went momentarily rigid next to me, as she felt this invasion of her rear. Her delicate hands tightened a little on my shoulders, then she relaxed and I felt the tight little flower of her arse open itself further to my incursions, as she submitted herself to my will. Beneath my grey peasant trousers a fresh ballooning spoke not only of the effect of the feel of that tight arse but also of the reviving powers of the food and drink I had been given.

My host noticed.

'You need to clear your mind,' he said indicating the bulge at the front of my trousers.

I nodded my agreement and with a swift sweep of my arm, whipped the young girl's body round so that, with a squeal of surprise and mock terror, she came falling into my lap.
I wasted no time. I turned her over swept the skirt, high above her waist and raising my hand brought it crashing down onto her ass.

It made a satisfying smacking sound and the tight cheeks wobbled from the force of the blow. The young girl let out a fresh squeal and her head came up, and with that I loosened the band of my trousers, extracted my erection, and putting a heavy hand at the back of her head pushed her forcefully to my middle. Once again her accommodating, warm, wet mouth opened to take my length, her lips wrapped securely round me and she began to work. With her mouth thus engaged I could focus my entire attention on the rosiness of her delectable ass. I paddled her hard, harder than I could ever remember hitting a woman and my host, himself aroused, suddenly joined in, so that as she sucked me and tried to draw in breaths of air, the young girl let out throaty, guttural gasps as her buttocks shuddered under the twin assaults, which only served to inflame us further.

Moments later, I felt the pressure building at the base of my loins. The head of my penis began to retract and as the first gushes of semen splashed inside the young girl's mouth, my friend reached out, prized the cheeks of her well-beaten arse apart to expose both the sweet lips of her cunt and the now reddened opening of her arse and, producing a meat bone from his plate, shoved it with a twist of his wrist into the latter. The blonde girl's entire body tensed at this. She tried to bring her head up, but I kept my hand on it so that she remained with her mouth impaled upon my dick and held her there until I was completely empty.

'Well?' my friend asked after I'd gone limp in the girl's mouth.

We both watched her as she slowly picked herself up

from my lap, wiped her mouth with the back of one hand, gently pulled the bone out of her behind and straightened her skirts to cover her delectable, little arse.

'I don't have a lot of choices,' I said, which was true. 'Time is running out quickly and the satyrs will find me sooner or later. I think now is the time to go on the offensive.'

'Agreed,' he said and put out one massive, hairy paw.

'Agreed.' I echoed and took it in both my hands.

Chapter 20

It was a simple plan we had conceived. Simple even by Calimba's relatively primitive standards perhaps. It required split-second timing, but if it worked it would be effective.

The hirsute man whose name was something between Chiang and Jiwing, depending on how many times you asked him to pronounce it gave me a crude map of a series of walled off passages and underground chambers which would take me under the street in front of the Governor's palace and then inside it, to where he usually slept.

'Not guarded inside heavily as outside," he had said, "and with the satyrs hunting you down everywhere I don't think there be many men waiting for you."

Boiled down to its simplest form the plan consisted of me undertaking the Test. All I had to do was survive another day. One more day, and release Chloe from the Governor's grasp and I would be free. More than that, not only would I be free to stay or leave as I wished but, if I really wanted to, I could crown myself the new Master.

I said it was simple.

But like most simple plans it was fraught with difficulties. For a start I knew already that the Master never really intended me to have a fair chance to win this game he had put in place. Secondly, unlike most other people in Calimba I knew that the Governor himself was more than a mere arbiter of the Test. He was meant to be the executioner - the one who saw that I never even got the opportunity to succeed. It was these thoughts more than the sleeplessness and fatigue which got to the core of my spirit and made my tread heavy in the dark.

The map Chiang had given me was written on some sort of leather skin dabbed on in luminescent ink. The moment I was away from the moonlight it glowed eerily in the dark showing me the massive range of underground passages which made up Calimba's subterranean side. For the first time since I'd woken up in Calimba I knew exactly what the stakes were. I knew what was being asked of me and, more importantly perhaps, I knew exactly what it was that I had to do. Significantly, for the first time ever I was also totally alone. Left unobserved and to my own devices. It occurred to me then, in my depressed state of mind, to just sit down in the dark. Curl up in a corner somewhere and let my weary body drift off to sleep and never waken. It was an appealing option. The option chosen by a desperate man.

Desperation, however, is a double-edged sword. It can bolster as easily as it can break a man. Alone, with my strange map in the bowels of a city that by rights should not exist, I found myself thinking, perversely, of Jemma Stones.

More particularly, I was thinking of my last time with her.

'You just won't believe this place Andy baby,' she'd breathed in my ear on the way to Paradise.

Paradise was a club she'd discovered on assignment in New York.

The occasion was our third year together. Three years during which Jemma had seen my career begin to slowly blossom as I started networking within the complex world of television.

Sexually too I was becoming more confident.

Jemma and I had experimented with practically everything, I had told myself. We had tried bondage and toys. Fantasy rape and role playing. There had been nights when full of booze and concentrated coffee I had spread-eagled Jemma on the floor of the flat we shared and had stayed on top of her for two hours at a time, pumping into the softness of her body until she was beaten into complete submission, ready to do whatever I ordered her to.

In due course, I had fucked Jemma from behind, used her mouth until her cheeks had grown too sore for her to suck me any more and come over her pretty face until her hair and eyebrows were plastered with semen and my seed was dripping in rivulets onto the upper slopes of her breasts and forming little crystal droplets at the apex of her long, erect nipples.

I had grown accustomed to Jemma and her little tricks and had become a little complacent.

And then she had taken me to Paradise.

We had flown to New York on purpose for the weekend. The club was an underground place just off Fifth Avenue.

'I don't think I'll need these,' Jemma had said on the way to the place. In the back of the yellow cab that was taking us there she had hiked up her long, split skirt to reveal her smooth, shapely legs, all the way up to the black lace of her panties.

Then, with me watching, she had proceeded to remove them, rolling them slowly down her legs until they were lying in a little crumpled heap on the floor of the cab.

'A souvenir,' she had winked at me, and had on purpose left her skirt up until I'd seen her shorn sex, the unguarded pink lips of her citadel looking shockingly vulnerable without the thin trim of fuzz that normally crowned them. The back of the cab was dark, and the driver was too intent on the road to notice what was happening with his passengers. Jemma's insouciance irritated me to the point where I reached across, got a handful of her rich, blonde hair and dragging her by it, pulled her head down on my lap.

She submitted almost immediately.

'Feel that pressure on your cheek bitch?' I hissed into her ear.

'Yes,'

'I want you to take it in your mouth and suck it.'

'I won't,' she said.

I could tell by the way her body was reacting to the pressure of my manhood against the softness of her cheeks that Jemma really wanted me in her mouth. A quick look at the driver told me that he had not noticed a thing, so the next moment I had unzipped myself, taken my erection out, so that it poked up from my black evening trousers like a rampant flagpole, and had pulled Jemma's head forward so that her lips brushed against the meaty girth of it.

'Begin licking bitch,' I ordered and just to show that I had, indeed, meant business, I had given an extra hard tug to her hair which had made her wince. Jemma's hot, obedient tongue began a slow, insistent dance at the base of my cock and started working its way up towards its tip. Her hot breath, stirred the coarse, dark curls at the base of the meaty pole and such was the passion she was inciting in me that, in my seat, I moved forward a little so that the entire length of it was now pressed against her face. Jemma's tongue, reached the top, probed momentarily inside my pisshole and then, her lips slowly parted to engulf me completely. There wasn't a lot of room for movement in the back of the cab so, instead, I just grabbed Jemma's blonde head with both hands and pushed her down so hard that I felt my cock lodge deep into the back of her throat.

Her throat muscles clenched, gripping it tightly and then I could feel the spasms as I just gushed and gushed and gushed inside her, lining her mouth and throat with sticky, viscous come.

'We're almost there.'

It had been the driver's words which had driven us

apart. Guiltily I had straightened up in the back, zipped myself back up again and looked out of the corner of my eye at Jemma who was busy reapplying her lipstick with the help of the mirror in her compact.

The cab stopped moments later and Jemma led me to Paradise.

The doors were shut and a man-mountain was blocking our way.

'No one passes though here tonight,' said the man-mountain.

He was black, bald and his body was reminiscent of a marble monument.

'We're not no one,' Jemma replied.

Before I could stop her she had gripped hold of my wrist, nimbly stepped forward and whispered something into the mountainous guard's ear. Seconds later the man had stepped aside and we were in.

Paradise is a fetish club.

Inside it is all decked out in leather and there are whips and handcuffs all over the place. Rumour has it, it was started by a couple from Ohio who were looking for a way to spice-up their sex life. She was into whippings and public showings and he was into slaves and corporal punishment. The result of all this, was Paradise.

The night Jemma dragged me in there, it was full almost to capacity. At the cloakroom I was given a drink and I watched as Jemma slipped off her cloak to reveal that the dress she had on was cut so low in the back that the cleavage of her round behind almost peeked out as she walked.

'This is a special night for us Andy,' she murmured into my ear, and I nodded my agreement. I might have been learning fast then, but at the time it was not fast enough otherwise I would have recognised the signs long before that night.

Jemma and I took a table.

'Whatever happens, this is what I want,' she said.

I nodded, not yet sure what she meant. My eyes kept looking around at all the women who were in various stages of undress. At the table next to us, half-hidden by shadows a young girl was being gangbanged by three beefy men.

They had her thrown over their table and her dress had been rucked up behind. Her mouth had been stuffed with a white, linen napkin and her hands were tied behind her back. No one seemed to be bothered and as I looked, eyes wide, one of the men finished, pulled himself from inside of her and made room for one of his friends to take his place. Jemma, next to me, was talking about something, seemingly oblivious to all this, but others apparently weren't. As I watched on and off, I realised that there was a growing number of men coming over to the table, fucking the girl and then leaving. The girl's head was hanging over the side of the table, her long black hair hiding her face, but every time she was entered a muffled groan would escape her lips and the guy riding her would grab hold of a long, thin strip of leather and slap away at her behind, adding the delicious sting of the leather whip to the pounding of her vulva.

Jemma kept filling my glass up to the brim and talking, her thigh occasionally brushing against mine and such was the hypnotic thrill of the place that I did not even notice the moment she was no longer next to me.

My eyes instead were on another woman at a corner further away. She was dressed in a body-hugging rubber dress, with openings for her sex and breasts and her hands were tied up in chains and fastened to her ankles so that she really was unable to move very fast at all.

A black rubber dildo had been stuffed deep into her mouth and secured there with a gag so that she could breathe freely only by concentrating on the way her oesaphagus opened and closed.

As I watched incredulously a thin, naked man proceeded to fondle this woman's breasts and cunt, turning her this way and that, until he had her pressed against a wall and unable to escape his attentions.

He then produced a whip, the handle of which was the longest I had ever seen. Totally unconscious of the crowd around him he had rubbed this all over the woman's rubber-clad legs and backside, and then had proceeded to whip her across her arse and the exposed lips of her sex and her breasts, until her body sagged into submission, her knees slightly parting to ease his access to her. He had then inserted the handle of the whip all the way up the woman, forcing it into her until its end had found the very opening of her womb and he was pounding her, eliciting such frenzied moans from her that even through the dildo stuffed in her mouth, I could clearly hear them.

Such was the scene in Paradise. Wherever my eyes fell women were being punished or taken, sometimes both at once. Some women were held rigid, in almost unimaginable positions, servicing up to four men at a time. Others were made to bend over and take five or six of them in quick succession, while others still appeared to be the exclusive property of just one man, who was intent on fucking them in as many different ways as possible in as public and degrading a manner as he could.

The smell of the place was one of women's secretions and men's semen and all around me women were being forced to their knees to worship at the temple of many a man's rampant manhood, and when they got up again their lips and chins would be covered with flecks of white, and there would be a satisfied gleam in their eyes.

I don't know how exactly Jemma happened to come across this place but the thought then of her being made to service a dozen men made me mad. I looked around me, taking this place in and that's when I met Tony.

Tony was Italian and very rich. He came towards me, his skin-tight leather trousers and black T-shirt worn almost like a uniform. One thin arm was wrapped round the tiny waist of a statuesque blonde who, that night was dressed in a flowing white dress which happened to be almost completely transparent.

Where the dress clung to her body, as she walked, I was given a very clear picture of her nipples, breasts, and hairless sex, between thighs which were made to be wrapped round a man's pistoning hips.

'My name's Tony,' he had said and then motioned towards the girl who was with him, 'This is Tanya. My slave.'

Perfunctorily I had shaken hands with the pair of them, my eyes scanning for Jemma. I was cursing the fact that I had allowed myself to be distracted and had not noticed the moment she'd slipped away.

'Jemma sent me,' said Tony and immediately he had my full attention. 'She wants to make sure that you understand what's going on here,' he said, 'Jemma says you're new to all this, not yet fully versed in it all.'

'Where is Jemma?' I asked.

'All in good time. All in good time,' Tony said and sat beside me, putting a friendly arm round my shoulders. The girl, Tanya, sat on the other side of me, her thigh pressed against me and, as the dress clung to her, I saw that she had not bothered with underwear at all and her hips were untouched by the sun and the colour of pure milk through the dress she wore.

'See I've known Jemma a long time,' Tony was saying, 'longer than you and I know exactly what it is she likes.'

'I'm not sure I-'

'Do you think Tanya's attractive?' he'd interrupted me.

'Er, yes but-'

'Would you like her to be yours for a night? Yours to do with exactly as you pleased?'

I had not been prepared for that question. I sat absolutely still, forcing my brain to work overtime trying to see what was happening and then the lights of the club had gone out.

'Don't panic,' Tony was instantly at my side whispering in my ear, 'just watch. Watch and learn kid.'

The darkness was split by a single spotlight. It fell in a narrow beam upon the stage where two steel pillars had been arranged. Chained between them, blindfolded and spread-eagled wasÖJemma!

'Don't make a sound kid,' Tony whispered in my ear, 'just watch.'

Mesmerised, heart pounding I watched as a savage drumbeat began from somewhere and two massive, black dancers appeared on stage. They were heavily muscled, their bodies dressed in tiny scraps round their middles and oiled, so that each muscle strand shone in the spotlight.

In their hands, the two men held black leather whips which they carelessly flicked as they twirled through their dance routine. The crack of the whips made Jemma's helpless body jump and shake and soon I, and everyone else, saw that the two dancers' apparently casual flicking of the whips wasn't casual at all, as rents began to appear in Jemma's dress.

'Look at the expression on her face,' Tony said and indeed, through the crack of the whips and glare of the spotlights I could see, from Jemma's face, that there was a carefully guarded delight at the prospect of having her body exposed and whipped in public. Her legs spread wide apart.

At the time I had still to get used to the idea that sex was a fundamental means of self-expression, a force which should liberate rather than bind and I was ready to spring to my feet and intervene. Tony however held me fast with his comments.

'Watch,' he said, 'how her back arches each time her body is caressed by the whip,'
Indeed, each time the whip touched Jemma's bound body it caused a new tear to appear in her thin dress. She let out a cry and strained against the chains that bound her to the pillars and the movement would cause her breasts to ride higher, push against the fabric of her dress, her nipples hard and clearly visible.

As the drum beat became faster and faster, more and more savage, the tempo of the two dancers increased in ferocity, their whips cracked again and again until Jemma's dress hung in tatters from her body, its curves exposed, the fullness of her breasts and the seductive cradle of her hips clearly visible to all.

Where the whips had scored her fair flesh, red lines marked their passage and there was a deliciously tortured yet abandoned look to her which aroused even me that time.

'Watch how the pain she's suffered and the anticipation of the unknown brought on by her inability to see how and when the next assault is to be inflicted upon her, have combined to heighten her perception of everything around her,' Tony whispered.

I nodded dumbly because it was true. At that moment the bound, near-naked, whipped Jemma Stones had more in common with a wild fertility goddess than the woman who had initiated me into the joys of sex.

Out of the corner of my eye I caught sight of Tanya, on the couch beside us, pressed into it face down. She was biting her lips against the charges of a man who had turned her over, shoved her forward, lifted her dress up above her waist and was now busy ramming himself into her, cramming her sex full of his meat while his eyes were riveted on Jemma up on stage.

As the music reached an even higher tempo the two black dancers threw away their whips, ripped at the thin material at their waists so that their members, erect, massive black poles stood fully exposed and let out a guttural cry in unison. A low, throaty gasp escaped many people's mouths the instant the two black men exposed themselves. They were truly enormous, with penises like rampant telegraph poles capable of stretching to the limit any girl's orifice.

They approached Jemma from behind and from the front, sandwiching her whipped, milky white body between them. My last glimpse was of her arms and legs thrashing violently against the chains and low, guttural cries escaping her as the two black men, goaded now by the cries of the audience commenced pumping against her, filling her up back and front, mauling her breasts, spreading her wide so as to be deeply penetrated. And her expression was of one of utter ecstasy. I was horrified; betrayed.

That was the image which came rushing to me in the darkness in my desperate hour of need and it served to remind me of the lesson I had learnt that night. Deep down we are all individuals who have unique, specific needs. No matter how common the path we take in order to find them, the same things have different meanings for different people.

The Master meant for me to lose so he could continue his dominance of Calimba.

The Governor meant for me to die and for Chloe to become his sex toy before she was sold off to some whorehouse where she would be used to service its rough clientele to the end of her days.

Chiang had told me of the anger the permanent loss of all Calimba women caused to the menfolk here. For our plan to work it was now imperative that I reached the chambers of the Governor and rescued Chloe.

***

In the dark, the passage of time becomes distorted. I don't know how long I spent inside the dark tunnels beneath Calimba, alone with my thoughts, loneliness and fears. My only comfort the fact that I had nothing really to lose, my only guide in the dark the strange luminous map with its crude sketch of the narrow passages I was negotiating.

Presently however, I noticed a slight change in the dank air. There were more smells, the temperature around me imperceptibly rose so that my teeth stopped chattering and faint noises began to reach my ears. I realised then that my steps were taking me nearer the Governor's residence, under his fierce guards' feet. I began to walk more slowly in case I made a noise and my heart began to hammer more loudly in my chest. Finally, my outstretched hands encountered a solid wall in front of me. I paused long enough to consult the map and confirm to myself that I was, indeed, at the Governor's residence. Then, as Chiang had told me to, I began to run my hands over the smooth wall in front of me looking for that tiny rise in it that would activate the lock. Sure enough, somewhere near the very top on the right, my hand encountered a slight ridge. I applied pressure to that and there was the faintest of snicks as the well-oiled mechanism engaged and the wall in front of me started sliding back.

The passage I found myself in was pretty poorly lit but by comparison to the complete darkness I had suffered it was like it was daylight. I stepped through revelling in the warmer air of the residence and waited until the portion of the wall had swung shut behind me before I went any further.

The residence was silent. Totally silent.

I consulted my map again to help me find my bearings in the strange house and then step by step I went up wooden stairs, past narrow hallways until I was in a single, dark passage which led to one room only. It was very quiet and I thought that I had got it wrong, that I had finally blown it and our plan had gone awry before it even had a proper chance to begin, but at last I heard a gentle sigh and a man's heavy voice and I knew instantly that no, I had made no mistake.

I was on the right path.

The Governor's chamber was just ahead, its doors wide open.

It was dark and dangerous in the passage, but I held my breath to quieten the loudness of my heartbeats and peered carefully round the corner.

In the gloom of the Governor's chamber Chloe's naked skin shone with a pearly translucence that made the breath catch in my throat. Her clothes lay in a puddle by her feet, on the floor, and she stood straight by the big fireplace. The smouldering embers threw out a glow that picked out the darkened tips of her proud breasts and the hidden shadows in the gentle curve of the plain of her belly as it vanished between her legs.

'Come here,' the Governor hissed and Chloe hesitated momentarily before taking one small step.

A hirsute hand lifted from the deeper shadows at the back of the room. A heavy golden ring momentarily glittered in the embers' glow and then vanished. But not before the fingers had moved, peremptorily motioned for Chloe to step towards him.

'It is time child, to do your duty by your betters,' said the heavy male voice.

Transfixed I watched Chloe comply. Her shoulders stooped, her proud young breasts momentarily sagged in defeat and she took the first real step towards the man who meant to ravish her. I would have done anything, given anything then to spare Chloe what she was to undergo, but it was important for the plan's success that I caught the Governor unprepared. Surprise was the one element, the only element of the plan that I was unwilling to sacrifice, so I pressed myself back in the shadows, a safe place to hide while still having a good view of the chamber.

Chloe, I saw instantly, had been fitted with a collar.

It was a wide, leather studded one and a chain hung from it.

'You have been spoiled by him,' the Governor said to her, 'I mean to see that you are properly trained. Come here!'

Chloe took a few timid steps, getting near enough for the heavy, black, hirsute hand to come out of the shadows, seize the chain that hung from the collar and, with a quick tug bring her down to her knees.

'You have no idea what I will do to you,' said the Governor and stepped out of the shadows.

He was naked, totally, and erect and such was the size and girth of him that at the sight of that erection Chloe let out an involuntary gasp and dropped her eyes to the floor.

'Now you realise why I'm called the Governor,' said the black man, 'by the power of this rod I rule,' and with that he moved forward quickly to grasp Chloe's chain, tug it upwards so that she was kneeling up and with a quick thrust, he fed his massive pole past Chloe's pretty lips and into her mouth. The first incursion snapped her head back and brought saliva out of her mouth.

'Steady now,' the Governor admonished her gently, scolding her, almost like a school teacher scolds his favourite pupil, 'suck on it gently first, make your throat muscles relax,' and with that he thrust harder against her. Chloe made a half-choking gulping sound and tried to disengage herself to gasp for air but the Governor held her fast.

'Take it deeper in your mouth slave,' he hissed and tugged at her chain so that Chloe's pretty head was forced forward, her face completely buried in his middle and as he thrust forward with those mighty hips Chloe made valiant attempts to contain him and I saw, in the glimmer of the few candles in the chamber, drops of saliva flow down her chin and glisten on her full, round breasts.

'We're going to have to stretch that mouth of yours little slave, if you're going to be any good in the waterfront. Men come off ships there, they want a woman who can swallow their length without any effort,' said the Governor in a matter-of-fact tone and continued to pump wildly at Chloe's mouth as she knelt in front of him, driving her pretty head back with each thrust and making her gag and choke.

'Just beginning, just beginning,' muttered the Governor oblivious to the young girl's discomfort. As I watched, curled up in the deepest shadows of the corridor, between a wall and some wooden boxes, the Governor pulled himself out of Chloe's mouth and hauled her up onto her feet, pulling at the chain round her neck.

On her feet, the twin, full moons of her buttocks featured prominently on the lush landscape of her body. She had the tiny waist still, of a young girl and the flaring hips as well that behind which would tempt a saint. The Governor turned her and I saw him study it. He put out a hand and felt a buttock, squeezed and kneaded it like he was buying meat.

'Hmmm, nice piece of ass,' he said to himself mostly, 'he gave an experimental slap to Chloe's behind, watched the way the solid flesh shook and jumped with the force of the blow. Satisfied, he tried it again, this time aiming at the other cheek.

'You have the kind of ass that really needs reaming,' he said to her and, reaching behind him, he pulled on a rope hanging from the ceiling of the chamber.

Somewhere inside the residence a bell went off. In the silence I could hear it clearly. 'Time to see what we can really teach you slave,' said the Governor and pulling on the chain he steered Chloe so that she was pressed, face first up against the wall of the chamber, legs apart, her sex, nestled in the tight space where the tight curve of her buttocks met the tops of her ripe thighs, clearly visible.

From one of the walls to his right, the Governor now took a thin dildo. It was black, like his erection and at least twice as long. Holding it like a sword he pressed himself against Chloe's unprotected body, forced her legs further apart with his knee and rubbed the business end of the dildo on the inside of a thigh, beginning from just above the knee. Chloe, let out a whimper as she felt the cold hardness against the tender inside of her thigh and tried to bring her legs together, trying in vain to protect herself, but the Governor held her easily against the wall with the chain and his knee pressed hard against her thighs, forcing them open again.

'Struggle? Now is that what you want slave?' asked the Governor and the dildo had now reached her sex and he was busy rubbing it up and down the open lips of her womanhood, parting them so that momentarily, the pink insides glistened wetly in the dancing candlelight, before the dildo was again rubbed back and forth. Chloe bit her lip against the torture, shook her head to make the anticipation more bearable and the Governor let out a low laugh, enjoying his role in this.

'I'll give you what you want you hot little minx,' he said and the dildo now began to ride higher, leaving Chloe's wet womanhood behind, riding the high, curvy hills of her buttocks. I watched as the Governor parted Chloe's ass with one hand, spread those firm, round cheeks wide and placing the dildo against her anus, drove it up into her with a violent twist. Chloe felt this sudden, savage invasion of her body. Felt the dildo force its way past the sphincter muscles of her anus and begin to explore the depths of her body and she let out a cry.

Immediately the Governor responded by slapping her ass, making the cheeks wobble. 'Shut up slave!' he ordered and gave her another slap, this time on the thigh, leaving the clear imprint on his hand on the ripe flesh of her leg.

With the end of the long dildo sticking out of her ass, Chloe tried to wriggle this way and that, but whatever she did, from behind, she was vulnerable. The Governor's massive hand on her chain held her fast and her writhings just made her bottom all the more delicious. Time and again thunderous smacks landed on the tender buttocks, making them quiver and shake. Every now and then he would give the dildo another turn or two and jam a little more of it up her. Just as Chloe's struggles were becoming frantic as the beating got harder and the dildo sank into her ass still deeper so that only its base was visible, footsteps were heard coming along the narrow passage outside his chamber.

Instinctively I sank deeper into the shadows and waited to see who was coming.

There were two naked men, walking fast, and my first guess was that they had responded to the bell that had rung when the Governor had pulled that cord earlier. So intent on reaching the chamber were they that they passed by me and never noticed me in the dark.

'You rang my lord?' one of them asked.

Their eyes darted respectfully from the Governor to take in the plush naked body of Chloe.

'Don't stand there fools,' he ordered, 'come here, I need you to teach this slave manners.'

Chapter 21

Hidden by the shadows I had a very clear view of what the Governor's idea of teaching manners really was. Dragging Chloe by the lead, he hauled her across the room until the hapless girl was on the bed on her hands and knees.

Another crack of his open hand on her buttocks forced her down, legs wide apart and instantly the three men were upon her taking it in turn to drive themselves into her cunt, spreading her wide so that she cried out, gangbanging her until her muffled gasps and cries subsided into quiet sobs.

Still not content with this they then grasped her by the arms and lifted her bodily. One of them lay on the bed, beneath her, erection pointed at the ceiling and they manipulated her legs so that she was lowered down to be directly skewered by him. Despite the soreness she must have been feeling at having been roughly used by the three men Chloe started to struggle. The three of them however were much too strong for her.

Soon she was impaled upon the prone man's erection, her thighs gripped and squeezed by powerful hands. The second man leapt on the bed behind her and yanked out the dildo which was still plugging her ass. Chloe's back arched as her the man penetrated her from behind and proceeded to thrust himself up into her, his thick, meaty pole plundering the tightness of her rear passage.

This double penetration made Chloe's head snap up, mouth open, ready to cry out again, and the Governor was waiting for just that reaction. He was standing on the bed straddling the head of the first man, his own rampant spear ready to thrust into her hot mouth and as her head came up he lunged forward with his hips and Chloe's unuttered cry was transformed into a deep, throaty gurgle as she struggled to cope with this fresh incursion into her. With all her orifices occupied, the poor girl was quite helpless as each of the men, in turn, came inside her and changed positions to penetrate her yet again, their hands in the meantime roamed the magnificent curves of her ass and cupped and squeezed her breasts.

Just when she must have thought that her ordeal just could not get any worse, it did. The Governor reached up and took three leather paddles from the wall at the bedhead. Each of the men grasped one and proceeded to let her have it in perfect unison with their thrusts. The smack of leather on heated flesh, serving to drive them into fresh heights of arousal so that their thrusts into Chloe's body took on a new, surreal quality, drove deeper into her than any girl or woman had been driven into before, touched the very core of her being and slowly, but surely, as the Governor had intended all along, began to transform her.

And all the while they beat her still. The man who was sodomising her let fly at her hips and buttocks. The one who was fucking her cunt landed crashing slaps on her breasts and stomach, and the one who was mouthfucking her rained blows down on her back. As they thrust themselves against her and paddled her flesh at the same time, Chloe's breasts and buttocks shook and jumped with the punishment she was receiving and this further inflamed the passions of the three men who were using her so that they prolonged their performance and attacked her with new vigour. Grunting with the effort, each time they thrust themselves upon her. Semen oozed from Chloe's pink pussy, where the men had come again and again and semen also oozed out of her ass and ran down the inside of her thighs. More semen still had spilled from her mouth where she had been unable to swallow the loads of come the three men had shot into her mouth. And there it had mixed with saliva and ran in rivulets down the magnificent pillar of her neck.

And still they used her, still they rammed themselves into her like she was a rag doll, throwing her about, spreading her legs and holding her to experiment with new positions which gave them better, deeper access to the hot, wet depths of her body.

They went on for a long, long time. Then, just as I was running out of patience I noticed a slight change in their behaviour. Their thrusts into Chloe lost a little of their vigour. Their remarks were no longer as snappy. And each of them now spent longer and longer on top of the bruised girl, holding her legs apart, knees bent towards her shoulders, ramming themselves deep into the middle of her, making her squeal with each deep thrust.

I began then to count the number of times they each took her. The Governor did it to her three times. The two henchmen he had called up did it to her two times each. Then the Governor was in the driving seat again, spreading her cuntlips with the size of his penis, forcing her to take him once again.

'Let's whip her now, give it to her again afterwards,' panted the Governor as he laboured on top of Chloe, driving her legs further and further apart with each thrust. One of his henchmen unwound a length of rawhide from a wall and proceeded to flick it her way. The Governor and the third man turned Chloe face down and held her arms spread wide. The long rawhide began to wreak its havoc on her back and buttocks. It snaked across the red patches the paddles had left and raised livid welts on Chloe's beautiful skin as it bit into her.

But even as she was whipped, Chloe's used, tired body was galvanised into fresh action, she writhed and wriggled, raising her buttock cheeks towards the whip, her vocal chords labouring to let out cry after cry. But now they were the hoarse cries of a woman transported by the unrestrained use of her body to regions where pain and pleasure had no separate identity. Calimba was working its spell on another of its women.

The Governor released her arms and knelt in front of

her head. Chloe made no move to escape from the whip but simply raised her face and with a deep moan opened her mouth wide so he could ram himself deep into it and thrust in time to the whipping.

It was clear to me now that the three men were tiring. From a deep pocket in the peasant garb I wore I took out the small wooden club Chiang had given me and waited for the trio to further tire themselves with further use of Chloe. Then, just as fatigue was beginning to slow their movements and dull their senses, just as Chloe's choked gasps and muffled moans became more laboured, I began to make my way out of the shadows. Crawling, like a snake, careful not to make any noise, I approached the bed upon which the poor girl was being put through yet fresh ordeals as the Governor held her head back and his two henchmen attempted to both cram themselves into Chloe's willing but exhausted mouth.

Judging the moment carefully, timing it for maximum effect, I leapt up when they were both in mid-rut and with two beautiful swings of my club I laid them out.

The thick wooden stock made a dry cracking sound each time it connected with the men's hard heads. The two goons stayed in mid-rut a moment longer. Then, as I watched, their eyes rolled up in their sockets and their bodies slumped forward. Freed from the erections of the two men who had filled her mouth to its limit Chloe lay back and suddenly took a breath.

Behind her, the Governor, who had held the chain while his two goons used the woman, looked at me like I was an apparition, and did not move.

'You have a name?' I asked.

'J- , James,' he said.

'Over here then James,' I motioned with the club for him to move aside.

He did so, his eyes looking daggers at me. With my free hand I released the collar from Chloe's neck.

'Master, you came,' she whispered.

Momentarily I spared a glance at her. There were dark rings of exhaustion beneath her eyes and there were bruises, fingermarks and welts all over her. Her lips were a deep red, where she'd bitten them against these men's rutting. But her expression was the same one I had seen on Jemma's face at the Paradise, a wild ecstasy that told of a body driven to the extremes of sexual experience where the primal gods reign.

'I wasn't about to let these goons have you forever,' I said.

'There's a plan to sell these women?' I said, turning to the Governor.

'Yes,'

'When?' I asked.

'Tonight. There'll be buyers coming.' He said and looked perplexed by my questioning.

'How are they coming?'

'I don't have to tell you that,' he said.

Without warning I moved forward and brought the heavy, wooden club down on his foot. The Governor let out a choked cry of pain and went down, face ashen.

'How are they coming?' I repeated my question.

'Helicopter. They're flying in.' He said at last. 'Why?'

'Where is the auction to he held?'

'In the main Chamber, same place you and the Master had dinner,' he said. 'Why, thinking of gate crashing?' he sneered.

I raised the heavy wooden club and was about to bring it down again, when at the last possible moment, I thought better of it and lowered it. Suddenly the Governor jumped sideways and lunged, hand outstretched for the far wall. Behind a hidden panel his hand caught some sort of trip wire because yet another bell sounded in the residence and steps and voices could be heard of in the distance.

'Damn you!' I yelled closing the gap between us and raising my club.

The Governor cowered in his corner, hands raised in

silent supplication as I was about to knock him senseless into next week. It was a move I never completed.

There was the barest hint of a footstep. The trajectory of my club was arrested in mid-air as if it had hit a brick wall and then I was lying on my side, head buzzing from a glancing blow.

I looked up and there, standing above me, towering over the three of us was none other than Matthew. I lay there, thinking how it was all lost now. I had come so close but I had failed to account for the physical power of the satyrs.

Matthew leaned over me, eyes darting between me and the Governor, club held in one hand and incredibly, he said: 'You'd better hurry up if you don't want to die Andy,' and put out one massive hand to help me to my feet.

***

Nothing happens by coincidence. The reason Matthew was there so quickly was because he had found Chiang and some of the others in one of the underground chambers and they had confessed when questioned that I had gone to kill the Governor and get Chloe back.

'The legend has to be respected,' said Matthew, 'all my life I've grown up with it. My father survived the judgement of the gods of the mountain and he was the one chosen to liberate and guide Calimba. When you came along I thought that the legend was true. My father was getting old and the gods had given us another successor. Someone who would take over and guide Calimba into the future. All the satyrs, each one of us long for that day. You came Andy. We all hoped you'd be the man we could obey. So you imagine our dismay when my own father reneged on the legend, secretly ordered you killed. And Chloe sold off.'

He went on and on, telling me these incredible things and, with each word, the Governor hung his head lower and lower.

'You're betraying your own father,' he said by way of defence.

'No, to go on would be to betray all he taught me,' said the satyr, 'to go on would be to betray the very same ideals we've all ruled Calimba with for dozens of years. To go on would be to betray our sacred oath. And you,' he raised a massive finger and pointed it at the Governor who was trying to get to his feet, 'you were bested anyway. If I hadn't come along your brains would be all over this floor. The blow-in has won the Test. By right he should be the new Master anyway.'

'Things are far from over yet,' I said.

'True, though I'm afraid there'll be no popular revolt Andy. We caught Chiang's people as they were coming out of the tunnels. They're all under lock and key and to let them out now, with the Master's visitors due so soon, is to court disaster."

'Maybe,' I said, ' but maybe we don't need to resort to a bloody revolt in order to stage a coup. Interested?'

Matthew perked up at this. 'I'm all ears,' he said.

'Then we just need to get to the Chamber by the fastest route possible and I'll explain the plan as we run.'

Chapter 22

Matthew knew a direct way to the Chamber of the Master and Chloe and I followed as quickly as we could, bringing the Governor with us.

The poor man looked broken, defeated, his entire reason for existence taken away from him. I could not help but reflect on the structure the Master had set up. The way he had structured society so that he needed people with the single-minded focus of the Governor and the muscle of the satyrs to keep it going.

'It all has to change,' I said to myself and Matthew stopped his running and turned around.

'What did you say?' he asked.

'I was just thinking how a lot of things need to change.' My words seemed to have a strange effect on Matthew. He suddenly went very thoughtful, became less jovial.

'The legend says that the new blow-in would bring a lot of change.'

The legend, again. I thought how ironic that the Master should be the victim of the complexities of his own mythmaking.

'Just take us to the Chamber right now Matthew. I'll see that the rest is done so smoothly as to make the transition not only bloodless but also amicable.'

Matthew looked at me strangely then but said nothing.

Already a new, complex plan was taking shape in my head. A plan which needed only a few Calimba women in order to succeed.

'Is there somewhere secure to hide in the Chamber?' I asked.

'Secure place to hide?' asked Matthew, 'the whole Chamber is one huge hiding place.'

***

We were in darkness again, and this left the mind free to wander. Matthew sat himself beside James, the Governor with the express intention, as he'd said, of snapping his neck the instant he thought of giving our presence away. I folded my arms around Chloe's delectable form, my hands forming a natural cradle for her buttocks, my face nuzzling in the deep valley between her breasts. I took in the natural aroma of her body, the musk of the ripe woman flesh and, despite the tightness of space in the small hiding hole Matthew had guided us into, I manoeuvred so that I was on top of her.

'We have a few hours,' I said, 'and my entire plan now

hangs on you. You should get some rest.'

'I will Master, I will,' she murmured her tongue flicking at my ear, 'but first if I can give you some releaseÖ'

It was what I was hoping she would say.

I moved so that my entire weight was now poised above her and as Chloe shifted beneath me and opened her legs to accommodate me, I let myself collapse, driving the entire length of my manroot, up her hot little love canal in one thrust. Chloe's breasts provided the ideal cushion for a session of tight fucking and as I moved upon her in the dark in my mind's eye there were replays of what she had already undergone at the hands of the Governor and his goons. I saw again the expression of pain in her face as they thrust themselves up her from behind. I saw her eyes widen in disbelief as she was forced to take them deep into her mouth. And again I saw that strange look upon her face at the end, covered in semen from all three men and the memory fuelled me so much that my hips became pistons of power and my hands taloned at hers and raised her higher so I could penetrate her deeper. Chloe strained to contain my strength. Her thighs wrapped themselves round me and I reached beneath her and grabbed a firm, round buttock in each hand and squeezed hard and lifted her higher so that as I crashed down I penetrated her that extra inch deeper which made me feel I was flying a mile higher.

When my release came it was a thunderous rupture that made my entire body go rigid and then limp, so that I felt completely drained. Rather than moving, in the darkness, I caught a few hours' sleep on top of Chloe, my cock going limp inside her. My head pillowing on her full breasts. And when dreams came, I dreamt of a city, high up in the mountains and of beautiful women and a life spent amongst them.

***

Slowly sound first, and then light filtered through to our darkness. I could hear loud music and the shuffle of many feet upon the floor and many voices.

It was my guess that the sale had started, or was about to start and that the Master and his guests were all outside.

'MatthewÖ' I whispered as quietly as I could.

'Right here,ÖI hear it too.'

'Do you think we can get out without being noticed?'

'Yep,' he was confident.

Our hiding place, luckily, was at the furthest point of the chamber from where the main attraction for the guests was being staged and this allowed us to quietly roll out without drawing attention to ourselves.

The very middle of the chamber, I saw, was now occupied by a troupe of dancers. I had never seen them before. The women were of the dark, willowy type with long legs and small breasts riding high on their chests. The men were muscular, slim but strong, of the type that can go on dancing all night if necessary. Instantly I realised that one of the reasons we had not drawn any attention to ourselves lay in the fact that the women dancers were dressed in short tunics which hugged their bodies and barely made it past the junction of their thighs.

As they leapt and skipped and gyrated the tunics moved with them affording tantalising glimpses of carefully depilated, young sexes, their coralled lips flushed pink from their exertions, inviting further attention. The lead female dancer was an exotic looking Asian woman whose breasts were more generously proportioned than those of her co-dancers. As the dance reached its climax, the male lead, grabbed the female lead and with a single, savage motion tore the tunic off her body.

The Asian woman let out a scream and tried to cover herself. It was a vain movement. She had a delectable behind, tight and slim, like a pre-pubescent girl's and the allure of it was only increased by the nakedness of her sex, shorn of all its crowning glory. The woman spread protective fingers over her sex, while with the other arm she tried to cover her breasts. The male dancer however gave her no opportunity. He backhanded her across the face hard enough to send her sprawling, legs opening as she fell and the audience surged forward, breath held as they caught tantalising flashes of the pink depths of her body and wanted to see more.

On the floor the Asian woman was scrambling on her hands and knees, trying to get away. The male dancer however was already upon her like lightening. He grabbed hold of her long black hair, pulling it up in one hand like reins. The movement arrested her crawling and as he made her straighten up her thighs parted so that from behind the lucky members of the audience were treated to the sight of her anus and sex in all their glory.

'Catch her,' voices urged from the all-male audience of buyers.

'Stick it to her,'

'Give her a good fucking,'

'Make her take you in her mouth,'

Held by the hair like that the hapless Asian girl was able to only go round in circles. Her round breasts, their nipples hard and pointy with fright, bounced and jiggled as she moved. Her slim legs worked hard to keep her from having her hair pulled too tautly.

Responding to the leering audience and taking the opportunity to experience some of the girl's delights for himself, the male lead stepped out of his trousers to display a long, thin erection. Holding the girl by the hair, he stepped round her and guided her head towards his middle. A collective sigh went up from the audience as they saw the long thin erection penetrate the soft, round oval of the girl's mouth. The girl made a choking sound as the male dancer's long penis vanished inside her mouth. Holding her like that, head buried firmly in his middle while he held her by the hair he was able to savour the pretty sight of her naked ass. Another male dancer now produced a horsehair whip and started flicking it at her, its end slapping against the taut, round cheeks of the ass.

Every time he hit her the girl's entire body would jump

and each muscle would be clearly delineated beneath the skin and her legs would go wider still and her sex would gape more openly and men would crane their heads and put their hands in their pockets to hide already burgeoning erections.

To fan the flames of desires and drive individual sex-slaves' price higher still, the Master had the remainder of the dancers circulate amongst the guests. More than once, from where we stood we saw a young woman seized by two, three buyers and denuded, her clothes ripped off her body. They then held her down on the floor, sometimes a man on each limb, and they would explore her depilated sex with their hands, thrusting their fingers deep inside her, working them in, trying to see who it would be who get a fist in there in record time.

On one such instance a young dancer tried to make a run for it, as we watched, but failed. She was surrounded by buyers who blocked her path with their bodies. She tried, desperately, to seek some help, but it was to no avail. Her duty, indeed, her role was to act as bait to inflame the mad desires of the buyers. Brought down on her knees she had her anus penetrated by one man and her mouth filled by ten others in quick succession, who sought almost instant relief from the arousal caused by the scenes on stage. The male lead's cock was still buried deep in the girl's mouth, the other dancer was still flicking at her with the whip and making her jerk and flinch with each blow. Her muffled gasps and the regular smack of the whip on her rounded buttocks was driving the audience wild.

From where our small group was I watched all this with growing interest sensing its timing, trying to get the moment right.

Just then I saw the Master. He was flanked by two younger men holding ledgers, which I guessed were where the book value of the slaves was entered, and he was talking to some buyers. Beyond the Master, in the shadows, I could see the lurking figures of two hulking satyrs. Heart pounding I quickly looked back at Matthew but he nodded me on, unconcerned. What was about to happen was probably the epitome of audacity but it was also the only way I could see where we could have an ousting of the Master without a bloody coup.

As the dancers finally managed to extricate themselves from their fans and run backstage, there were a few moments of relative quiet while the buyers gave a thought to the merchandise they would like to see.

It was just the moment I had been waiting for. Running between two groups of buyers, I made it to the band of drummers and with a curt signal told them to cut the drum beat out. It was the same effect as if someone had suddenly thrown the television in your average house, out of the window. The silence was startling.

The Master looked up and saw me. An angry frown creased his brow and he gave a signal to the satyrs to get me, but just as they started to move towards me the Governor's voice rang out:

'Let him be. He has things to say I think we should well listen to.'

The satyrs looked decidedly confused. One of them looked from the Master to the Governor and back again. Just then Matthew stepped out from the shadows behind the Governor and added his weight to the argument.

His presence alone was enough. The Master looked first confused and then slightly worried. He honestly had no idea that he was heading towards disaster.

'Thomas Powell,' I said and the acoustics of the chamber made my words reverberate.

The Master now looked genuinely angry. I guess not many people knew who he really was. 'Thomas PowellÖthe game is up! You've wasted enough lives. The game now must stop.'

'I don't know what you mean,' the Master tried to brazen it out.

'I've survived the Test. The legend is over. I am now

your official replacement.'

The buyers looked from one to the other, sensing that here was change, but not radical change. It had little to do with them. Things would go on much as before.

'I'm not ready to go,' said the Master and clicked his fingers.

At that satyrs moved from all around the room, but I had been prepared and I knew exactly what to do. I looked over to where Chloe sat waiting and I nodded. Then I nodded towards the band.

Instantly a new rhythm started. A savage, guttural beat that gripped you by the viscera and did not let you go until the last note had been played.

Chloe sprinted to the centre of the room, slid round in a tight circle and then pirouetted to where I was. On our run from the Governor's chamber we had been able to find her some clothes, and now they were to play a crucial role. The thin, full, skirt she had on flared out as she moved so that the clear, ripe outline of her thighs was visible all the way to the hip, exposing the fact that under her dress Chloe had no underwear. It also exposed the crusts of dried semen on her skin and the marks of the whip and the paddles. This was clearly a slave who could take whatever a master wanted to hand out.

As everyone in the room held their breath Chloe flicked from man to man, dancing for each alone, learning to know them, learning what they liked, making each one feel special. There was not a man in that room that night who did not dream of owning this slave for himself, who did not want to have those legs spread wide at his command, who did not wish to have those luscious breasts to play with, to have this hot, woman-flesh on her knees in front of him, willing to do anything, anything at all, to please him.

It was as masterly a manipulation of heart, mind and body of the buyers as anything the Master had to date managed to achieve, and it was no accident. It was, instead, the fruition of half a lifetime's development. The lone, sometimes meandering and sometimes straight road which I had embarked on when I'd first met Jemma Stones and which had finally culminated in my being there, in Calimba.

At the danger of replicating the Master's mistake and believing in the potency of mythology which was entirely of my own design, I truly felt, that night, that nothing which had happened to me, had happened entirely by accident. Each of the myriad little things which had happened to me in my life, from that fateful night in Paradise, when Jemma let me know she had had enough and wanted to move on, to the many small and large relationships and sexual encounters which had led, each in its own way, to the development of Andy Meyer. The man who had decided to go alone up strange mountains and then had woken up in Calimba. Each event, in turn contributed to my actions and decisions in the Chamber in Calimba that night.

It was as if suddenly the surface of things was completely stripped and I could clearly see every man in there, not as a mass of inner conflict and uncertainties, but as pure motivation.

I could see the Master, scheming, lonely and manipulative, managing a city which was becoming increasingly more difficult to manage, having little choice other than to resort to greater and greater levels of oppression in order to maintain control.

I could see Matthew, burning up with the desire to believe that what he was, what he had become, a gargantuan warrior of massive appetites who knew no restraints was in the service of a higher cause. Something far greater than the feeble mortal coil of the Master and the lush flesh of the vessels he commanded.

I could see every satyr in there that night, caught in a state of ambivalence, torn between loyalty to the Master who'd helped make them and the man who commanded them, uncertain whether they should really believe in the power of the myth they all served and accept me, or go along with the Master and destroy me.

I saw the Governor, a man whose life had been built around a function he never thought he would have to fulfil. But now he was required to fulfil that role the only way of proving himself lay in a course of action which refuted everything he had ever believed in.

There was Chloe, a vessel, one like no other. Wanton to the extreme. Wanting to serve, to be subjugated to a greater cause than her own desires.

And there were the buyers. Rich mortals, tried by life in various forms. Seeking just some small part of the flame, the great flame of being encapsulated in the hot flesh of the uninhibited women of Calimba.

I could see all that. I was at its hub. I controlled it - somehow. And beyond it, beyond the primitive rooftops of Calimba's stone buildings and the snow-capped tops of the Andes, I could sense two worlds. The common one of humans and everyday life, a world ruled by misunderstandings and jealousies, inhibitions and false emotions and a greater one, lying beyond it.

In that other world there was no cold, or fear or hunger. There was no false emotion. There was no conflict, but similarly there was no real identity. No individuality. It was like a wild sea. Beautiful and restless. All encompassing and all powerful. A universal sea of sorts. And weÖwe were just droplets. Divorced from it. Savouring our individuality but for a brief time before the sea came back to engulf us, to ask us to join it.

And we longed to get back into that sea. We longed to drive ourselves once more into its bosom. And it was the wild message of that sea, its magic allure of oneness and harmony which drove us mindlessly into the cradle of women's hot bodies. For only at the moment of rupture when some sort of release was achieved, could we hope to recapture a little of the essence of what we had lost.

It was a sad thought that. And a potent one.

It burdened my soul that night, pinned it to the floor of the Chamber just as securely as if a great big, rusty nail had detached itself from the night sky and plummeted through the Chamber's domed ceiling and skewered me.

I took the pain that night. Opened myself to the realisation that Jemma had loved me, more than I had been capable of knowing. And that what had made her force me to leave her was the realisation on her part that at the time I was just not ready to understand.

The plan I had hatched then was workable.

I affirmed that in my head, and within instants, I had made the decisions necessary to confirm to everyone present that night that the mantle had moved on and I was now the real Master.

As Chloe danced her full breasts jiggled and bounced with every movement and she twirled skilfully round each prospective buyer in turn, fanning the flames of their desire, forcing them, unwittingly to rise to a higher level, one where what I would say would be better received. One put a hand up her skirt and stole a feel of her round ass. Chloe's erotic dance was working its magic. The prospective buyers were engrossed. As everyone watched her gyrate hoping for a peek of her more intimate parts, Thomas Powell wasted no time in running up to me.

'Why are you doing this?' he asked.

'Doing what?'

'You know perfectly well what. You lost the Test.'

'I'm still alive,' I reminded him, 'I evaded capture, even turned the satyrs and freed my slave. I have fulfilled the entire part of my bargain.'

He spluttered a little at that. 'You have no idea what you are toying with,' he hissed at me, eyes wild. But without his satyrs he was like a tiger without any teeth, his claws clipped to the bone.

'Watch,' I said, 'observe, learn and then perhaps we

shall discuss whether I know what I am toying with or not.'

Certain of the way each person in that room worked, I spread my arms wide, became the centrepiece of attention, and caused every eye to focus my way.

'Satyrs,' I said, 'remain where you are,' I clicked my fingers at Chloe and she understood. The band started playing a different rhythm, something more primitive, their eyes on me and I nodded my tacit approval.

Chloe then went into a wild spin, her eyes more luminous, their focus slacker, as if a more primitive force than her own suddenly worked through her. The buyers crowded her.

One of them reached out and grasped a piece of her skirt and there was the clear sound of thin cloth ripping. And it was as if a signal was given.

Another one moved and reached out and clutched and Chloe gyrated away and there was the sound of ripping again. And then another and another. And each time Chloe span out of reach more and more of her delectable body was visible, so that her legs now were uncovered almost to their full glory and there were maddening flashes of her breasts.

A proud, dark nipple peeked through a hole in her tunic and the tight, roll of her haunches was no longer completely covered. The buyers went mad at the sight of her. They chased her round, running after her as she danced and gyrated driven by a music and a primal energy not entirely of her own control. They howled as they ran after her, and started tearing at their own clothes, exposing their soft, flabby bodies and thin legs. And one of them caught her, or Chloe just decided the moment was right and span towards him instead of away from him.

They bore her to the floor, their hands crawling all over her, cupping and squeezing her full breasts, insistently rubbing at her nipples so that they went even harder. Imprisoning her arms, pulling her legs apart.

'I have never allowed them to do anything like this in here before,' Thomas Powell said by my side. He was pale and shaking, unable to comprehend the kind of energy he was witnessing being released.

'Quiet,' I admonished. 'Observe.'

We watched as someone took hold of Chloe's pretty head and turned it towards him, offering her his erect penis. Chloe, spread-eagled, unable to resist, opened her mouth wide to take him, relaxed the muscles of her throat, controlling the gag reflex as the man, driven by a desire akin to madness, thrust blindly at her, ground his hips into her face, mouth-fucking her like she'd never been mouth-fucked before.

Chloe took him in all the way, letting her mouth fill with his hot semen as the instinctive sucking she began caused the man to come off like he'd been on a hair-trigger. She had barely had time to swallow before someone else had taken his place and a fresh meaty pole was being fed into her mouth, its bulbous head plunging down the depths of her throat.

'This is madness!' Thomas Powell said beside me. He was wringing his hands with anxiety and his eyes were darting all over the place looking for some kind of escape. 'You cannot control them if you let them do this. You cannot do anything then, you will have to use the satyrs eventually and some of them will get hurt. Then there will be retribution. These are powerful men. Calimba will be wiped out. We will really cease to exist.'

I felt sorry for him because he really could not see.

'Can you really not feel what is going on here?' I asked him, 'are you really blind to what is really taking place in front of you?'

He turned to look at me, eyes wide. 'Who are you?' he asked, and then shook his head as if berating himself for his stupidity. 'What is happening?'

Instead of replying I bade him look once again.

Someone now lay between Chloe's spread legs. There was a man on each leg, holding them wide apart, running greedy hands up and down the supple flesh, pinching and pulling at the tender inside of each of her thighs. With her legs held so wide apart, the lips of her sex gaped open, the pink depths inside revealed. There was a sweet flow from her body, the wetness winked and glistened in the light of the Chamber and the man who was about to plunder her and taste that sweetness for himself, momentarily hesitated, his eyes feasting upon it.

Then, with a guttural yell he was charging her, plundering her, pumping himself like a maniac, plump wide buttocks pistoning up and down against her Chloe's lush, straining body.

'It is madness, madness!' intoned Thomas Powell, pacing in ever decreasing circles, reluctant to stay and watch; incapable of going. Unwilling to surrender the mantle of his title, to relinquish control just yet, and yet knowing that suddenly he no longer understood how the society around him worked and operated.

Impassive, like statues made of flesh, the satyrs watched this carnal frenzy, their eyes occasionally darted towards me, turned to the immobile figures of Matthew, their leader, and the Governor and then returned back to me, taking in the slow unravelling of the man they had once called Master, and who now was clearly, once more, nothing more than Thomas Powell.

'They will kill her! They will kill her! There are too many for one woman to take, too wild,' Thomas Powell was saying beside me, his eyes wildly taking in the unfolding tableau.

Chloe had been turned to lie on her side now. Her head was held in a strong grip by one man and he was busy ramming himself in and out of her mouth. Each time he pushed himself in, her eyes grew wide and her cheeks hollowed as she sucked at him with all her might. A man was lying over her from behind, his hands greedily feasting on her perfect breasts, and yet another was holding one leg up from behind, exposing her arse, his erection buried to the hilt in the tight, red-rimmed opening of her rear canal.

A fourth man was lying facing her, one hand fondling her breasts, the other one at his hip, helping to push harder inside her, his rod rammed in the centre of her where each thrust now squeezed from her body the mingled love juices of her own secretions and those who had poured themselves inside her.

'They will kill her! You must stop this!' Thomas Powell kept saying. I shushed him with a curt hand signal.

'They would kill an ordinary woman,' I said and he looked at me like I had gone mad. I noticed that the satyrs standing guard heard my words and exchanged quick glances.

'Chloe right now is no ordinary woman.'

'You are mad!'

'No. I was mad. We all were. Now I'm sane.'

We both watched in silence, each having totally different thoughts of his own, as the quartet of men using Chloe satiated, removed themselves from her body to be replaced by another four.

Chloe was like a being possessed, her mouth opened wide to accept, one, two cocks at a time, her throat worked to swallow the splashes of thick, coagulating semen being poured down into her mouth.

Semen had coated her face, mingled with sweat and saliva there, and thick white specks of it clung to her hair.

Her breasts rose and fell, as she laboured to breathe deeply, her hips gyrated, driving against the incessant pounding directed at her from all sides, her ass wobbled and moved and thrust against the plundering that was being inflicted. She was totally without any inhibition, she was lust incarnate, divorced from the limitations which normal bodies are constrained by, capable of satisfying entire armies if need be.

Matthew watched all this enthralled, in awe of the power he was being permitted to witness. At last this was what the satyrs had been born for. This was exactly what they had been created to protect. Here, in front of his eyes, was a raw example of the power the satyrs felt when they went into battle. Here was the same force which put them beyond fear, beyond harm, beyond even the need for weapons. What weapon could possibly match, let alone surpass the intensity of such power?

Our eyes met briefly over the tableau of rising and falling bodies and guttural grunts and half-choked cries and he nodded his understanding and, from a distance, bowed his head to me signalling his total surrender to my authority. The movement was seen by the rest of the satyrs and they too, suddenly bowed, their heads inclined as they recognised the transition of power from Thomas Powell, to me.

'Have you all gone mad?' asked Thomas Powell, his voice reedy and plaintive, stripped of all power. 'Has he got you all under his spell?'

I ignored his pitiful ravings and focused instead on the Governor, the man who had been bred with no other mission in life but to kill me. A deep air of dejection hung about him as he witnessed the display in front of him. He finally knew and understood the limitations of what he had been given to do. He knew he had failed and, to his eyes, there stretched no other road ahead apart from oblivion.

The Governor, I saw to my consternation, was preparing to die.

Chloe had now been turned to kneel on all fours, her mouth stretched to the limit by two cocks at a time. Hands clawed at her thighs and hips as two men rammed themselves inside her from behind, one testing her back door, while the other plundered her vulva. It was nearing completion I saw. Even Chloe was now beginning to tire, the power which flowed through her was beginning to ebb, the goddess of lust having satiated her desire, returning to the darkness of the remote dimension she called home. To my amplified second sight everything was as clear as if it had been inscribed in blood upon a marble white slate.

I judged the moment finely, waited until the instant the last shot of come was splashed on Chloe's unprotected face, I waited until the last male erection was withdrawn from her body and the scene around her was more reminiscent of a battle-field than a carnal feast. Bodies lay all around, with her as the epicentre..

I waited until the urge for self-annihilation which had been gradually building up in the Governor had reached its apex and was about to break out. I waited until the incomprehension and fear and uncertainty had finally worked their trick and Thomas Powell had been reduced to a blubbering imbecile, given to making inane remarks which bore no relevance whatsoever to what was happening, and then, only then did I clap my hands sharply. Once.

Instantly the band stopped playing and put down their instruments.

After the music and the madness and the wild orgy that had followed the Chamber seemed oddly empty.

'You all deserve an explanation,' I said at last.

And every eye was on me.

I looked at everyone individually, carefully gauging my pitch, fine-tuning it to their reaction.

'What you've just witnessed, what you all felt in here tonight is the power of Calimba,' I said and the buyers blinked and tried desperately to understand. 'You will go away empty-handed tonight,' I said and there were a few hissed intakes of breath, 'what's more you will leave your money behind. The same amount of money you intended to spend here in the first place.'

Some exchanged looks of alarm at this suggestion.

'I know exactly how you feel right now,' I said, 'what's more I know exactly how you felt while you had Chloe. I know that in the past you have come here and gone away with Calimba women. Vessels which you have called your own. I now tell you this, you will never again own a Calimba woman.'

'You have gone crazy!' Thomas Powell hissed beside me, but no one paid him the least attention. All eyes were riveted on me, Matthew was grinning, his big head nodding encouragement and even the Governor had stopped concentrating on his willingness to die and was trying to understand what I was doing.

'No one however,' I continued, 'will ever stop you from coming here and buying the rights to a Calimba woman.'

I paused and surveyed them all. Matthew was beaming.

'We don't understand,' ventured one of the buyers. He was younger than the rest, his face was perplexed.

'It is simple,' I explained, 'we will undertake a new training programme for our women. A truer one than the one we have been adopting,' I cast a pointed look at Thomas Powell and he cringed and looked furtive, 'you will still be able to come here, pay us money and take a woman away with you. That woman however and - I promise you this- each one of them will be of the same quality as Chloe, whom you've just enjoyed,' I could see this caused a stir amongst them, 'each of these women will belong forever to Calimba. What you will be able to buy, is the rights to them, a lease if you like, for an agreed length of time. Then they will have to return to us. Return home.'

Matthew was grinning broadly.

'We will train them hard, rigorously, to please you,' I said. 'We will appoint a special man in charge of the training programme,' I let my eyes rest on the Governor and could almost sense a palpable shift within him as he realised whom I meant. 'A man whose entire life will be dedicated to producing women like Chloe,' I said, 'what we expect from you in return is payment not just in money, but also in silence and trust and technology. Calimba will cease to exist, except in myths and legends and the half-forgotten memories of back-street prostitutes. We will no longer take in women from outside, but breed our own instead. Do I have your agreement gentlemen?'

It was a strange scene.

These wealthy men had been allowed to taste a glimpse of the beyond, to experience a sacred taste of what lies beyond the world of mortal men. It was a powerful experience, one which they would take away with them forever and prize in their memories and when they were alone, at times, and the hour of need was upon them, out would come this strange memory and they would then grasp it in their minds and hold it up to the light of logic and carefully examine it and try desperately to understand.

Needless to say they all agreed upon this to a man.

They went away that night, empty-handed and poorer and Calimba became a changed place.

The satyrs released all the prisoners. A greater integration was achieved with the menfolk of Calimba sharing in the complex training of the women. The Governor became very important. He was the one charged with that training. His days were spent in constant consultations and experiments and trials with different techniques and he always had a guard of satyrs with him, not because he was ever in danger but to mark his importance. Matthew became my close friend and confidant. The man I knew I could trust my life to if necessary.
Chloe was mine. Even from the very beginning, she was always mine, except neither of us knew it then.

Though she will always be a slave she is no longer for sale. Her art is practised only with me these days. Her body is the temple which I visit often, to worship at the altar of the goddess of love.

The buyers have multiplied. Word of mouth has spread and now we have as much wealth and modernity in Calimba as anyone could possibly wish for anywhere on the planet. Rumours are that internet chatrooms are frequented by some strange men and women whose cybersex techniques are incomparable and whose net-presence exudes a quality many find disturbing and very few ever forget, but these, of course are only rumours and

I am not going to give much credence to them.

When the cold wind at night comes down from the snow-capped mountain tops of the Andes it swoops low over the rooftops of Calimba and whistles its eerie news as it flies down the narrow passageways that mark this tiny, forgotten city. Of course the thatched rooftops have long gone and the hovels retain their character on the outside only.

Thomas Powell, I hear returned to his family, the people who so long ago had given him up for lost. A mystery still surrounds his disappearance all those years, one he has never tried to shed light on.

He is, I hear, a sex therapist now, one specialising in women.

I have agents out there who tell me Jemma Stones has still not married. She still occasionally takes the red-eye to New York to visit Paradise, though I am told she is less and less inclined to become the centrepiece for a night's action these days and prefers instead to keep to the fringes, scouting for younger men to initiate.

I still keep my eye on her. She was the one who first brought me into this world, even if she refused to, or was incapable of taking me any further.

I am sure that one of these days our paths will cross again. Until that happens I am happy where I am, being what I am.

Andy Meyer, the TV executive sadly died in the mountains. His Land Rover was found but not his body. That is still to be recovered. Who knows? In years to come, he may show up again, one day, just like Thomas Powell.

Then again, Andy Meyer, might just remain missing, presumed dead, forever.

- THE END -

And now follows a preface and the opening of next month's title "Tales from The Lodge" *by Sean O'Kane & Falconer Bridges*

The Lodge - not its real name of course! - is an exclusive club dedicated to the delights of submission and domination. By great good fortune the authors Sean O'Kane and Falconer Bridges have been allowed access to some of the staff and members to record their experiences. 'Tales from The Lodge' gives a fascinating glimpse into a world inhabited by fabulously wealthy men and beautiful, submissive women.

This extract is the beginning of Lolli's story, in which she tells Falconer how she came to be a housegirl at The Lodge. These are remarkable insights into a world where SM dreams come true...........And this is just the beginning!

LOLLI

"I think she's in the Common room," Alan Masterson told me as he led me along the magnificent first floor corridor in the west wing of The Lodge; probably the most exclusive and discreet club in the country. He pushed open a heavy, oak pannelled door and ushered me in. I found myself in a long, high ceilinged room, four tall sash windows were spaced out down one wall and the afternoon sun flooded in on richly upholstered and luxurious chairs and sofas. On the walls were many portraits in oils and in between them, where you might have expected to see crossed halberds and muskets in a fine old house like this were tasteful arrangements of whips and canes. There were scourges and flails, bull whips, crops, tawses and paddles; short canes, long ones, slender ones and thicker ones. And tucked away round the edges of the room were frames, bars and benches on which were arranged all the restraints and chains one could wish for.

I registered all this in a quick glance which also told me that the room was empty apart from an elegantly dressed, tall, dark haired man lounging casually against the arm of one of the sofas. He waved at us a little distractedly, and I couldn't blame him because kneeling in front of him was a dark haired girl in a long, blue satin dress. Her back was towards me and the low cut of the dress revealed the marks of what must have been a fairly recent beating. Her head was moving slowly and rhythmically backwards and forwards at the height of his waist. With something of a shock I realised that she had his penis in her mouth.

"That's Lolli," Alan said, "watch her. She's a real artist."

My initial embarrassment was quite overcome by the two men's casual acceptance of what was going on. But then, this was The Lodge after all, I reminded myself.

So I followed Alan over to another sofa which gave us a side view of Lolli at work and we settled down to watch. He was right, Lolli was indeed an artist at fellatio. Her pretty mouth moved slowly and lovingly up and down the thick rod of the man's sex. Every now and then she would take her mouth off it completely and allow her tongue to lap lasciviouly across the engorged glans which stood, huge and shiny in front of her face. And she didn't just lick, she put her tongue right out and made sure the man she was pleasuring could see exactly how carefully she was caressing him. When she went fully down on him I couldn't help noticing that she managed to fit in an extraordinary amount of the rigid shaft. After a few minutes we heard a small gasp from the man and his hand came down to rest on the back of her head. At once her head ducked down towards the hand which held the base of his sex and as he bucked his hips forwards as the spasms of his orgasm ran through him she took every drop without even swallowing, she obviously had the knack of opening her throat completely to whichever man wanted to use it.

Although she must have seen us from the corner of her eye she took plenty of time about making sure she licked the man clean of every last trace of sperm before tucking the softening cock back into his trousers. The man waved casually to us once more and left while Lolli got to her feet and came over to us, only to kneel down once more after carefully raising her skirts and then settling back on her heels.

"This is Lolli," Alan said getting up and preparing to leave. "No-one will want this room till after dinner so you've got plenty of time," he told me, and then turned back to Lolli. "I shall expect to hear that you've looked after our guest properly Lolli."

"Yes Master." She said.

Alan left the room and I looked at Lolli. She was very attractive, full breasted and pale skinned. Her dark hair falling in waves round her face framed a soft and sensual mouth and dark eyes which sparkled with intelligemce.

I took out my notepad and prepared to start the interview, but I was finding it difficult to put out of my mind the scene I had just witnessed.

"Well. . . . Lolli," I began, "Is it. . . I mean. . . How did you get that nickname?"

She laughed immediately, a pleasant musical laugh.

"No it's not because of that! Although I am reckoned to be pretty good! I'll tell you why. . . . . "

It was an experiment.

And she was part of it. Girls at one of the most diehard traditional boys' public schools? My God no! The Colonel Blimps said the fillies were just a bunch of loose moraled little whores and they didn't want their precious progeny mixing with an army of such precocious delilahs. Lolli thought the old buffoons were scared that the randy little buggers would take after their fathers and spend all their time peeping through keyholes or spying on the showers trying to catch the girls naked. Their studies would suffer, or even worse, they'd be so busy fawning over the temptresses that they'd lose interest in the playing fields and the first fifteen would disappear straight down the pan. No, they were adamant, it wouldn't do at all.

But it did do and the blimps lost the argument. However they did gain one major victory. They were insistent that discipline was the purpose of a good school. Iron discipline, in turn to be learnt, endured and respected and girls must not be allowed to threaten tradition. So it was decided that in the matters of obedience, and correction, all would be equal. The wenches were to be treated no differently to the young gentlemen and there was to be no deference to their feminity. If a thrashing was called for then a thrashing they would receive.The only reservation being that in their case no corporal punishment could be administered by a prefect. A caning targeted on the firm, but tender milky white buttocks of a maturing nubile could easily unbalance an impressionable adolescent experiencing the first white hot flushes of sexual awareness. It could set him on the wrong track or lead him to seek out esoteric pleasures before he could properly handle them.

So the senior prefects were done out of one of their major perks and they weren't at all happy. They'd been full of it from the day they'd heard the girls were coming to the school and talk of the chance to sniff some fanny and inflict a damn good thrashing on a juicy arse had filled their conversation. They'd still be allowed to beat their male fags and juniors of course, that was normal acceptable behaviour. And a little bit of buggery never hurt anyone either, it was a part of everyone's schooldays, like the tuck shop.

No, the task of administering punishment to pupils of the non-male gender, that's how they put it, had to be vested in more responsible hands. But there weren't too many responsible hands that wanted the assignment. They either couldn't bring themselves to beat a girl, or more usually, they much preferred to get their jollies bashing the botties of the little boys. And so the onus for ensuring discipline was maintained at the highest level amongst the girls fell mainly upon the shoulders of one particular master. The girls were all terrified of him and Lolli in particular looked upon him as some kind of horrid ogre. The sight of him striding along the corridors with his robe flowing made her knees tremble.

In the event he was her very own housemaster and he treated his duties with extreme seriousness. Punishment was meticulous and strict. Tender little bottoms were beaten for the slightest of misdemeanours, their only protection being the thinnest of shorts. She steered well clear of trouble and avoided his clutches only to be thrown into the lion's den by a shit of a prefect, who for no apparent reason had it in for her.

Talking in assembly, that was her crime apparently. The prefect hauled her out of the congregation, humiliated her in front of the whole school and put her on report. The consequence was never in doubt, it was an automatic six lashes of the strap. From then on she had to work very hard to avoid the trips down the echoing corridors to stand outside his study and await punishment. But for the most part she managed as well as any of the other girls and boys. And that was really the point because however cruel and unfair, it was the same for all of them. They all lived with the same cruelties and injustices; and the same certainties.

Lolli looked down, analysing her thoughts, before her eyes swept upwards and fixed my own.

"I suppose it made a big impression on me," she continued, "broken home and all that; father abroad all the time. I was always scared of punishment but I always respected his scrupulous attention to the school's disciplinary code."

But then it all changed.

It happened at a stage of her development when there were so many hormones sloshing about in her that even the sex life of plants in Biology left her hot and bothered. The same prefect who had had it in for her all along got her for having taken a short cut on a cross-country run. Again she was hauled out in assembly and put on report. But this time it was too much. A few weeks past her sixteenth birthday and made to bend over again like a little kid? She wasn't going to take it any more. She raced back to her dormitory and pulled on four more pairs of knickers before reporting to the Housemaster's study.

As usual matron was there to see the rules adhered to, but on that occasion she was dismissed and Lolli was alone with him for the first time. And it came as something of a shock to her to find that he wasn't really old. He made her bend over his desk, pressing her budding breasts flat against the surface, her hands stretched out and grasping the edges. By the fifth form, short pleated skirts had replaced shorts and she felt the material ride up her long thighs. He made her stand on tip toe to push her buttocks up further and she knew that if she were naked her virgin sex would be pushing back towards him. And at that moment the dread she had been feeling evaporated to be replaced by a strange tingling feeling. It was anticipation.

But on his part, what should have been a tight little bottom thrust up for punishment was blatantly padded and he spotted immediately that she was trying to cheat.

His voice was cold. Controlled.

"I am not often called upon to strap fifth form girls," he said, " but even I can see that you are attempting to avoid your full punishment. Now stand up and remove the extra knickers or whatever they are."

Bright red with humiliation but still tingling in the pit of her stomach, she stood up, slowly hitched up her skirt and wriggled each pair of knickers down and stepped out of them. All that was left was the briefest pair of satin ones that matron would allow.

"Ah. . . . Humbert. . . . . Humbert. . . ." She heard him whisper as she smoothed the skirt down and resumed the punishment position.

And then he beat her, administering the lashes with much greater severity than ever before; the penalty for trying to cheat, she learned later.

As she knelt at my feet, Lolli's overpowering sexual presence was prompting a stirring of activity in my own loins. I found my thoughts distractingly running over Alan's parting instruction to her, hoping against hope that looking after me 'properly' might include the same consideration she'd been been showing to the man on our entrance into the common room. That she did, after the conclusion of her tale, go on to provide me with one of my most potent sexual experiences remains a vivid memory. Her tongue, her lips and her throat all combined to bring me to a shattering orgasm, relegating any acts of fellatio before or since to an almost banal level of amateurism. The wonders of her own, very special oral talents, spoiled me forever, leaving me endlessly debating whether it wouldn't have been better if I'd never entered that particular corner of paradise.

"When I think about it now," she said, "I can't believe I was so stupid. But I'm glad I was. If I hadn't been, he would never have leathered me so hard and I would never have experienced the joys of submission, bondage and correction. It stings, it hurts, sometimes it bleeds, but the pain that comes with the thwack of the cane or the slash of the whip is Heaven."

But then it was a new experience. She'd felt something other than discomfort, but exactly what emotions had been aroused in her she didn't know. And apart from that, who was Humbert? The other girls were as baffled as she was. What had he been talking about? The prefect cleared up that mystery the next time he put her on report and after that Lolita became required reading in the dorm after lights out. Her friends took to calling her Lolli and 'nymphette' seemed to be the buzz word amongst the prefect and his cronies every time she came across them.

She was quite proud.

She had many encounters with the housemaster after that, but he never beat her with such severity again. In fact he never spoke to her, except to discuss her academic progress or to comment on the reason why her rebellious nature resulted in so many referrals to him for corrective discipline. Even though by now she was committing every and all punishable offences just to get close to him, every beating was administered with clinical adherance to the school guidelines. After that one time the matron was always there to witness the absolute propriety of the the enactment of the sentence, and she hated that. It felt like an intrusion on something very private.

She herself was never happy because all she cared about was him but it seemed that in his eyes she was just another rebellious teenager. And it went on like that right up until her eighteenth birthday.

She was still there, at the school. Her father was still abroad and so she had nowhere to go. She'd done well and was up for Oxford. Her father had a long distance chat with the Head and sent him a pretty hefty cheque to use in any manner he saw fit and so it was agreed between them that she could remain on campus throughout the summer break. So there she was one night, taking stock of herself and posing in front of her mirror. Not bad, she thought. Pretty fair boobs, hat peg nipples, a good backside and a mouth no man with a serviceable rod could possibly refuse. And then out of the blue the summons arrived. He wanted to see her.

That threw her. She'd spent years pining for his attention but secretly she'd long given up hope that she might one day become more than just an errant shoolgirl in his thoughts. What was she to do? Now the opportunity had come she wasn't going to miss out, that was for sure. She thought it over for about two seconds and then pulled out the suitcase that she'd packed ready for college. She opened the lid and took out the short silken sheath she'd bought with the cash her daddy had telegraphed as a salve to his conscience. That dress was a statement. It said that she was grown up, sophisticated and alluring and its purpose was to make her the Belle of the Freshers' Ball. Now it was going to have a different destiny.

It wasn't cold but all the same she was trembling as she knocked on his door. She heard footsteps approaching and then the door swung open. Beyond the door the room was dimly lit. There was music. Roxy Music. 'Slave to love' it was, and that music itself signalled that here was a very different man from the crusty denizen of the classroom. A fleeting thought whisked through her mind that maybe the song was intended to convey some sort of message. He beckoned her inside and his private rooms were like nothing that she could have imagined; intimate, tastefully decorated and not at all the lair of a soulless bachelor. And as for him, now devoid of his shoolmasterly trappings, he was as maturely rugged as in the portrait she'd painted in her dreams. The threadbare gown was gone; the mortarboard non existent, the chalk dusted fingers an illusion. In their place was a dinner jacketed sophisticate who exuded all the sex appeal she had ever dreamed of. He closed the door behind her and ushered her in by placing a hand on the small of her back. Lolli shivered at the touch, hot shivers, then shivered more as his hand slipped down to rest very softly, but somehow possessively, on her hip.

A table was set with two places. Candles flickered, wine flowed and the food was prepared by Aphrodite herself. He was charming, eloquent and above all, although he was firmly in control of the proceedings there was no condescension, he treated her as an adult. She was swept by an elated, triumphal gratification that he should see her as a desirable woman and she determined to play her part to the full. All thoughts of the schoolroom were banished, no longer tutor and pupil, they were now seducer and willing victim. His conversation flowed along with the wine and she fell ever more deeply under his spell as his words wove patterns of magic into the fabric of her impressionable, eager young heart.

It seemed an eternity before the dinner was over and they finally rose from the table. This was the moment she'd been longing for, the fulfillment of her dreams and he didn't have to lead her to the bedroom, she couldn't wait.

She was in a hurry. All those frustrating years of yearning piled themselves into a mountain of urgency. She started to throw off her dress but he caught her arm and slipping the silken fabric back over her shoulders he motioned her into stillness. He held her at arm's length and spent several agonizing moments devouring her body with hungry eyes. He slid his palms over her hips and down her thighs, following the lines of her suspenders until he reached the lace tops of her stockings. The silkiness of the material allowed him to feel everything as if there was no barrier between his hands and her yielding flesh. He explored the ridge where stocking gave way to naked thigh and then his hands slipped around to caress her bottom. Sensitive fingers traced the perimeter of her French knickers and after working their way back lingered on the mound of Venus, gently probing her womanhood.

She was in a frenzy of arousal. She couldn't help herself and pushed herself against him. A stinging slap came from nowhere, reddening her cheek. Then he gently pushed her back to arm's length. She learned quickly. She was to submit to his desires only and must make no moves herself. Any sexual release she craved could only come with his express permission. She tried to stay calm. Again he caressed her intimately and despite herself she shivered in delight as he found her proud nipples and cupped her breasts.

"How long have you waited for this moment Lolli?" he asked.

She was both surprised and thrilled that he'd adressed

her by her nickname, the name she'd been endowed with because of that incident in his study all those years before. He must have heard it whispered furtively around the corridors but she wondered if he'd ever connected its origin to his own lips.

"Forever," she whispered as a shiver of anticipation flowed downwards from her shoulders, rolled over her eager breasts, tingled down her spine and after lingering over the soft insides of her thighs, surged into the ever moistening depths of her vagina.

She was devoured by lust, the hunger in her soaking sex was unendurable and unable to control herself she reached out for him.

He threw her grasping arms aside and roughly spun her around.

"No! Do nothing until I instruct you," he ordered. "You must learn obedience."

A slap, much harder than the first, exploded on to her thinly protected bottom causing her to gasp in an involuntary exhalation. And then another. And another. Tears welled into her eyes, not just tears of pain but tears of euphoria. At last her dreams were coming true, she was suffering at his hands, enduring correction as she'd imagined it so many times. He turned her around to face him again and taking several steps backwards stood surveying her once more. Her knickers were drenched now and it took all her self control to stop herself from putting her own hand down to massage her hard little clitoris. He was aroused too, that was obvious from the impressive bulge that was straining his trousers. She wanted the cock that was throbbing inside that tent, she wanted it desperately and she couldn't tear her eyes away from it. He looked down to view the object of her attention and she thought that he was surprised himself at its highly visible proportions.

"Insolence will not be tolerated," he snapped, "didn't you learn anything in the classroom?"

In firm tones he told her that voyeurism was his prerogative, his alone to enjoy and savour. She was never to display any emotion, curiousity or reaction to his personal physical state. In view of her disrespect, punishment was called for.

"Is that not so?" he questioned.

She was incapable of answering. A hurricane of need raged through her entire being, turning the pools of love juice lubricating the slit of her sex into a raging turmoil of molten lust which left her weak kneed and helpless.

"Answer girl," he raged.

"Y . . yes," She stammered out weakly.

"Speak up," he ordered. "Let me hear you. And it's still Sir, or do I have to punish you for forgetting that too?"

"No," she bleated.

His fury increased.

"What!" he bellowed.

"I mean yes," she sobbed in frustration.

He stepped forward, lifted the hem of her dress and smacked her smartly across the expanse of milky thigh that lay exposed between the tops of her stockings and the lacy edges of her soaking gusset. A cherry red impression of his open palm flashed over her yielding flesh and burned itself into her skin.

"Yes what?" he roared.

"Yes, Sir," she managed to croak out through lips that were still trembling from the impact of his stinging slap.

"Make up your mind," he ordered, "or is that as wet as your crotch? First it's yes, then no and then yes again."

She tried to explain that yes, she deserved to be punished for her insolence and that no, he did not need to correct her for failing to address him in the correct manner, unless of course he considered her lapse sufficiently serious to warrant chastisement. He replied that he found her explanation lacking in conviction and that in the circumstance a sound thrashing was his only possible response. Her own response was a marked hardening of her nipples and an almost crippling spasm in the inner muscles of her vagina. It was unbearable, almost more than she could endure but she knew she had to fight to control her reactions or risk turning him away.

He pushed her firmly down into a sitting position on the bed and, after instructing her to stay where she was and keep silent, walked over to an elaborate old seaman's trunk that lay against one wall. He heaved open the heavy lid and levered it upwards. She was unable to see into the dark interior of the chest and as he plunged his hand inside she could only wonder what instruments of agony lay hidden in its depths. He fiddled around for a few moments and then seemingly satisfied, he withdrew his arm and turned to face her. She saw that in his right hand he clutched a thin cane. He took the tip of the cane in his other hand and flexed it into a tight bow before swishing it cuttingly through the air in a whirlwind of slashes.

This was going to hurt, she knew it. This was going to introduce her to the ecstasy of exquisite pain and submission and there wasn't a nerve in her body that wasn't raging in anticipation. She'd touched herself up and masturbated herself into a frenzy time and again just re-living those relatively minor teacher and pupil floggings in her mind and now the real thing loomed. Her whole belly was on fire and an ocean of foam couldn't have put out the flames. Her prayers were about to be answered.

One entire wall of the bedroom was mirrored from floor to ceiling, although it wasn't until he slid one of the panels aside that she realised it was actually a giant fitted wardrobe. He stepped inside, pulled out a high four legged stool and slid the panel back into position so that the wall once again appeared to be one seamless expanse of mirror. He carefully positioned the stool a couple of feet from his reflection and when he was sastisfied that it was in perfect alignment he returned his attention to her. She shuddered at his gaze. Her heart thudded, her breasts felt full and tight and her sex lips quivered. She was panic stricken, in her state of arousal the slightest stimulation would thrust her over the edge. He leant forward and pulled her from the bed. As she rose she caught sight of the patch of dampness that had leaked from between her open lips, soaked her knickers, sodden the back of her dress and had marked the bed covers. She despaired, there was no way she was going to get through this without climaxing.

She sobbed. He mistook her tears for fear of punishment, not for the fear of failure they actually were.

"Pull yourself together girl," he rasped. "This is for your own good, you'll thank me for it when it's all over."

When it's all over! She could have ravaged him there and then. Leapt on him, plunged his wonderful swollen cock deep into the roiling tube of her vagina and sucked every ounce of his seed from his body. Never had her obedience been tested to such limits.

"Over here," he said, "in front of the stool."

She did as he bade, noticing that the seat was deeply padded and the front two legs had leather wrist straps fastened about half way down their length.

"Now, bend over the seat," he ordered, and once again she responded to his command.

He pushed her stomach flat down to the padding and looped a thick belt under the seat and up over the small of her back, buckling it not too tightly, so that she could raise her buttocks a few inches but could not escape from its confines. Her breasts hung lush and full over the opposite edge of the padding and she prayed that his hands would not brush against her tingling nipples as he leant over to secure her wrists. His slightest touch would have spelt disaster, she'd have come off with all the power of an earthquake. To have come that far and then fallen at the final hurdle was a humiliation she couldn't contemplate. This was one battle she was determined not to lose.

He stepped backwards and commanded her to turn her head towards the mirror. She did as she was told, although as she was strapped to the stool her head hung halfway to the floor and locks of her hair fell across her eyes partly obscuring her vision. It was exceedingly uncomfortable and her neck strained to support her head in such an awkward position. Instinctively she tried to straighten up but was constrained both by the thick belt wound around her back and the straps that held her wrists. She yelped in pain as a slap from nowhere stung her taut bottom, and through tearful eyes, in the mirror she could see the satin softness of her dress clinging to her backside where his palm had struck.

"Did I give you permission to move?" he asked, and without awaiting a reply answered his own question. "No, I did not. Any further misdemeanours will result in stricter retribution. Do only as I order, is that understood?"

She understood alright. She was striving with all her being to obey without reaction but it was all so hard. She was desperate to meet his standards, his conditions, but she couldn't stand it, she wanted him to shag her. NOW!

She bit hard on her lip, drawing blood as she fought to bring her wayward emotions back into line. He ordered her to keep looking in the mirror and whisked the hair away from eyes so that she could see clearly. She watched as his own eyes roamed over her projecting rear, taking in every feature and contour. The stool was of such a height that although the heels of her shoes were skyscraper high she was forced to stand on tip toes and although this again caused her discomfort, she was thrilled to see the angle at which this necessarily tilted her rear towards his gaze. Behind her, the hem of her dress was rucked up over the tops of her stockings and she shuddered as he slipped his hands between the inside of her thighs and caressed them. He took great care not to allow his fingers to graze her dripping sex. Her knickers were plastered to her slit and the juice trickling down her thighs had given him sufficient warning of the precarious state of her arousal. He was not going to risk any premature orgasm.

He withdrew his hands, took the hem of her dress in

his fingers and flicked it up over her bottom, revealing the whole expanse of her thighs and the white stockings that clung to them. Her knickers were so wet that they'd become transparent and his eyes stayed glued on the leaking labials to which they were clinging. He hooked his thumbs over the ribbonned edges of her knickers and slowly eased them down over her hips. The smooth satin slid easily past the tops of her stockings and down to her knees but no further. He didn't take them off but left them hanging for a moment and then bending down to place his palms on the insides of her calves he pushed her legs apart until they were wide enough to stretch the fabric tight.

He stood back and admired his handiwork. In the mirror she could see the proud moons of her buttocks jutting upwards from the stool, framed between the upper band of the suspender belt around her waist and the suspender straps themselves. He frowned, something wasn't right. It was the suspenders, they were in the way and might obstruct the proper application of the cane. He stuck a finger under the middle of the belt and tugging it upwards disengaged the hooks and then, after unclipping her stocking tops he pulled the entire belt from where it now lay trapped between her stomach and the padding of the stool. The stockings were essential though and he made no attempt to remove them. It was lucky, she thought, that despite the belt she was wearing hold ups.

She was finding it increasingly difficult to remain on tip toe and fidgeted uncomfortably. She saw him catch her movement and braced herself for the inevitable punishment. It did not come. Instead he once more slid the mirror aside, entered the wardrobe and stepped out carrying two wedge shaped wooden blocks. He slipped these beneath the heels of her shoes, instantly giving her the support she needed to remain positioned according to his desires. He was satisfied, and with one final glance at her now glaringly exposed sex, he stepped over to the bed where he'd carefully and almost ritually laid the cane. Once again flexing the cane in his hands he positioned himself behind her, and half in dread half in excitement she steeled herself for the forthcoming onslaught.

"Remember madam," he said, "no reaction and no blubbering; this is not the schoolroom. And don't take your eyes away from the mirror, it's my duty to ensure that you see as well as feel every stroke. Now, are you ready to take your punishment?"

She managed to squeak out a reply in the affirmative but in the mirror she saw her body shudder visibly as he laid the cane across her buttocks, selecting a site for the first stroke. She was hungry for the feel of that first slash and whether or not his coolness and slow method of procedure were designed to inflame her passions she couldn't say, but the tension was driving her senses into overload.

"Six strokes, as always," he said, "but you will find this somewhat different from what you've experienced until now."

And with no further ado he lifted his arm high and dealt her a stinging, swingeing slash that catapulted an uncontrollable scream of pain from her shocked lips. She gasped, blinking back the tears and her stomach sagged on to the supporting surface of the padding. Her heart sank, she'd failed. Her first test and she'd flunked it, the flash of agony had been so much greater than she'd expected.

So, it was over.

And then, surprise of surprises.

"That outburst, my disobedient young lady, will cost you another six strokes later. Discipline must be maintained. Prepare yourself."

She couldn't believe it. He was giving her another chance to prove herself. She put up her defences and now knowing what was coming she suffered the next stroke without crying out. Each succeeding stroke, though no less agonising, stoked a rising tide of arousal that matched the pain in its intensity. When he was done both her buttocks were fiery plains of torment. He'd laid three strokes across each one and the mirror displayed vividly the parallel weals that flashed out from the tender abused flesh of the single moon facing it.

He laid the cane back on the bed and resumed his stance behind her. He took off his jacket and the image of the trouser bursting erection that she saw captured in the silvered glass took her breath away. She'd never seen his cock of course, but she knew it would be magnificent and there it was, imprisoned in his pants. She was crazed with lust. Her nipples were diamond hard studs of desire, her breasts strained against the constraints of her dress and the lips of her sex peeled even wider open in spontaneous waves of expectation. Via the mirror his eyes fixed hers. She was hot, flushed and erupting with frustration. And she was still bound to the stool, immobile and helpless.

He reached for his zip and very slowly began pulling it down. She watched, open mouthed as he freed his straining manhood and prised it clear of his underpants.

Do dreams come true?

One look at that glorious dick told her that they did and her eyes devoured every inch of its thickly veined shaft. He looped his palm around it and, loose gripped, ran his fist backwards and forwards over his bulbous bell end. He moved closer to her straining rear and pointed it straight at her lusting hole.

"You want this, don't you?" he demanded.

Oh God, did she!

"Yes," she blurted out. He waited expectantly.

"You're not making a very good start, my girl," he said. "At the moment your report reads 'Must do better'." Christ, she'd done it again.

"Yes Sir," she blurted out in what was practically a shout.

"That's better. Now, keep your eyes on the mirror," he ordered.

Almost insane with need she obeyed his instruction and was horrified to see him take a step backwards.

"Naughty girls don't get their goodies," he said. "Naughty girls require discipline. And you're a naughty girl aren't you?

She strangled on her reply. She knew she should agree, that things would go badly for her if she didn't, but she was delirious with lust. She was a tart. She had to have him.

"NO!" she cried. "Don't leave me. Fuck me Sir . . fuck me please!"

His eyes turned to steel and he addressed her coldly.

"We have further to go than I imagined," he said and gripped his penis as if to return it to its lair. He stopped in mid action, seemingly having changed his mind. "No, on second thoughts, part of the punishment for your inexcusable insolence shall be to observe exactly what it is that you have placed in jeopardy."

Once again he brought the engorged and shiny glans close to her twitching and grasping sex lips, but not close enough to touch. In disbelief she watched as he began slowly stroking and caressing his shaft along its entire length. He was masturbating! He really was going to leave her unfulfilled. Gradually, with unhurried motions he increased the length of the strokes. Even she could smell the musky odour of her own arousal as her sex exuded desperate need, but he resisted the summons and instead of plunging his gorgeous manhood into the welcoming depths of her vagina he carried on. Faster and faster in perfect rhythm the strokes intensified.

An elephant could have fucked her at that moment and she would have welcomed its gargantuan proportions, but no such relief was at hand. Wide eyed and open mouthed she watched as the strokes became a frenzy. His eyes never left the glistening pink gash of her dripping sex which strained back towards him until at last he clasped both fists around his jerking manhood and directed the stream of his ejaculation straight onto her gushing hole.

She was devastated. Sobbing uncontrollably in frustration she dropped her eyes from the mirror. Almost instantaneously she felt his still throbbing weapon slap up against the weals on her backside as he leapt forward, grabbed a fistful of her hair and jerked her head back upwards. She was to keep on watching, he had not given her permission to stop. She had committed yet another punishable offence. He untangled his fingers from her hair as her neck took over the support of her head and she saw herself in the mirror. She was a mess. Her eyes were puffy and red rimmed, black streams of mascara ran down her cheeks, the stripes on her buttocks were livid and sticky trails of semen dripped from the swollen lips of her sex. She'd wanted that thick fluid pumped deep inside her, smashing down the walls of her womb and there it was collecting in puddles on the already soaked surface of her knickers.

This was a punishment far greater than she could bear.

"There's always a salve for physical pain but mental torment is the cruellest form of torture," he told her. "And there will be no release for you until you learn obedience, which for the time being means remaining as you are whilst I consider the next step in your tuition." He did however allow her to drop her head and peering backwards between six legs she watched him tuck his softening sex back into his trousers and leave the room.

It seemed like an eternity had passed before she heard him come back. Although her legs and her back were aching and protesting violently against the intermittent cramps that gripped them, she had not moved an iota during his absence. She was learning, and although her emotions had calmed somewhat she was still crazed with need for him to take her. But she wasn't about to foul up again. She'd had her eyes closed and opened them to see him approaching her carrying a bowl and a towel. He laid the towel across her back and put the bowl down on top of it, instructing her not to move; if so much as one drop of water was spilled there'd be extra punishment. He lifted a sponge from the bowl and after wringing it out carefully cleaned his emission and her love juice from the insides of her thighs and towelled them dry. He didn't touch her sex though, he knew how aroused she'd been and he was going to stretch the agony of her frustration to its limits. He moved around to the front of the stool and once again raising her head by clasping her hair he sponged her face. He told her he could deal with a disobedient girl, but not a dirty one and now that she was a little more presentable he could carry on with her education.

Carrying the bowl he left the room, returning almost immediately, empty handed. He picked up the cane and stalked the room, whipping and slashing the air. And there it came again. She couldn't stop it. Just the sight of him and the cane in action was enough to kickstart the engine of her desire. Her nipples stiffened and once again she felt the moist heat of wanting spread up from between her legs. She shuddered and then cursed inwardly. He'd seen. She felt the springiness in the cane as he laid it lightly on her rear.

"Come, come girl. Self control remember?" he said and in a lightning move pulled back his arm and with a single stroke lashed her smartly across the backs of both her tender white thighs. The breath rushed from her lips but she didn't scream. He gave her a moment and then whipped another cutting lash from on high to twin up with the first. She gasped again and although tears welled into her eyes she managed to remain silent.

"Very good," he said, "A Plus, for effort."

The blows had stung like the devil but the glow radiating from the livid raised weals was as nothing to the glow of satisfaction that flushed through her body. At last she'd passed a test, only a small one but it was enough to give her hope and strengthen her resolve. She determined to meet every demand he made of her, to take her punishment and to be the most obedient pupil possible.

Her dress was still pulled up over her buttocks, the enticing entrance to her sex staring him straight in the eyes. He bent forward and for one heart stopping minute she imagined that he was about to fasten his lips to her glistening slit. No such luck! He reached down and after telling her to close her legs he slipped her knickers down and lifting each foot in turn slipped them off. They fell to the floor and inserting the tip of the cane into their elasticated waist he lifted them into the air. Flying like a pennant from the thin willow, he transported the soaking silk over her back and then, slipping them from the cane, he bunched the knickers in his hands and fed them to her, pressing them against her face. A wide lace edged knicker leg covered her eyes and her nose was buried in the sopping gusset. The smell of sex was overpowering, his sperm and her love juice mixed into a cocktail of intoxicating eroticism. She puckered her lips and sucked in the fabric. Bliss. Whether he liked it or not, she'd finally got something she wanted: his sperm in her mouth.

He whisked the underwear off her face. She was apprehensive but his demeanour was unchanged and he did not admonish her or threaten additional punishment. Instead he stood in front of her and trawling two fingers along the inside of the knickers' gusset scooped up the sticky juice still clinging there, he pushed the fingers into her mouth ordered her to suck it off. She worked on his fingers as though they were his cock, licking, sucking and sliding them over her tongue. She wanted him to know what pleasure lay in store should he decide to fuck her mouth. His face betrayed nothing and when his fingers were licked clean he withdrew them and inspected them as though scrutinising a manicure. He made no comment so she must have performed satisfactorily. Her breasts were hanging loose and pendulous, her nipples sticking out like bolts. Trapping the cane under an armpit he slipped his hands inside the neckline of her dress, slid them downward and after lingeringly stroking his open palms over their iron textured tips, tested their full weight in both cupped hands. In order to do this he had necessarily moved much closer to her, so close that through the fabric of his trousers the bulge of his rekindled erection brushed against her mouth. This was another test, she knew it. The pressure increased as the bulge travelled back and forth along the length of her desperate lips. She couldn't help herself, delirium seized her and out of control her mouth clamped itself over his constrained penis. The taste of cloth attacked her senses. This was not what she wanted, she didn't want her mouth filled with a mixture of wool and man made fibre, she wanted it stuffed with cock. His cock.

Instantly he backed away, tugging his hands free of her breasts and roughly pulling them out from inside her bodice. One hand went straight to the cane and wrenched it from his armpit.

"That, my girl," he said icily, "was gross misconduct. Inexcusable, deliberate disodedience."

She had displayed a total lack of deference to her master's wishes and completely ignored his instructions. The resumption of her education would cease temporarily whilst he considered exactly what punishhment befitted her crime. He was angry, really angry this time. Not raging, but coldly infuriated and for the first time she felt real fear. And now that her dread was one hundred per cent genuine any wants, desires and thrills she'd felt before were as nothing. Her lust increased a hundredfold, her sex lips rippled, muscles contracted and she burst into an instantaneous sweat which flooded from her ankles, her legs, and her armpits, to trickle down across her breasts and even her hair flashed into flood. She was dripping from every part of her body.

She had been bound to the stool now for a considerable period and she was aching for relief, both sexual and physical. She'd expected an immediate thrashing but it didn't come. After some deliberation he approached her once more and she was surprised to see that despite his anger he was still displaying an impressive erection. He positioned himself before her and with the cane held firmly in his right hand he laid it on the back of her shoulder. There was hardly any sensation of weight but she knew better than to succumb to the idea that perhaps next time it wouldn't sting quite so much. With his flies directly in front of her open mouth his left hand moved to his zip.

"Now, absolutely no reaction," he instructed. "You must do nothing unless I so order."

The zip slipped slowly down its track and when it was fully disengaged he slipped his hand inside and uncaged his penis. It sprang skywards and laying his palm over its upper surface he pushed it downwards until it lay rigid but horizontal. It pointed straight at her hungry mouth. So, she thought, he was going to continue with the mental assault, knowing full well by now that she found that even more unbearable than physical torment. Correction by psyhcology, it was inhuman and she wanted to scream at him to whip her instead, but she took a grip on herself and held her tongue.

He pushed his glans closer. Her emotions were rising dangerously and she gripped the legs of the stool tightly and her back pushed against the constraints of the strap as she fidgeted, trying to bring them to order. The cane whipped away from her shoulder and a cutting lash ripped across thc top of one of her buttocks. She couldn't help herself, she screamed as the singeing pain bit into her.

"That's two misdemeanours in one go," he said, "not good enough."

She heard the swish of the cane once more as it cut through the air on its flight to her tortured bottom. She managed to stifle the scream that had rushed to her lips as the impact seared another weal into her delicate flesh. She couldn't see these fresh stripes but she knew they'd be in perfect symmetry, leaving enough space to accommodate the four which must now surely follow. She froze her muscles and remained immobile as he waited for any reaction. When none came he returned his attention to his member. His palm still lay across the top holding it down and she saw the blob of fluid which now trickled from its eye. It wasn't the real thing, she knew that, just some sort of lubrication or something but she was mad for the taste of it. Her tongue refused to obey her brain and rolled out in eager anticipation and at the exact instant she realised her transgression her senses were stunned by the impact of the third lash.

"Get a grip girl, control yourself," he barked. "Or are you just being wilfully disobedient?"

"I can't help it sir. It's too much to bear," she squeezed out through clenched lips.

"Well then, you'll just have to learn to bear it, won't you?" he said. "We will now resume the lesson. And take care, I will not continue to be so lenient if your flagrant insubordination continues." He pressed his bulbous glans up against her closed mouth. With the greatest effort of will she checked herself and managed to keep it clenched shut as he wiped his bell from side to side along the join where her lips met. He brought it to rest in the centre of the cupid's bow that shaped her mouth and prodded her lips as if trying to prize them apart. Sidelining the frenzy that was building in her crotch she did not respond.

"Very good," he congratulated. "You're not such a backward pupil after all. I think it's in order to proceed a little further." He told her to open her mouth, wide, but to make no contribution to what he might do. Again he impressed upon her the necessity for absolute obedience, she must only react when expressly ordered to do so.

He pushed his glans through the portals of her lips and laid it to rest on the salivating surface of her tongue. Only his bell had entered and he left it lying there, its girth stretching her lower jaw to its limit. He remained perfectly still, just a slight throbbing on her tongue indicating his heartbeat. He had a pulse in his cock, she never knew about that, but he had said she'd got a lot to learn so perhaps it was normal. Normal or not, the power of those pulses seemed to strengthen and they directed waves of stimulation coursing all the way down to the centre of her frustration. It was all too much. She couldn't keep still and her mouth leapt to devour his wondrous cock.

He was out in an instant. Her mouth gaped and her tongue lolled out, rolling around shamelessly seeking his shaft. She wriggled her backside, struggled against her bonds and cursed the impotence of her actions.

He was livid.

"A giant step backwards, after we'd come so far," he said. " You've received three strokes already during this session, perhaps another three will help you remember."

She said nothing.

"Well, will it girl?" he barked.

He was right, they had come a long way but she was beginning to despair. And yet she had to keep on trying.

"Yes Sir," she answered.

"You are a tart, a whore and a brazen hussy," he hissed as he commenced to circle around her, the cane continually slapping into his open palm. In passing he flicked one of her steel hard nipples with the tip of the cane.

Lolli stopped for a second, discontinuing her story and addressed herself directly to me.

"Compared to a good thrashing that may not sound much," she said, " but the pain is exquisite. And you've got to be a woman to really appreciate how agonising a blow to an inflamed nipple can be."

I glanced down, and saw that she herself, very clearly appreciated it. Her nipples were pushing the satin of her dress into hard little mounds, just at the memory. She caught my glance and smiled up at me. She really was an enticingly enchanting girl, that smile alone catapulting my pulse rate into the danger zone. She didn't miss the signals, laying a cool, smooth palm on my thigh to heighten my tension as she resumed the tale.

He completed several circuits, prodding here and there, never landing a full blown lash but tormenting the nerve ends of her bottom, her thighs, her breasts and even her sex with cutting flicks of the cane.

"Discipline must be maintained," he said, as much to himself as to her, "and I will not tolerate your rebellious, ungrateful behaviour. You madam, are a trollop and I find myself in two minds as to the wisdom of continuing your training. In fact, to put it bluntly I feel you are something of a lost cause."

The atmosphere was tense, taut with his indecision. All her sexual passion flashed out of existence as iced water replaced the blood in her veins. Her clitoris subsided and retreated within its hood, the walls of her vagina relaxed and the previously warm musky flood bathing her intimate parts cooled into an uncomfortable stickiness that dripped coldly from the strands of her pubes. Her vagina might have frozen but her pulse raced, her heart thumped and she could hardly draw a breath. How long he stood deliberating she had no idea but in her tangled senses it seemed an eternity. At that moment she came as close to total emotional breakdown as she ever had, before or after. She couldn't lose him now, it would mean the end of her world, paradise lost and the shattering of all her dreams. She determined that if he did cast her aside she'd end it all, if she was not to be his slave then she'd rather be dead than be a slave to an empty life without him as her master.

Eventually he addressed her and in detached icy tones asked if she had anything to say which might influence his judgement. A torrent of grovelling apology poured from her lips; she cried and she pleaded. She said she was sorry that she was just a foolish fallible girl, she'd never be disobedient again and she begged for one more chance to prove herself. He silenced her with a tap of the cane, and as he deliberated, for one agonising moment she thought she'd failed in her arguments. But then the verdict was announced and the sentence delivered.

"Very well, young lady," he said, "I'm prepared to make one final attempt to continue with your tuition but the slightest lack of adherence to my orders and you will find yourself dismissed from my presence, immediately and forever."

The relief was orgasmic in its scale. Muscles relaxed, her pulse slowed, and she managed to get her breathing back under control. She flopped into an ungainly heap over the stool, she was in heaven, and as long as he continued to test her, that was where she would stay.

His first recognisable pronouncement was that before they could proceed any further she must receive the outstanding three lashes due from her last indiscretion. She indicated neither acquiescence nor rebuttal, wisely opting for silence. She really didn't care what retribution he chose to extract, she just thanked every deity in the universe for her salvation. He circled her, very slowly one last time, firstly allowing the cane to slide along the groove of her vagina, then introducing it into her, finally flicking mercilessly at her swollen labial lips. That stung like the very devil. She didn't scream, or even utter a sound, but her involuntary wriggling betrayed her. Taking good aim he laid several swift, stinging strokes right across her sex and stood, awaiting her reaction. She squealed inwardly but with an effort of self control she didn't know she possessed, she held it in check, no sound passing her lips. He seemed satisfied, turning his attention to her breasts. Using the tip of the cane, he molested her protesting nuggets, flicking up, down and from side to side in small, swift swishes. It was agony. Her nipples burned and her vulva pulsed in injured protestation. Then the blunt end of the cane probed the secrets of her anus.

Both sphincter muscles clamped shut in shocked surprise at the first ever penetration of her rear. But it was an erotic sensation and here was something she'd never before considered. Could something as slender as the end of a cane be the harbinger of future delights? Replace the cane with his throbbing cock and she'd be practically ripped apart. She thrilled at the prospect and the first stirrings of re-arousal rang alarm bells the length and breadth of her body. Calm down, stay cool, think of anything but sex she told herself. But that was far easier said than done, her anus welcoming the pushing, prodding willow, and heigthening her already savagely intensifying emotions. This was another danger point and when his intimate exploration ceased and he pulled the cane from her bottom with an audible plop, she uttered a silent prayer of thanks.

TITLES IN PRINT

Silver Moon

ISBN 1-897809-17-4 Bikers Girl on the Run *Lia Anderssen*
ISBN 1-897809-23-9 Slave to the System *Rosetta Stone*
ISBN 1-897809-25-5 Barbary Revenge *Allan Aldiss*
ISBN 1-897809-27-1 White Slavers *Jack Norman*
ISBN 1-897809-29-8 The Drivers *Henry Morgan*
ISBN 1-897809-31-X Slave to the State *Rosetta Stone*
ISBN 1-897809-36-0 Island of Slavegirls *Mark Slade*
ISBN 1-897809-37-9 Bush Slave *Lia Anderssen*
ISBN 1-897809-38-7 Desert Discipline *Mark Stewart*
ISBN 1-897809-40-9 Voyage of Shame *Nicole Dere*
ISBN 1-897809-41-7 Plantation Punishment *Rick Adams*
ISBN 1-897809-42-5 Naked Plunder *J.T. Pearce*
ISBN 1-897809-43-3 Selling Stephanie *Rosetta Stone*
ISBN 1-897809-44-1 SM Double value (Olivia/Lucy) *Graham/Slade**
ISBN 1-897809-46-8 Eliska *von Metchingen*
ISBN 1-897809-47-6 Hacienda, *Allan Aldiss*
ISBN 1-897809-48-4 Angel of Lust, *Lia Anderssen**
ISBN 1-897809-50-6 Naked Truth, *Nicole Dere**
ISBN 1-897809-51-4 I Confess!, *Dr Gerald Rochelle**
ISBN 1-897809-52-2 Barbary Slavedriver, *Allan Aldiss**
ISBN 1-897809-53-0 A Toy for Jay, *J.T. Pearce**
ISBN 1-897809-54-9 The Confessions of Amy Mansfield, *R. Hurst**
ISBN 1-897809-55-7 Gentleman's Club, *John Angus**
ISBN 1-897809-57-3 Sinfinder General *Johnathan Tate**
ISBN 1-897809-59-X Slaves for the Sheik *Allan Aldiss**
ISBN 1-897809-60-3 Church of Chains *Sean O'Kane**
ISBN 1-897809-62-X Slavegirl from Suburbia *Mark Slade**
ISBN 1-897809-64-6 Submission of a Clan Girl *Mark Stewart**
ISBN 1-897809-65-4 Taming the Brat *Sean O'Kane**

Silver Mink

ISBN 1-897809-15-8 The Darker Side *Larry Stern*
ISBN 1-897809-21-2 Sonia *RD Hall*
ISBN 1-897809-22-0 The Captive *Amber Jameson*
ISBN 1-897809-24-7 Dear Master *Terry Smith*
ISBN 1-897809-26-3 Sisters in Servitude *Nicole Dere*
ISBN 1-897809-28-X Cradle of Pain *Krys Antarakis*
ISBN 1-897809-32-8 The Contract *Sarah Fisher*
ISBN 1-897809-33-6 Virgin for Sale *Nicole Dere*
ISBN 1-897809-39-5 Training Jenny *Rosetta Stone*
ISBN 1-897898-45-X Dominating Obsession *Terry Smith*
ISBN 1-897809-49-2 The Penitent *Charles Arnold**
ISBN 1-897809-56-5 Please Save Me! *Dr. Gerald Rochelle**
ISBN 1-897809-58-1 Private Tuition *Jay Merson**
ISBN 1-897809-61-1 Little One *Rachel Hurst**
ISBN 1-897809-63-8 Naked Truth II *Nicole Dere**

*UK £4.99 except *£5.99 --USA $8.95 except *$9.95*